MELTWATER

Fiction and Poetry from The Banff Centre for the Arts

KRISTIN ANDRYCHUK
JANIS BARLOW
BRIAN BARTLETT
VEN BEGAMUDRÉ   CURTIS GILLESPIE
ASTRID BLODGETT   SUSAN GOYETTE
RONNA BLOOM   GP GREENWOOD
STEPHANIE BOLSTER   GAIL HELGASON
MARY BORSKY   GREG HOLLINGSHEAD
MARY CAMERON   SALLY ITO
WARREN CARIOU   DAYV JAMES-FRENCH
MARLENE COOKSHAW   JANICE KULYK KEEFER
                     CATHERINE KIDD
                     BILLIE LIVINGSTON
                     YANN MARTEL
                     JULIE MASON

Meltwater

LYNN DAVIES
JAMIE DIAMOND
MARILYN DUMONT
DEIRDRE DWYER
MICHELLE DESBARATS FELS
ANNE FLEMING   ALLY MCKAY
CYNTHIA FLOOD   BARBARA NICKEL
REBECCA FREDRICKSON   ARMAND GARNET RUFFO
BILL GASTON   JAY RUZESKY
JOANNE LEAH GERBER   JEAN RYSSTAD
                     DIANE SCHOEMPERLEN
                     JOAN SKOGAN
                     MICHAEL WINTER

BANFF CENTRE PRESS

Edited by Edna Alford, Don McKay,
Rhea Tregebov, and Rachel Wyatt

CANADIAN CATALOGUING IN PUBLICATION DATA

Main entry under title:
Meltwater
"Fiction and poetry from the Banff Centre for the Arts."
ISBN 0-920159-55-9

1. Canadian literature (English)—20th century.* I. Alford, Edna, 1947– II. Banff Centre for the Arts.
PS8251.M44 1998   C810'.8'0054   C98-910946–1
PR9194.9.M44 1998

Cover and Book design by Alan Brownoff
Cover photography by Don Lee–The Banff Centre for the Arts
Printed and bound in Canada by Hignell Book Printing Limited

We gratefully acknowledge the support of the Canada Council for the Arts for our publishing program.

BANFF CENTRE PRESS
The Banff Centre for the Arts
Box 1020-50
Banff, Alberta Canada T0L 0C0
http://www.banffcentre.ab.ca/Writing/Press/index.html

THE CANADA COUNCIL | LE CONSEIL DES ARTS
FOR THE ARTS | DU CANADA
SINCE 1957 | DEPUIS 1957

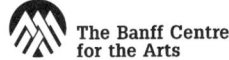

The Banff Centre for the Arts

CONTENTS

RACHEL Wyatt

INTRODUCTION

TWO YEARS AGO, I was sitting at dinner in a Halifax restaurant with several writers. They had all attended the Banff Writing Program but in different years. One of them, obviously a trouble-maker, said, "Rachel, you told us we were the best group ever." Looks were exchanged and then from the others came cries of "But she said that to us." "No. We were the best!"

I had been found out. Not in a lie but in the kind of truth that can get you into trouble. And what is fiction but a kind of dangerous truth? What is fiction indeed? There is no easy definition. Fiction is. Poetry is. And for five weeks in the mountains, The Banff Centre for the Arts is alive with words. The mountains, Rundle, Cascade, Sulphur, Norquay, echo with images and visions, characters and scenes. Wandering elk and malicious magpies are witness, or would be if they cared, to a remarkable flourishing of talent.

Poets and fiction writers from Newfoundland and British Columbia and all points in between come together to complete a novel, to work on short stories, to put together a manuscript of poems. Or to be inspired by that amazing and thaumaturgic view to write something entirely different. It is not unknown for a poet in this atmosphere to take to prose or for a novelist to turn out a fine sestina or ghazal.

For nearly seven decades, writers have been gathering in the shadow of these mountains to learn from various masters. One of the first teachers was Hugh MacLennan and one of those early students was Robert Kroetsch.

In 1972, W.O. Mitchell became director of the Writing Program. It was, he insisted, to have no element of the creative writing programs being set up in universities, no formality. At Banff, writers were to write "without the pressure of performance." Like a mediaeval scholar, he gathered writers around him and talked to them and showed them ways in which to free their captive ideas.

It was a summer program then and high-school students as well as mature writers came to sit at the feet of the master and to work their way into the craft and art of writing. Poetry and prose, drama and writing for radio, all had a place and all, with variations, continue to thrive in Banff.

Adele Wiseman agreed with W.O. Mitchell's view of formal writing courses. When she took over as director in 1987, she brought her own distinct ideas and built onto what was already in place. Her vision was primarily to create a community of writers in what had become the May Studios. Working individually with editors, writers would be encouraged to be independent artists confident in their own voices. Adele had a sharp editorial eye and was often able to make invaluable suggestions to a writer but always with the admonition, *Remember, this is your work.*

When she was offered the directorship of the program, Adele called me and said, "Would you like to go to Banff?" The Banff Centre for the Arts, specifically the Writing Studio, had been till then a kind of Mecca for other writers who knew a secret password that would never be revealed to me. I had been given a ticket to the Enchanted Kingdom.

My first view of the mountains as the car passed by Lac des Arcs confirmed this. The "Welcome, Rachel" banner that Adele had hung over the balcony in Lloyd Hall was a sign of the future; my three-week assignment turned into a twelve-year relationship. Due to ill health, Adele was only present as director of the program for three alternate years out of her six-year term, but she set her mark on the program in that short time.

There were days when I felt like saying to Adele, "'This is another fine mess you've gotten me into.'" But most of the time it has been a wonderful experience and, after all, a writing program without some problems would seem to be out of touch with that reality from which we all write.

When, four years ago, due to accommodation problems, the program was moved to the fall, some feared it would wither and die. As if perhaps the long dark evenings might drive writers to mayhem and madness. So far, mayhem and madness have largely stayed away. These years have been extremely productive and many remarkable writers have been able to take time out from busy working lives, in the home or out of it, to pursue their creative goals. Of the group of twenty writers in the 1996 program, eleven have subsequently had books published or accepted for publication.

"My book has been accepted!" It is a joy to hear these words on the other end of the line. And the writer who speaks them knows that across the country many others will truly share the pleasure in that moment of triumph.

As important as the new work that is written here, the ideas that fall into place, the leaps forward, is the support from others in the group. It is easy for a writer who has till then worked alone to think that all the other writers in the program, the country, the world, come to their desks fresh each morning and produce a masterpiece a day. What a comfort then to discover that it is the same for everyone: writing is a struggle; a wastebasket full of discarded pages is nothing unusual; sweat and tears are normal.

It is impossible to praise highly enough the men and women who have given up their own writing time to come to Banff as faculty members. Without them, their honest critical work, their careful, sometimes painful-to-hear suggestions, their gentle attention to problems of all kinds, there would be no Writing Program. They have made it what it is and given the program its now international reputation.

The effect of the Banff Writing Program can't be measured in the number of books published or the acknowledgements on the first pages of those books. But it might be measured in the letters we get and in the "conversations" that continue long after the mountains are left behind.

Over time, the Banff Centre has changed. New buildings stand where once were trees. More programs and more conferences take place than ever before. One year, writers were startled by shrieks beneath their windows. Members of a management training course were jumping into one another's arms from the trees. On another occasion, I was startled to see a minotaur tethered near the theatre building. It was not a figment of an over-stimulated imagination, but a Brahma bull brought there to grace a western-style pancake breakfast. Another conference brought Stephen Hawking to Banff and we were able to sneak into the back of the room to be inspired by the man himself and the poetic language he used in his discussion of "black holes." That same evening Cleo Laine gave a concert in the theatre. Such days and nights!

Amid all this and the good sounds of musicians practising, the Writing Program goes on in its quiet and, to some, mysterious way. And writers emerging like spring bears from their rooms after a long day at the keyboard, can go to a fine concert, the opening of an art exhibition, or walk to the Sundance Canyon.

The Writing Program would be chaotic affair without the support and help of the staff and administration at the Banff Centre. Nothing seems to be beyond the capacity of the co-ordinator or the people in the Community Services office. In the past few years, cries of "Where can I get a new typewriter ribbon?" have been replaced by "The printer needs new toner" or, "I can't read my disk." All these and many other needs are responded to with due speed. For the writer used to working against the demands of ordinary life, it is like being cared for by a flock of kindly aunts—of both sexes.

All across Canada and now in England, Australia, and the United States, there are writers who met one another at the Banff Centre and who are friends for life because of those weeks in the mountains. They know that there are people out there who understand, who share their struggles and their memories of walks up Tunnel Mountain, of volleyball games, Hallowe'en goblins, and the great bargains at the downtown church rummage sale.

"It was the best experience of my life," the letters say. Or as one faculty member put it, "I came home feeling there were new worlds to conquer and I believe the writers went away with the same excitement."

And what kind of people are they who come to spend five weeks in the mountains and write? Men and women, married and single, just out of college or ready for retirement, they have one thing in common. And that mysterious *thing* is caught here between these covers: stories of family life, of travel, of other worlds; poems with visions and styles as varied as the poets themselves.

There would be no book had it not been for the generous and rapid response of these writers from the program's past twenty-five years. To all of them, whether their work is included here or not, the editors would like to express deep gratitude. It has been a true pleasure to read so much fine writing, to re-discover old friends, and to be delighted by new work.

I am writing this soon after W.O. Mitchell's death and six years after Adele Wiseman passed on. To them and to all those fine faculty members who have generously given of their time, their knowledge, and their skill to help and encourage so many writers, this book is a dedication and a tribute.

DIANE Schoemperlen

STRANGER
THAN
FICTION

ANY NUMBER OF PEOPLE will tell you that truth is stranger than fiction. They will usually tell you this as a preface to the story of how their Aunt Maude was frightened by a bald albino juggler at the East Azilda Fall Fair when she was six months' pregnant (the juggler, himself frightened by a disoriented cow that had wandered into the ring, lost control of five airborne bowling pins, and one of them hit poor old Maude square in the back of the head) and later she gave birth to a bald brown-eyed baby, Donalda, who was allergic to milk and her hair grew in so blonde it looked white and now she's unhappily married to a man who owns a bowling alley in downtown Orlando.

Or they will tell it to you as an afterword to the story of how Rita Moreno appeared to their best friend Leona's first cousin Fritz in a dream, doing the Chiquita Banana routine and feeding the fruit off her hat to a donkey, and sure enough, the next day, Fritz, who was an unemployed actor, got his big TV break doing a commercial for Fruit of the Loom underwear and he was the grapes.

Oh sure, lots of people will tell you, and with very little provocation too, that truth is stranger than fiction. But I, now I have got THE PROOF.

I was writing a story about a woman named Sheila. Apropos of nothing, the name Sheila, I discovered, is an Irish form of Cecilia, from the Latin, meaning "blind." In the story, Sheila was thirty-two years old, slim, attractive, and intelligent with blue eyes and straight blonde waist-length hair. (I often give my fictional characters blue eyes and blonde hair because I have brown eyes and brown hair and I don't want anyone to think my work is autobiographical. Also, my hair is naturally curly, short.)

Sheila was married to a handsome brown-haired man named Roger, a bank manager, and they lived in a ranch-style bungalow in Tuxedo Park. Sheila amused herself by taking aerobics one afternoon a week, doing volunteer work at the senior citizens home, and having long lunches a lot with her friends. She and Roger got along well enough, although every once in a while Sheila would remember that they hadn't had a meaningful conversation in four years. They lived an easy life, gliding gracefully and politely around each other like ice-dancers.

So then I made Sheila unhappy in her heart of hearts, because what's a good story without a little angst?

The thing was, Sheila wanted to be someone else. Sheila wanted to be a country-and-western singer. She knew all the words to all the best songs, which she practised by singing along with the compact disc player while Roger was away all day at the bank. She had a special secret wardrobe stashed in the back of her walk-in closet off the master bathroom. On the cover of her first album, she wanted to see a picture of herself in her chaps astride a white horse in the wind. Having never been much bothered by either self-doubt or self-examination, it did not even occur to her that she might very well be crazy or untalented.

Then she met a man named Carlos in a specialty record store called Country Cousins. Carlos bore a startling resemblance to Johnny Cash in his younger days. Of course, they hit it off right away because they were both looking for that old Patsy Cline album with "I Fall to Pieces" on it. They went for a beer at The Hitching Post, a nearby country bar where, as it turned out, Carlos's band, The Red Rock Ramblers, was playing. They were only in town for the week, having just spent two months on the road, and now they were heading home to Saskatoon. Feeling gently homesick, Carlos talked a lot about the prairies, which Sheila had never seen, about the way they'll change colour in a thunderstorm or a dangerous wind, the way they'll make you think of things you've never thought before, because you can see them forever and they have no limits. So by the time he got around to telling her he had a wife and three kids out there, it was too late to turn back now, because he already had his hand on her thigh and his tongue in her ear.

I was having a bit of a time of it in my own life right then. Three-and-a-half weeks earlier, I had fallen in love with a man named Nathan who was from Winnipeg and also married. This was in July and it was hot, humid, and hazy; it was hard to concentrate. I was downtown Friday night having a drink at The Red Herring, an outdoor patio bar with a magnolia tree, orange poppies, handsome waiters, and blue metal tables sprouting red-and-white umbrellas advertising Alfa Romeo, Noilly Prat, and OV. The regular clientele consists largely of writers, painters, and jazz piano players who are just taking a little break in the sun. Nobody ever really gets drunk at The Red Herring: they just relax, recharge, and have pleasant, informed conversations about postmodernism, Chinese astrology, and free trade. They are intense and innocent.

Nathan was drinking alone and so was I, leaning against the stand-up bar inside. I'm not even sure now how we first got talking, but, lo and behold, the next thing you know, he's telling me that he's a writer, too! Well, you can just imagine my joy at discovering we had the whole world in common. He wrote poetry, mind you, whereas I write fiction, but I was willing, for the most part, to overlook this minor discrepancy. He was in town for a weekend workshop at the university. He was dynamic, sensitive, intelligent, funny, clean-shaven, tall, fairly well-off, very supportive, unhappy in his marriage, and he'd even read my books. So what else could I do? (Caught now in the act of recollection, I recognize how flimsy all this sounds, but at the time it was compelling.)

We found a table on the patio and drank a bottle of expensive white wine while talking about our favourite writers, books, and movies, our favourite foods, colours, and seasons, and the worst reviews our respective books had ever received. We congratulated ourselves on being so much alike and ordered another bottle of wine.

He did not talk about his wife, except to say that she wasn't fond of wine, and her name was never mentioned. (I already knew from Sheila that a married man who does not call his wife by her name is pretty well ripe for the picking.) So it was easy enough, sad to say, to keep forgetting about her.

I forgot about her as we walked back to my house arm in arm at midnight, singing a slow country song, and he was the slide guitar. I remembered her as he undressed me in the living room, but I forgot about her again as he took me in his arms and his skin was so cool. I remembered her when he sighed in his sleep, but I forgot about her again in the morning when we had a shower, some coffee, and he read to me from *The Norton Anthology of English Literature*.

Then I read him the story of Sheila so far and he said he really loved it. I took this to mean that he loved me, too.

Afterwards, he told me about his teacher one summer at a writers' workshop years ago in Edmonton and how this teacher was a big influence on him, always telling him, "Life ain't art." I wasn't sure how to apply this apparent truism to my own life/work, but I agreed eagerly, as if it were something I'd known all along.

It was shortly after this that Carlos in the story began to look less like Johnny Cash and more like the young George Gordon, Lord Byron. He admitted that when he retired from the music business, he might take up writing. Sheila recalled, but did not relate, the story she'd heard of a writer and a doctor chatting at a cocktail party and the doctor said, "When I retire and have nothing else to do, I think I'll take up writing." So the writer said, "That's a good idea! When I retire and have nothing else to do, I think I'll take up brain surgery."

Carlos told Sheila that everybody has a book in them somewhere just waiting to be written and Sheila wondered, briefly, where the book in her might be right now: lodged behind some major organ perhaps, her liver, her lungs? She had this recurring dull ache, sometimes in her left breast, sometimes in her right. It worried her occasionally, usually late at night, and then she would lie in bed beside Roger, feeling her breasts through her pink cotton nightie, looking for lumps, holding her breath. Roger, who, she was convinced, could have slept through Armageddon, sighed dreamily and draped his left arm straight across her breasts by accident, so that she lay there pinned and pleading with God. She had come to think of this pain as her "heartache," but now she wondered if it might just be a book trying to get out.

I told Nathan this pink cotton nightie of mine had belonged to my mother, who was dead now, of lung cancer, though she'd never smoked a day in her life. He said he understood my not liking to sleep in the nude and I was relieved, as this is a point some men get funny about, as if it were an insult to intimacy or their masculinity. I told him that I might like to write a book about my mother someday, as she had led an interesting life, and he assured me that everybody has a story worth telling and I'd have no trouble finding a market for that sort of human-interest thing.

I told him how my first boyfriend had convinced himself that he would die young, tragically, in great pain, and alone. His name was Cornell and he suffered from migraines and whole days during which he could not climb out from under this escalating burden of impending doom. I felt guilty for dumping him, but I could not let go of my own romantic fantasy of growing old beside my one true love and we would bring each other freshly fluffed pillows and cups of weak tea as the time drew near.

Sheila touched her breasts and felt nothing. Roger in the morning was always cheerful and animated, so she never told him about the pain and the sad certainty of something that would come to her at five in the morning when the earth shifts imperceptibly on its axis and everything changes or begins to be the same all over again. When she told this to Carlos between sets at the bar, he said how his six-year-old daughter often woke screaming from nightmares in which she was afraid of everything and then he would lie beside her all night while she sighed and foundered feverishly.

At five in the morning on Sunday, Nathan got up to catch a plane and I kissed him quietly goodbye without asking how old his children were.

I am comfortable enough with the derivative aspects of Sheila's story in relation to my own. I am accustomed by now to this habit fiction has of assuming the guise of reality. I am no longer surprised to go out one night for New York steak with baked potato (medium rare, sour cream, and bacon bits) and the next day my characters are enjoying the very same meal (well done, mind you, hold the bacon bits, yes, I'll have the cheesecake please). I no longer find it unsettling to see the woman beside me in a bookstore leafing through a paperback called *How to Live with a Schizophrenic*, and when I get home, the next thing you know, there's a schizophrenic in my story and that book is really coming in handy.

So the whole time I was putting Sheila through her paces, I was also thinking, with some other side of my brain, about Nathan. I wasn't seriously expecting a letter or anything as incriminating as that. I did hope that he might get very drunk some time and call me up in the middle of the night, begging and reciting love poems. I knew this wasn't something he ever could or would do sober (considering his wife, his kids, the prairies, and all). This just shows you how little I wanted, how little it would have taken, how very little I was asking for.

But then again, in a different mood (more confident, more optimistic, very nearly jaunty), I was also thinking: Well, why not? Why couldn't he, after sleeping with me just that one weekend, go back to his bungalow in Winnipeg, pack up his word processor, leave his wife, his kids, the dog, and the algae-eater, and come back to me with tears in his eyes and a lump of love in his throat? I would pick him up at the airport, of course (all good romantic fantasies should incorporate at least one airport scene or maybe a bus station at midnight, or rain, high winds, a blizzard, a taxi at the very least, with a surly, silent driver and the meter running), where we would float across the mezzanine and fall into each other's well-dressed, tingling arms, while all around us dark-skinned foreign families wept on each other and tried to catch their luggage on that stupid whirligig.

Well? Why not?

Stranger things have happened. Which is another of those truisms that people will present you with just before they tell you about the time they picked up a hitch-hiker on the highway halfway between Thunder Bay and Winnipeg and he turned out to be from Wabigoon where their friends, the Jacobsens, used to live, and he didn't really know them but he'd heard of them and he'd seen the same flying saucer they'd seen in 1975, August 17, 11:38 P.M.

Many of these stranger things are duly documented in the weekly tabloids I buy occasionally at the A&P when I think no one is noticing. I take solace from the headlines, tell them to my friends, and we all laugh, comforted to know that:

MICHAEL JACKSON WAS THE ELEPHANT MAN IN HIS PAST LIFE
FLEA CIRCUS GOES WILD WITH HUNGER AND ATTACKS TRAINER

MARRIAGE LASTS FOUR HOURS—GROOM WANTED TO WEAR THE
    WEDDING GOWN

TERRIFIED TELEPHONE OPERATOR CLAIMS, MY HUSBAND TRAINED
    ROACHES TO ATTACK ME

HUBBY WHO GAVE KIDNEY TO WIFE WANTS IT BACK IN DIVORCE
    BATTLE

MEN FIGHT DUEL FOR GIRL'S LOVE WITH SAUSAGES

So yes, stranger things have happened in the past. And the future, on a good day, extends eternally the promise of more.

About the time I got Sheila to the point in the story where she was actually going to get up on stage at The Hitching Post (Roger thought she was at a Tupperware party) and sing "I Fall to Pieces" (she had her satin shirt on, her fringed buckskin jacket, her cowboy boots, and everything), I accidentally thought of a girl named Sheila Shirley Harkness who was in my grade nine history class. She was not a friend of mine. In fact, I avoided her, because the one time we did have lunch together in the cafeteria, she ate half my French fries right off my plate and told me the story of how her Uncle Norman had killed himself by slamming his head in the car door. Sheila Shirley Harkness was older than the rest of us because she'd failed grade eight twice. Her mother was that woman who walked around the neighbourhood in her curlers and a mangy fur coat, twirling a baton, singing to herself, and waving her free hand like a flag. My mother said Mrs. Harkness should be ashamed of herself, acting like that in public, as if this bizarre behaviour were something we all secretly wanted to exhibit but we knew better.

Sheila Shirley Harkness was so fat she had to sit in a special desk. And she smelled, although this was something we girls never discussed among ourselves, because maybe we were afraid that we smelled, too.

Sheila Shirley Harkness gave birth to a six-pound baby boy eight days before final exams. She was one of those girls sometimes written up in the tabloids who says she never knew she was pregnant. She thought she had something wrong with her: cancer, gas, or a blocked intestine. When the baby's head came out in the bathroom at three in the afternoon, Sheila thought she was dying, turning inside out before her very own horrified eyes. She dropped out of school then, out of sight, and kept the baby, Brian, at home. There was surprisingly little speculation about who the father might be. It was not unimportant; rather, it was unimaginable. Immaculate conception seemed more likely than Sheila in bed with a boy, any boy, moaning.

This first Sheila (or this *second* Sheila, according to your perspective on such matters as fact/fiction, life/lies, and the boundaries or dependencies like veils hung between them) has receded fuzzily into my memory now and so was probably not quite the girl I remembered anyway, was probably less frightening, less doomed, and might well be working at this very minute as a high-level executive for a major advertising firm, living in a harbour-front condo with an original Matisse in the loft, brass end-tables, and a marble Jacuzzi, rather than lying around all day in her underwear (yellowed or grey, the elastic shot), eating maple-walnut ice cream, and watching *I Love Lucy* reruns while her mother bangs her head against the wall in the basement and her illegitimate children run rampant through the neighbourhood in their dirty diapers, as we all, in the grip of our mutually hard-hearted shiny-haired adolescence, assumed she would end up.

Either way, the first Sheila was not at all like the second, like *my* Sheila, as I had come to think of her. *My* Sheila was, among other things, friendly, cheerful, clever, clear-skinned, well-educated, long-legged, ambitious, and sweet-smelling. Her last name was Gustafson and her middle name was Mary, although neither of these names actually appeared in the story. Her parents, for the sake of simplicity, were either dead or living on Ellesmere Island and so didn't bother her much any more.

Being a fictional character, my Sheila was not obliged to explain herself to anyone or to divulge her darkest fondest secrets to total strangers. Unlike myself (with my disarming or disturbing tendency to spill my guts, to tell the worst about myself to anyone who will listen), unlike myself (me having yet to accurately determine the difference between revealing and defending yourself), unlike myself (me having only recently figured out that most people don't tell the truth about themselves, not even *to* themselves, because they don't know it, like it, or remember it), Sheila knew when to keep her mouth shut.

Nevertheless, my Sheila started to subtly change. She started feeling sluggish all the time. She wore the same old dress three days in a row. She bought a baton. She ate two cheeseburgers, a large fries, and an order of chili and toast at one sitting in a greasy spoon in a bad neighbourhood. For a minute there, she questioned the meaning of life, if there even was a meaning, if there even *should* be one. She sniffed her armpits in public. She was on the verge of a transformation, threatening to rewrite her whole life, not to mention the story. I was having none of this.

For fear of exactly this sort of thing, I try never to call my fictional characters by the names of people I have really known, even just in passing. So I tried to change her name in the middle of the story. First, I tried to call her Janet, then Beth, then Brenda, Delores, and Laura.

But no. None of the new names would do:

Janet was too responsible.

Beth was too timid and kept threatening to die of scarlet fever.

Brenda was too easily satisfied.

Delores was the name of my friend Susan's Irish setter bitch and her hair was red.

Laura was the woman who came to demonstrate a talented but over-priced vacuum cleaner all over my living room for an hour and a half one Wednesday afternoon and she was sorry she'd never heard of me, but she didn't get much time to read any more what with this new job and her two-year-old twins, not to mention her husband, Hal, and did I know Danielle Steel personally? When I said I didn't have two thousand dollars to spend on anything, let alone a stupid vacuum cleaner, she said, "Now, that's funny. I thought all writers were rich."

So Sheila stayed Sheila and I struggled to keep her on the right track, would not give her permission to gain weight, pick her nose, or stay in bed with her head covered up till three in the afternoon. I would not allow her, much as she tried, to dream about babies born in bathtubs, buses, or a 747 cruising over Greenland at an altitude of 22,000 feet. Against my better judgement, I did allow her one nightmare about her mother having joined a marching band, playing the bagpipes with a sound like a cat being squeezed, and the parade stretched from one end of the country to the other, but at the very last minute her mother turned into Tammy Wynette and everything worked out all right.

Sheila got a little surly with me sometimes but that was understand-able, considering her situation, her frustration, and human nature being what it is.

One Friday afternoon, when I'd manoeuvred Sheila around to the place in her life where she either had to shit or get off the pot, I decided to go down to The Red Herring for a drink instead of writing. Sheila had been a big hit at The Hitching Post. Carlos had professed his love and offered her a job with the band. She hadn't vacuumed the house all week and Roger hadn't even noticed. Two things remained unclear: what was Carlos going to do about his family back in Saskatoon and why was Roger so dense? Now, Sheila either had to pack up her buckskin and join the band (Carlos was waiting outside in a cab with the meter running, off to the airport any minute now), or go home and cook a tuna casserole for Roger (who was stuck in rush-hour traffic at the bridge, fuming, sweating, and listening to the stock-market report on the car radio). To the naked eye, this would seem like a simple choice, but Sheila didn't know what she wanted to do. I wanted to make her live happily ever after (if only because I thought this would bode well for Nathan and me), but happy endings have fallen out of favour these days—modern (or should I say postmodern?) readers being what they are (that is, intelligent, discerning, and slightly cynical), they find happy endings just too hard to believe, too much to hope for, fake. Could I really hope to convince any of them that stranger things have happened?

I was tense and thought a drink or two might do the trick. Going to The Red Herring in the afternoon is not like going down to, say, The Sunset Hotel, where they have table-dancing, four shows a day, and the regulars, in the manner of serious drinkers, gaze deeply into their glasses of draft between mouthfuls, dredging there for answers or hope because they don't know where else to look. Some woman in gold glitter high-heels and pink short-shorts is dancing by herself and the old guy in the back booth is sleeping with his head on his arms, having just wet himself or thrown up under the table.

The Red Herring, on the other hand, is a classy place, and having one or even two or three drinks there in the afternoon, especially on a Friday, is an acceptable enough thing for a real writer, even a female one, to do. I imagined that as I sat there sipping, my writer's block would be hanging off me with a certain attractive, highly intelligent sheen.

I mean, what can you expect of writers anyway when they are prone to sitting around all day with their heads full of events that never happened to people who never existed while conducting conversations that never took place in carefully decorated rooms that will never be built?

Besides, it was at The Red Herring where I first met Nathan, so that was another good enough reason to go there. If I am fortunate enough to get the same table (towards the back, to the left), I can imagine that he is sitting across from me, we are drinking dry white wine and smiling, holding hands, and making plans. In this fantasy, his wife is not, as you might expect, dead, confined to a sanatorium, or cheerfully giving him a divorce—she has simply vanished, vapourized, dropped off the face of the earth like rain. She might even be alive and well on another planet, having assumed a whole new identity, with the papers to prove it, living out her life like a pseudonym.

So I fix my eyes on the empty chair and construct long loving conversations with Nathan, who is always wearing the same navy T-shirt and white cotton pants because that's all I ever knew him in. Sometimes I get carried away and catch myself nodding and moving my lips, smiling away to beat the band. I can only hope that the other patrons, on seeing this, take me for one of those independent strong-minded women who is always inordinately pleased with her own company. But then I remember that Ann Landers column where someone complained about always being told to smile and Ann reminded her that people who walk around smiling all the time for no reason are often followed by unsmiling men in white coats.

No such luck that day though—the only empty table was one to the right just beneath the magnolia tree. Our table was occupied by four cheerful young women in straw hats and lacy sundresses. They were eating elaborate beautiful salads and toasting the glorious day with Perrier and lime. I had no reason to resent, dislike, or envy them, but I did anyway.

I ordered a peach schnapps with orange juice, which is called a Fuzzy Navel, so of course, the waiter and I had a chummy little chuckle over that. Then I sat back to nurse my drink and read an article by John Berger in *Harper's* called "The Credible Word."

At the very beginning, he wrote: "Today the discredit of words is very great."

And in the middle: "A scarf may demand more space than a cloud."

And finally: "The pages burning were like ideal pages being written."

I took this to be a validation of sorts and flipped through the rest of the magazine feeling light-hearted, encouraged, and close to inspired. (It is, I have frequently found, much easier to feel inspired in a nice restaurant, facing up to all that good cutlery, fine china, fresh pasta, and crisp lettuce, than it is in my office, facing up finally to the typewriter and all that blank paper.)

Skimming next through the "Harper's Index," I could not help but feel secure and confirmed in the knowledge that the number of brands of bottled water sold in the United States is 535, the number of fish per day that a Vermonter may shoot in season is 10, the price of an order of sushi at Dodger Stadium is only $4.50, and the number of Soviets in Petrozavodsk who were crushed to death in liquor-store line-ups last year was 3.

I felt myself to be having, after all, one of those dizzying days in which everything can be connected, all ideas can be conjugated and then consumed whole, sense and significance are dropped into your lap like gifts, and the very cast and camber of the air on your cheek is meaningful.

Stranger things, yes.

I ordered another drink and an appetizer, the liver pâté and some French bread.

I eavesdropped intermittently on the couple at the next table who were talking about their old dog, Shep, who was going blind, poor thing, about their new vacuum cleaner, and a misguided woman named Lisa who was looking for trouble and she was sure going to get it this time, couldn't she see that guy was no damn good?

I felt a tap on my right shoulder. I was feeling so happy and self-absorbed that I thought, without wonder, that it must be Nathan or God. It was a woman in a pale pink pantsuit, carrying one small grocery bag and a white wicker purse. She looked to be in her sixties. She said, "Please may I join you? There's nowhere to sit."

What could I do? I nodded as she took the chair beside me. She ordered a screwdriver and some escargots in mushroom caps. She said, "I like a long lunch with my friends."

I could see right away there was something *good* about her, something motherly and kind. A pair of bifocals lay on her chest, hanging from a golden chain, and she'd put a blue rinse in her white waved hair. I thought of my own mother once saying that sometimes all she really wanted was a place to lay her head, but why was it so hard to put it down there in the first place? This was after my father had left her for a younger woman.

I was glad enough for the company of a stranger. As opposed to family and friends, strangers will believe anything you tell them and they are less likely to ask you what's wrong right when you thought you were doing just fine. They will not tell you that you look tired on a day when you thought you felt terrific. A stranger will tell you any story as if it were true. Often I have envied total strangers on the street: just the inscrutable look of them makes it obvious that their lives are better than mine, more normal, more simple, and perfect, yes, perfect ... perfect strangers.

"Hello," the woman said, "my name is Sheila."

I, rendered helpless in the face of coincidence, said, "Hello." It was the kind of thing that if you put it in a story, nobody would believe it. I recovered myself quickly enough because, after all, what possible harm could there be in exchanging pleasantries on a pleasant afternoon with a kind woman who happened to be, through no fault of her own, named Sheila?

It made little difference that I'm no good at small talk because this third Sheila (or was she, chronologically speaking, because of her age rather than her advent, the *first* Sheila?) proved to be exceedingly talkative. In the course of the conversation, I had to tell her very little about myself, virtually nothing in fact, except to say once, when her momentum was interrupted by the arrival of dessert (chocolate almond cheesecake) and her story was stalled, that I was a writer, single, no children, said to be successful.

She told me with detailed delight about a recent trip to the mountains she'd made with her younger sister, Serena, who had the glaucoma, and how you see things differently, more clearly, more brilliantly, bright, when you have to describe and explain them to somebody else, the blind, or a child.

She confided that one of the hardest things about getting older was the feeling that your body was turning on you, falling to pieces one thing at a time, and also the hair, which got thinner and thinner and she never ever wanted to become one of those sad old ladies that you can see through to their pathetic pink scalp. In high school, she said, she had been much envied for her hair, which was long and lustrous, a deep burnished red that swung and bounced, beautiful in the soft sun, when she marched in the school parade twirling her silver baton.

She talked about her children, three of them, two boys and a girl, who were all grown up now and living in other cities. She understood that, but still, she missed them.

Mostly she talked about her husband, Victor, who had died tragically in a car crash in a snowstorm in December 1963, four days after they'd bought their first home, a brick bungalow on Addison Street downtown. She still lived in that house and every day she thought about her Victor, wondered if he'd have liked the new wallpaper in the bedroom, the beige shag carpet in the front room, the placemats, the blue towels, the new tuna casserole recipe, the microwave.

No, she'd never remarried. Things were different in those days: a new husband had never occurred to her. With her Victor gone, she just figured she'd had all she was ever going to get of or from love, for better or worse. She was satisfied, she said. She'd lived a lovely life, she said. For some things, yes, she agreed, yes, it was too late now. It was too late now to turn back. It was too late now to turn her back on what she had created: three children, the house, those long-felt heart-held memories of her Victor who, like all the young dead, had never aged, never betrayed her, never ever broke her heart again. Why would she want to change anything after all?

Why indeed? Why did I find all this so hard to believe: me with my constant chronic longing, my searching, my secret sadness at those moments when I should have been happy, me with this annoying ache always stuck in my heart or my head? "Why create trouble where there isn't any?" I'd asked myself often, asked myself now.

"Now I have this pain," she said unexpectedly. "This funny pain, *here*," she said, pressing the palm of her hand to her breast, which was draped with a silk scarf dramatically patterned with bright large tigers in various predatory poses.

My own hand twitched with wanting to reach across and touch her, but I was afraid there would be nothing there ...

... no woman

... no breast

... no scarf

... no tigers

... just air

... the palpable eloquent air pushing down from the swollen storm clouds gathering above us.

The patio was emptying quickly under the threat of rain. All around us, women were scooping up their purses and packages like prizes, gaily preparing to just disappear.

I walked slowly back to my car in the underground parkade where I'd left it.

I was tired suddenly and rested my head for a minute on my arms wrapped round the steering wheel. I thought of a morning not long ago when a navy blue Oldsmobile had pulled up suddenly in front of my house while I sat at the breakfast table in my nightie, hovering over my third cup of black coffee. The driver, a stranger, a bearded young man in a plaid shirt, sat there for a full five minutes with his head like this on the wheel. Then he drove slowly away, leaving me alone again, alone again to speculate in the dappled, moted sunlight.

I hesitated as I left the parkade, not sure which way I wanted to turn, which route home I wanted to take. A man in a baseball cap in a brown van behind me leaned so hard on his horn that my eyes filled in an instant with angry, insulted tears.

I turned left into the rush-hour traffic and drove on.

Sometimes on my way home from The Red Herring these days, I can imagine a car (red with black interior, air scoop, chrome, shining) running the red light at 100 kph, rocketing through the intersection, hitting my car on the driver's side so that I am flung up and over, flying, then finally coming down face-first on the asphalt, so mutilated that no one will be able to identify me. I can imagine this so clearly that unconsciously I brace myself for the impact, for the sound of ripping metal and breaking glass, as I roll through each intersection.

Sometimes I imagine that I am one of the poor pedestrians in the cross-walk at the time. I am mowed down right alongside the rest of them ...

... strangers

... young woman, Wendy, pushing baby in stroller, pulling toddler in harness, has a headache and hates the way her hair looks like straw in this heat

... bank teller, Jane, on lunch, carrying roast beef on rye with pickle and cheese in small white bag while worrying about varicose veins, humming sad song about cheating and hearts

... old man, Ed, with white cane and dog, wishing he was dead or his wife was still alive or his children, at least, would call

... businessman, Martin, with briefcase, nice teeth, green tie, has not a thought in his head, no reason to suspect that anyone else has either

... stranger things have happened.

Sometimes I imagine that I am the driver of the car, with the radio on and my foot to the floor, and the bodies scatter from me like pages or petals, unleashed. Or then they are not bodies at all but balloons, of all colours, full of wonder, words, and hot air, bobbing up and away, bouncing off asphalt, the roof-tops, the pain, and a cloud.

SUSAN *Goyette*

THIS
TOWN

There should be a troll beneath the Black Bridge
at the edge of this town. A voice that stops people
on their way to mini putt with a warning:
Do you know about this town? The troll should ask.

And there should be an emergency seamstress.
Someone who could whip up a little fire-resistant number
to wear to the bowling alley blaze. A catcher's mitt
and knee pads. A welder's goggles and a bullet-proof vest.

There should be a posture master or a contortionist
at the foot of the mountain who'd lean backwards
from a tree all the way down to the path and who'd look you
in the eye and recite the dangers of mountain climbing
before you even start.

And there should be a referee at recess, someone
with a whistle and a wagon full of sticks and stones. Someone
who has a sense of fair play and knows about personal
fouls. Who can count and keep track.

The town needs more magicians, maybe one behind every house
turning artificial flowers into birds, girls into warriors.
I'd lie down in any box, watch my legs and neck
being sawed apart, if it means I'd feel more like myself.

And it needs more stop signs in living rooms, in kitchens,
a spell for calling exit ramps, doorways, black holes.
It needs women named Dolores working in the dépanneurs,
because Dolores means lady of sorrow
and sorrow should be available twenty-four hours a day.
The train whistle should mean more.
And the sky, the sky over this town shouldn't be so cloudy,
so close to the trees.

SUSAN Goyette

THIS STONE OF KNOWLEDGE

There are things you'll need to know. There is a god for soothing
waves. Pray to him, it has to help somewhere. And in some language
there must be a word for this distance, find it and write it over and over

on the back of a train schedule. Mail it to me and I promise to answer.
I've been reading that there might once have been a stone of knowledge:
check Ryan's rock collection, he's been gathering them for so long.

And I say your name, when I ride up in elevators, when I plug in the kettle.
Say mine too, the way you do, all the way to the 'n.' I've also read, to gain love
you must sprinkle the person with the powder of dried hummingbird.

Aren't you glad we've been through all that? The hair of hyena brushed
against lips, the full moons. We have anniversaries now, so many days
we have in common. And remember to write down where you plant

the tulip bulbs, the hyacinths. There's nothing worse than coming home
to a strange garden. But that's not all I'm afraid of. There's that day
in August, we were camping by the ocean and early morning I went

down to watch the sunrise. The beach was littered with people panning
for gold, crouched over their pans and the water. Behind them, right behind
them, the sun coming up all over the rocks. Remind me often of our alchemy.

It was seven hours on the train. Elsie lay on the floor between us. Dark windows, a dim yellow light. We kept her on the blanket with Gerve's sweater packed under her head to staunch the flow. We had never been this far east.

You boys should have put her out.

She moaned on every bump. At least Gerve had given up on that. There was just us and Rory Trask and Berta Jesso and Ellen Jesso in thick clothes with seven five-gallon buckets of partridgeberries, and Sam Tobin who was also after grouse. The women had tough fingers. Rory Trask shaking his head, kneeling.

That Al Lakie's dog. You Al's? She been like that how long?

But he poured a cap of whisky on the wound, which made her tail knock. He tore off a strip of duct tape and wrapped it over her eye. From eight that night until three in the morning, sharing the clear whisky with his two women and Sam Tobin under the yellow strip light. They were all looking at Elsie as if to say they wouldn't have put her on the train. They would have finished her on the barrens and it's a misery to keep her like that. They were looking at us shameful. Beautiful dog, the blue belton. They hated to see something that good go to waste. The women sang to cover the moans and Rory pressed his concertina. His brown fingers against the leather straps. Elsie's moans were like how large trees will creak standing still. They came from deep inside.

We pulled into Grand Falls at three A.M. and Rory Trask woke up the vet. We slid Elsie and the blanket into the back of Rory's green pick-up. His red brake lights burning hot. Gerve and I sat on the bright lids of the seven buckets of partridgeberries. Rory and the two women rode in the cab, shoulders squeezed. Our shotgun barrels looking too long in the bed of the truck. And by four, she was under an anaesthetic. Dr. Ted Eriksson said he couldn't get all the pellet and he wasn't sure if there'd be any damage to the brain. There was no way he could save the eye.

I said to Gerve, Vet wants to tear off a bit of our faces.

Elsie didn't stir until the sun was full off the trees. Dr. Eriksson wrote out a pale blue bill and left us in the clinic, for it was Sunday. Gerve was lighting smoke after smoke.

She looks bad, Joe.

The vet had the socket sewn up and three other patches of black stitching on her forehead and jowl. It looked like she had a pile of ants mashed on her face. She lay with her head on her front paws beside Gerve with just her tail swishing. It was seventy-four dollars for the work on her face.

How you paying that off, Joe?

Rory Trask pulled up with Ellen and Berta Jesso. They came in with a plate of muffins and a Thermos of tea. They took a look at Elsie. They checked her eye and said she's still smart.

You boys did fine. You leave that here when you're done.

And they piled back into the passenger side.

Those jackie tars, Joe. Man, they live up there.

We waited in the clinic until noon, until our red car with brown primer on the fender pulled up.

We had been sitting next to the rails. Elsie growling into the gravel. The creosote from the ties seeping into the ground. Gerve had his topographical map of the Gaff bent over his knee. The railroad and the barren hills. Some of the transmission poles had been sawed down for fuel. All that's left is the tops hanging to the wires.

Joe, I'm going to get some land off George's Road. Build a log house. There's some big spruce in there. I'm going to be a helicopter mechanic, there's money in that. I can work on the base in Stephenville. Or a bush pilot. Lou must be outfitting in Labrador. How much you figure land is in Labrador?

Uncle Lou's a busher. Dad said to us when Lou went missing that at some time you have to return to the ground that owns you. But he hasn't come down yet. It's twelve years and he's still up there, hovering in the present. They haven't found him, so up there he is and I figure he doesn't mind it one bit. When a plane flies by, Gerve will say, There goes Lou.

What do you think he's doing?

He's doing the kippers.

He's going to kill you.

She didn't heel.

Oh, so it's his fault.

Dad curing fish in the back yard. An elbow of aluminium pipe connecting the old bathroom sink cabinet to a barrel. Fresh herring, laid out in rows. Splits of wild cherry, smouldering. It's as good as hickory. The joke that he is smoking heroin.

Training Elsie with a partridge wing.

Fetch it, Else.

Elsie never pointing, just fetching.

You should shoot her, Joe.

She's all right.

She's fucking bleeding to death.

You want me to shoot her with a number four?

I got a slug, Joe.

We tried to keep her head up with Gerve's sweater. The ground had no give. Just stone and caribou moss.

Why you got the slug?

I got three. You never know, Joe.

He had them wrapped in a turn of newspaper.

A caribou come out of that blaze, bang.

She got half her face tore off.

We didn't know the schedule. We took turns stroking her. Sometimes, she wanted to paw at it and we had to keep her hind leg down. She bit me lightly each time I stopped her. Her jaws circled my wrist and she tugged, but it hurt her face to do any more. She looked puzzled, as if she kept forgetting what was wrong. Those teeth around my wrist like a bracelet.

The wind rose because we were on the Gaff. That was good to keep off the blackflies. The burgundy bushes were turning blue and then the sun sank over Saucer Hill. Gerve broke open his flask of silk tassel. We waited six hours for the train. We kept talking to her, good girl Elsie, come on Orelse. But we were getting tired of it. We were fed up with her moaning and the wound wouldn't coagulate. The barrens had turned to the colour of tattoos with grey patches of outcropping. There was no moon. It had trailed the sun by an hour.

It's three hours to Howley and there's no vet there. Steady Brook, four hours.

Gerve said he couldn't if I said no, but if I wanted he could with the slug and then we could take the body with us any time. We had to be together on this. He said we could stay another day then and it wouldn't matter. We could put her in one of the fertilizer bags.

You going to paunch her, too? Or just let her blow up.

You're an asshole, Joe.

And then we felt the vibration in the rails.

The sound's behind us.

Must be bouncing off the Gaff.

The beams of light arcing from the wrong direction. From the west with the wind.

Fuck.

Gerve grabbed Elsie by the collar, to keep her there. How Dad would rub her nose in her mess if she did it inside.

We're going to fucking Grand Falls, Joe.

Gerve has a scar on his belly under the stomach. He's never trusted me since. I was cleaning trout in the lake in the dark. I had the flashlight trained on a spot of water. We had paddled up to Shoe Brook in the canoe and they were leaping around the old stump. A beaver slapped at the mouth of the brook. We fished until after dark. There was a whole moon they were jumping for. Casting the line over deep dimples. The caribou bug tied in the basement. The belief in what lies underneath. They were leaping against a curtain of bulrushes. On the way back, the lights of cabins trickling over the surface, snipe tickling the shoreline. A loon was crying. The trout gave a thump on the floor of the canoe. The fibreglass drawing four inches so that the fish were under the water-line.

I like cleaning them. Dragging my thumbnail over the spine's zipper to scrape out the black. I was rinsing one and it gave a jerk. I had it gutted, but something in the muscles made it twist. With another, I was looking at the shameful load of orange roe. Then a movement behind me. A deep, low growl. I twisted quick, punching.

I was fucking joking, boy.

Gerve man Gerve.

I had the knife in a good inch. He was wearing a cotton shirt.

You're fucking manic.

The lake catches over as I freeze with the knife in my brother. We are ice-fishing on Finger Pond. The auger chipping through eight blue inches before the hollow plunge of water. Dad scooping off the slush with a bare hand. We are careful with a slice of bacon in tinfoil. And when we have a trout caught, we use its eyes, a piece of its face.

Elsie watching the lynx cross the frozen bog. She is biting off the baubles of snow on her belly. Chewing the ice from between her webbed toes. We check out the lynx's trail. I wear my plywood snowshoes with holes punched through on my father's drill press. My father places my bare hand inside the paw print. He holds my wrist, guiding me in. My fingers touch the points of its claws.

The knife touches no organ.

I have never seen my father teach. He takes Gerve and me to his school on the weekends. He rolls in the piano from the music room and plays while Gerve and I prepare the fibreglass matting. The obscure drawings on two green chalkboards in my father's hand. The angles and degrees, the front, vertical, and side views of gun racks. My father playing Chopin.

Holding the blueprints for the cabin, Dad says there is a map of the world larger than the world itself. It exists in a computer, an enlarged model of the earth's skin at a thousand to one. It meshes real photos from the space shuttle with a satellite geography of the earth. You can research any square inch of the earth's surface. There are people frozen in the act of crossing a street, he says. Sunbathing, fixing television antennae. You can zoom in on spring chives punching through crisp brown leaves. The migration of land mammals. The carving out of rain forests. It took six days to collect all the pictures, but they make it appear as one day. As if you could nail down a day, he says. The whole earth in perpetual daylight. No dark side. Maybe we're in the map several times, Gerve says.

We had cornered a covey of grouse on the bluff. Elsie pointing stiff. We were creeping up the sides. They were like moving rock, speckled granite, some of the oldest rock on earth. The wind flinching their feathers so you could see the down. The oldest thing I've ever touched, Gerve says. Rock from the ocean floor.

We shot low just as they were lifting, before they had any speed, their wings up, so the shot could hit the breast. Aiming a little ahead, into their future. That chuckle they give as they lift. And then it was Elsie filling up my sights.

She's not moving.

Elsie.

Fuck Joe fuck.

She didn't heel.

You were aiming at the fucking ground.

I was at the grouse. You said low.

You fucking nailed her.

She was lying on her belly, her head straight out.

She's breathing.

Come on, Elsie.

She was trying to crawl away from us.

What kind of name is Elsie. You can't go shouting Elsie over the barrens. You need a one-syllable name.

It was Elsie.

Orelse. That's what Gerve called her.

You'd better do it, Orelse.

At least it was her bad eye.

Elsie the runt. She had stumbled over the tall grass in Mr. Dawe's back yard. Tripping towards her mother. Her brothers and sisters already taken.

It'll clear up in a few months.

I don't like her to have a rheumy eye.

I can knock down the price.

And there's no papers.

You can trust me, Al. The bastard's pure.

My father holding our chilled feet. We are hunting ducks in October. He tugs off our boots and damp socks. Gerve says he's okay, but we're all a little numb. Dad blows in his hands and then cups my foot as if hiding it. He rubs the air in. He wiggles each toe, polishes my instep, the heel. Toes I had forgotten return to life. He is pressing the tingle of circulation back into them. It is his breath he is rubbing in.

As we lie in the tent, my father says all lit moments are recorded in the distance of light. Every moment frozen in speed, beaming away from the earth. These moments exist in a solar wind. In the continuous flow of charged particles, moving farther from the reflected surface of earth. But things in the night, things hidden from windows, remain unlit, are unknown. Us lying here in this tent by the beaver dam. We're safe from history.

He says, slowly, that there is an island in Grand Lake called Glover Island. And Glover is the largest island on the island of Newfoundland. And on Glover there is a pond. And on that pond there is a smaller island. I want, he says, to paddle up Grand Lake and portage over Glover Island. Get to that pond and cross to the island and spend a night. He says there is only one other island in the world with a lake holding an island, and a pond on that island with an island in that pond, and that place is in Sumatra. And if you took a globe and put a finger on Newfoundland and another finger on Sumatra, you'd see they're pretty much on opposite sides of the earth.

The joists were numbered in white chalk. We had built the cabin in the industrial arts room. Taken it up in sections on the train. Gerve had found a good station on the transistor. You could get everything up here. There were three grouse from the afternoon around a hill called the American Man. Elsie had frozen on a patch of creeping juniper and I flushed the grouse out while Gerve nailed them with his over and under. The grouse were still brown, even though it had snowed a little on the way up. They won't turn until October when it's good and white.

Our father was cleaning fish when we left him. We took the train and the dog in from Steady Brook. He was wearing the plastic apron I wore to bathe Elsie in the enamel sink. His chest covered in cod blood.

Before you shoot, have a look in the distance. Know where your brother is.

The huge astonished heads of the cod, their innards hanging on to the skull like a root. Holding the filleting knife sharpened on the grinder. The light board for worms. The scales cutting the fish into two-pound bags. The deep freezer full of stiff wild meat.

My father told us he had visited Uncle Lou, when Lou lived in Florida. And he'd heard the twin sonic booms as the space shuttle landed at the Cape and on a clear day you could see it rise.

He said Lou had been living illegally in Orlando, working for a garage at four American dollars an hour. This was before your aunt, he said. He came back for Aunt Myrtle. But Lou had a woman in Orlando he thought about marrying in order to stay in the States. But she was a hard person to get along with, Dad said. She had views. They'd been living deep in Orlando, and yet Uncle Lou noticed something had been eating his tomato plants. Something wild. They were pulling into the driveway and caught a pair of eyes in the high beam. A possum. The middle of Orlando. They eat possum in Tennessee. Lou took a shovel and followed the possum into the hedge.

Gave it a pat between the eyes and threw the carcass in his landlord's back yard. It must have been thirty pounds of meat.

But the space shuttle. My father noticed it glinting in the daylight as it orbited. He figured it was dead over them, mapping the interior. Lou had some quotes for inland property, which was pretty cheap even compared to Newfoundland.

When Gerve telephones, I imagine my father's careful hands scooping water over his elbows, leaning in to rinse, the water trickling down the backs of his arms into the pink sink. The elevator movement of his triceps, a soft muscle under the skin. The hair beginning at the elbow and ending at the bald knuckle of his wrist. My father cannot wear a watch. His body stops them. My father in a white vest when the phone rings. It is six in the morning and he is about to start his Sunday. He has shaved, the smell of his beard burning on the hot motor. His glasses still folded against the mirror ledge. The only time I imagine his eyes closed. His small blue eyes like white water. Yes, he tells the operator. You're where? Who shot her? Oh you ... fools.

It takes him five hours to drive the Trans-Canada. He packs a Thermos of tea and a bag of dogfood and stops at the Buchans turn-off for a cup of coffee. He sees three moose in the marsh by Pynn's Brook. He urinates in the ditch while log trucks roar past to the pulp mill. In Grand Falls, he stops once for directions. Gerve opens the clinic door. My father with the tips of his fingers in his front pockets, as if he is about to shove his hands in or take them out. It gives his shoulders a little rise. He holds his mouth firm. He looks at the empty muffin plate and the Thermos. His dog.

Where were you and where were the grouse.

I point at the magazine rack about ten feet from Elsie.

And Elsie.

We map out the scene on the floor. Gerve by the washroom, I am near the exit. Elsie where she is. My father standing alongside of me. You can follow the path of the grain, how the spread caught the dog before it reached the grouse. You can tell the distance between my father and Gerve and me.

You better put her in the back.

He takes the bill from my brother's hand and reads it. Then he folds it twice and pushes it into his jeans.

We sleep through most of the unfamiliar territory. Our father nudging us to show the turn-off for the mine and the road leading north to Gros Morne. We tell him of the Jessos and the muffins and he says what good people they are and how we should notice how they live in the land. He says the narrow-gauge railway will be gone soon and the Jessos will just hike in like they've always done. They're selling the trains to Chile and the rails are going as scrap metal. The ties are used in flower beds. The entire railway lifted out of the land. The black line in the meat of a lobster tail.

A transport truck is tilted into the ditch. The trees and hills are much like the trees and hills we are used to. The Howley turn-off is the first thing I recognize and suddenly the land becomes warm.

Gerve and I are trying to come up with the largest number in the world. A million, a billion, a zillion and four. Perhaps, it's the bill. Gerve says there's always a number larger. The windows are misted and Dad says there is one number larger than the rest. It is a special number that few know about and we should take care of it. And in the mist on the windshield, he draws a sideways eight, like a racetrack. It is a number we have never seen before and my father names it.

A rise in the pavement means ten more minutes to Steady Brook. The town is built on a holm that floods every few years. Elsie moaning at the quick drop in altitude. We pass the bend in the Humber where we first fly-cast from the boom. Our blue raincoats. The difference between salmon peal and trout marked on the boom with a charred stick from the fire. The forked tail, the speckles along the belly. But we forgot. There were so many trout, dozens, flicking them with a back cast into the long grass on the shore. Their bellies wriggling for water. We had them lined up on the boom. And the warden with his cream vest, waiting for our father, who was fishing upstream. Each salmon peal, Mr. Lakie, could be a fine of two hundred dollars.

The water rushing to meet the paper mill at the Humber mouth, where deep grilse hold the ferocity of the sea in their muscles. Racing to the shallow force of river with the pulse of milt.

How many falls to make water pure?

Three, we say, together.

All three of us.

THE STORMS ARE
ON THE OCEAN

ALLY | *McKay*

It was the year Buzz Richardson pulled his blinds, went to bed, and didn't get up again. Next morning his neighbour, Mrs. Martha Swiss, affronted by those still-drawn shades, remarked in town that Buzz wasn't worth the powder and flint to blow him to hell. All the time, he was in there dead, oblivious to her petty assassination. It was also the year I started thinking about a lot of things I hadn't thought about before. I was obsessed with talent that year. A craving for originality, a desire for brilliance blew across my life. I lusted for a gift, some mark of genius that would make me special. I felt stifled and forgotten between a charming princess older sister and the world's most precious baby brother.

I think of Dar and Winnie this way, and will until I die, because my mother used these words over and over as she explained to me how charming Darlene needed extra privileges and precious Winston deserved favouring because he was so new at the game. To be fair, I believe my mother meant to encourage me when she praised my maturity. For a while, I stood up very straight at these moments, thinking maturity was like good posture, and what a big help I was to the family. But I knew I was not my mother's pet, and deep inside, some precocious sense of justice was offended. That year, not by any specific deed, but by a slow erosion of trust,

I felt a gaping chasm stretch between my mother and myself. Into it, her explanations and my comprehension tumbled and were lost.

Besides me, only my grandfather acknowledged the gulf. I heard him defending me one day in the soft sad tone he used with my mother. "Don't be so hard on that child, Jo. You can't make her go away by ignoring her."

My grandfather's second childhood and my first coincided. He was just past the prime of life that year, a vigorous old man who had conquered the demons of his middle years and come full circle to youth once more. A few years on, he would be an infant again, tottering through the house, gumming soft foods, and stammering to me in garbled, disjointed sentences. I remember him best, though, at the apex of his life, when pleasures he had never before allowed himself—hunting, poker, sleeping in, friend-ships with children—were all he lived for. A man who had worked hard all his life, he savoured retirement. "They've turned me out to pasture," he joked, "and I've become a colt again."

Sunday evenings, to redress a balance gone awry and because he enjoyed an easy mark, he played cards with me before bed. Poker was the favourite game, five-card draw, nothing wild, or seven-card stud, two dummy hands to make the odds less ludicrous. He played as earnestly against me as with his buddies. "Plenty of time for you to win when I'm cold and in the ground. Another couple of years, you'll be thinking, candy from a baby."

I broached the question of talent during one of these sessions.

"Well, child, it can't be as bad as you say it is. Just isn't possible that everyone but you has something special about them. You're special to me." He picked up the cards I had dealt him on the draw, smiled. "Have to practise my poker face a little more. You're gettin' too big for your britches about this game." His weathered hands clutched the cards close to his overalls, as if I could see through them.

"Do you have a special talent?" I searched his pale blue eyes, then the lines around his mouth for clues. "I'll stand pat."

"Pat, will you?" He scowled at his cards, trying to scare me into a give-away. "Some people would say my special talent is makin' life hard for them. But you now. Seems to me you did a pretty good job singing those Brenda Lee songs around here last year. Almost drove us crazy with that little catch in your voice. What's wrong with that for talent?" He pushed some change to the centre of the table. "Five."

"It's not the same, copying someone. No one noticed." I meant my mother. I looked at my hand again, clicking through the combinations, avoiding the old man's eyes. "I need something of my own, something I can do better than anyone. Who knows, I might be a genius." I counted out the pennies. "See you, raise you five."

He put his cards down, his face serious for a moment. "Look, short-stuff, I'd say you better just try on a lot of hats till you find one that fits. Talent ain't like lightnin', you know. It don't come through the window and strike you. Some folks never find it. Ain't interested or don't have time." He picked up the cards again, glanced at me, then at the pot. "Call."

I turned my hand out on the table, fanning the cards so he'd see how pretty they were. "Straight, ace high."

"Sorry, kid. Full house. Kings over treys."

I wasn't sure I was in the right place to be looking for talent. We lived in Pennington, in the heart of high-plateau farm country between the Rockies and the Pacific mountain ranges. Because they depended on it, to one degree or another, the minds of the people of Pennington were focused on the soil, on its uninterrupted fertility, on rain and sun and snow all in good time. They were proud of leading predictable lives, neither as eccentric as folks on the edges of the continent, nor as bland as denizens of the prairies, nor as crazy as fools in cities east or west. Their minds were on getting the grain in before the mould hit, or on raising kids on cannery wages.

They didn't give much thought to talent.

Still, there were people around Pennington for whom regularity was anathema. Most of them lived on the outskirts, leading lives more marginal and more ambiguous than people in town, working patches of poor land, cultivating truck gardens. One of these places was Hoecake Row (so called by locals, though its recorded name was Hoelk Road, for a German settler who found paradise there). Homely, weathered houses lined the hard-packed dirt track that ran out parallel to the branch line. Weed-choked fields and shallow gullies separated the properties, leaving room for softball and hide-and-seek between the houses—close enough that the clink of lemonade glasses floated from one porch to another on summer afternoons and in the winter, family arguments seeped through the windows. We lived there, among the cannery workers who had lost their jobs, the Indians who had lost their land, and newcomers who had lost everything somewhere else before drifting into the area looking for a fresh start.

Living out on Hoecake Row made it hard for me to develop my talent. It was nearly four miles from our place to the centre of town and the ballet and music lessons. Once the afternoon school bus dropped us off, I was stranded, my grandfather in the cardroom at the Temple Hotel or in the fields with a shotgun, my mother at work at County Hospital.

In the summers, Pennington seemed close. My bicycle, built from junkyard parts, churned up the alkali dust as I raced in to the swimming pool or St. Joseph's skating rink. But autumn came quickly to the plateau farmland, heralded by a morning when, as if by a sign, the leaves on the sycamores and the alders turned orange and beet, and then another day when they dropped, catching in webs spun beneath the branches, falling in haloes around the trunks. In October, the bus had its lights on as we headed home on the back roads, the fields turning lavender, then flint grey. The cold moved in with the dark and the bus scared up bobolink and pheasant from the ditches as we broke through frozen potholes. My bike hung in the barn, tires deflated, chain smeared with axle grease, seat covered with a flour sack, waiting for April and my mother's permission.

I dreaded those autumn afternoons. The ditches that ran along the sides of Hoelk Road seemed like tracks that went to school and back and nowhere else. All the town girls were at Miss Fraser's, practising jetés (jettys, they said next day, poking out their hips, leaning on one leg, toes pointed as they imagined ballerinas doing), or at Mrs. Swaggert's, tying knots and baking chocolate cake. Even Dar managed an afternoon or two a week in town, riding home with our neighbour, Edgar Swiss. Cheerleading practice and Girls' Club were some of the encouragements my mother gave my charming sis.

Briefly, a family with a girl my age moved into the cook shack on the edge of Mrs. Swiss's land. For two weeks, I jumped from the bus hollering, "Come on, Juanita, come on!" We raced to the barn, batons in hand, and twirled while I told her about school. I taught her the tap dances I'd learned from Dar the year before: "Hop, shuffle back, flop step-step. Hop, shuffle back, flop, step-step. Hop, shuffle back, flop step-over." I yelled at her, prodding her through the formula, while the swallows wheeled and cried above us as we flung out our arms and cocked our toes on the pallets below.

"Why are we doing this?" Juanita eventually wanted to know. She was hopeless at dancing, worse at twirling, and usually cold. "Why can't we just go inside and play paper dolls?"

"I'm looking for talent," I answered her. "I'm trying on hats." Our friendship slumped even before Juanita's folks moved on, unable to find work.

I decided to learn to play the piano. The fact that we owned no instrument, that we were unlikely ever to have one, and that there was not a single piano on the whole of the road did not deter me. Ambition fuelled my inventiveness. From cardboard, glue, and crayons, I fashioned a model of the keyboard in the school auditorium, hiding it in the space behind the window-seat in the room I shared with Darlene. Concealment was instinctive: the contraption fit my mother's definition of fantasy, not to be indulged for fear of getting one's hopes up.

I sat at the library table in the front room, the keyboard spread beneath a window that gave me a clear view of Hoecake Row in either direction. I picked out tunes—"Silver Threads Among the Gold" and "Drink to Me Only with Thine Eyes"—from a book I found among the Christmas decorations and photo albums in the back closet. I marked the keyboard and book with musical notation and pressed the keys, sharp and flat, imagining I could hear the melodies. My feet hung down just to the rail of the mahogany table, and I pumped an imaginary pedal as I'd seen girls do at school recitals.

The results were not satisfying, and in only a few days, I knew this was not the answer. That was when I met Buzz Richardson. Attention focused on the keyboard, I heard a sound at the window and raised my head, expecting to see Dar's laughing face. Instead, Buzz stood there, not ten feet away. My foot stopped pumping, my fingers froze on the table. Oh, Jesus.

"Your grandpa around?" he bellowed through the glass.

"Pheasant hunting!" I reached over and opened the window.

"When's he due back?"

"Suppertime."

"What's that you're doing, kid?" Buzz's voice was quiet and curious, with a slight drawl.

"Plain enough for you to see." Frustration made me cranky.

"Plain enough you're playing a piano that's lost its voice, and not havin' much fun to boot, that's all." A slight blush flashed across his face, then a grin. He was making fun of me.

"What do you know about music anyway?"

He smiled at my sassiness. "You're your mother's child all right. Didn't mean to step on your feelings. But now you've hurt mine, I've got a right to ask another question. Right?"

Pacified, and convinced the worst had already happened, I stepped closer to the window.

"Don't get mad again now," he joked, "but can you hear any music when you play that tongue-tied board?" He was leaning on the sill. "What's it sound like?"

"Outside, it's quiet. But the song is there, somewhere. I guess it's just me singing inside my head." I moved away and began folding the keyboard. "I'm giving it up anyway. Guess I'm not a genius."

"What's your grandad say about this?"

"He says I've got to keep trying things out."

"He's right. No use giving up so early. Something will come along." He peered behind him into the failing light. "Guess I'd best be going now. See you."

From the opposite direction, my mother was carrying Winston home from the baby-sitter's. His legs were wrapped around her waist and she stumbled as she neared the house. Winston's dad had left us before Win was even born; of my father, and Dar's, nothing was ever said. I went to put the kettle on.

As my mother drank her black tea, I thought about Buzz. He had come back to the road the year before when his mother was dying. I knew him only by sight. Like most of the men around Pennington, he was thin and weathered from outdoor work, and he wore the local uniform: Levi's, a pearl-snapped gingham shirt, a denim jacket, and scuffed western boots. But Buzz's clothes fit him badly, as if he'd bought them for a larger image of himself. His pants were held on his thin flanks by an old leather belt caught in front with a trophy buckle. His hair was sandy under the Stetson; I'd seen him once or twice without the hat, bent over in his garden on the other side of the Swiss's house. His eyes were hazel, like mine, but duller, as if a light was going out; his skin was like ivory wallpaper. He must have been close to my mother's age. Could they have gone to school together, this old young man and my mother?

Mrs. Swiss, on one of her news-passing Sunday visits, claimed that Buzz and his mother were hillbillies. By this she meant drifters, dull-witted outsiders whose good faith was not to be trusted. My grandfather scoffed at her, saying that the Richardsons had lived on Hoecake Row most of his life. "Your own folks, Martha, came from back east, didn't they? And not the richest part neither, as I recall."

I sat at the library table the following week, the paper piano abandoned, imagining myself there until spring.

Years before, my grandfather had purchased the original Hoelk property. The old farmhouse had burnt down, but the barn still stood and the well was sweet. Our house—an angular relic known as the Rackam place—was moved from the other side of the county and set down on the old foundation. The trees and shrubs old Mr. Hoelk had planted wrapped the Rackam house like a mother welcoming a lost child; the German left us a legacy of red and black currant bushes, lilacs, gooseberries, three colours of iris, day lilies, great clumps of rhubarb, raspberry canes, and a small patch of asparagus. The ground around the house was richer than most on the row—the gift of chickens and pigs long since dead. Only Buzz Richardson boasted a better garden. Mrs. Swiss said it was because the man did nothing but scrabble in the dirt all day. She was quieter when the harvest from his half-acre was distributed up and down the row.

I believed I could remember the day the house was moved. From my seat at the library table, I watched the farms and fields float past as the house and I were pulled slowly, carefully up Cabbage Hill, past McKenzie Reservoir, along Split Creek where cutthroat trout stared stupidly up at us from the gorge. Temporarily stripped of its porches, the lanky house dipped and curtseyed on the flatbed, signalling goodbye—to the Rackam fields, to the foothills that had filled its windows all these years, to its siblings along the road. Gravel squeezed out from beneath the wheels. My mother insisted I could not remember this event. "It happened long before you were born. It's just a dream."

The fantasy lingered as I watched Buzz Richardson turn off Hoecake Row onto the grass. He waved through the glass at me, hollering, "Hi, kid." He was carrying a grey suitcase, and I wondered if he was leaving town, but he thrust the case up at me almost before I could get the window open. "Here, stop daydreamin' and have a look at this." My face must have betrayed my bewilderment. "Don't worry. It won't bite you." I heard a faint jingle in the box as I lowered it onto the table. "I'd better get on now. Tell me what you think about it tomorrow." His hand chopped an abrupt goodbye; my attention was on the case.

I carried the box into my room and unhooked the silver clips. The hinges creaked as I pushed open the lid to reveal, nestled in red velveteen, an instrument strung on the front like a guitar. Thirty-six graduated filaments flared from the widest part of the base and were caught by silver pegs at the narrow end. Ten wooden bars, marked with symbols and musical chords, intersected the strings, a button topping each one. Just underneath the strings, lettered in gold: "Autoharp."

I ran my finger lightly across the strings. The sour sound echoed sweetly back to me. I tested the weight of the harp, lifted the pegged board, and discovered a small, frayed notebook. The name Richardson was printed on it, and in a scrawled hand, "How to Play the Harp." The waxy wood smelled of moss and roses, and I knew what I would say to Buzz. I closed the case and slid it under the bed, praying Darlene wouldn't pick that night to lose a shoe. I took the notebook to the library table until my mother came home.

The next afternoon, I waited for Buzz on the porch, the notebook clasped in my hand. In my eagerness, I almost ran to him.

"Well, I guess you're going to be a harp player."

"I haven't tried it yet," I blurted. "Can I hear you play it? How do you hold your hands?" I felt my face flush. The afternoon seemed too short a time to ask him all I wanted to know.

I retrieved the harp and we settled down on the back porch. He hoisted the autoharp into his arms, cradling it against his left shoulder like a child. He slid his fingers into metal picks—the jingle I had heard when he'd given me the instrument—adjusted the harp, and began to play. The fingers of his left hand pressed the buttons as his right hand played a guitar rhythm, then strummed across the strings. Buzz's thin face softened, his sunken cheeks seemed to fill out. I forgot to notice the bony prominence of his knuckles and wrists. He played melodies I hadn't heard before, mountain music, humming along, singing a line or two. Then he lifted the harp off his shoulder and passed it to me.

I took it up, all fingers and elbows, trying to play as he had done. My fingers weren't strong enough to hold the chord bars down, but through the mangled notes, I could feel the cadence building up in my right hand.

It seemed so natural, so magical, I lost myself in it. When I looked up again, he was rising from the rocking chair, a little unsteadily.

"I'll be around again soon. Read the book. Sing the songs out loud. Keep at it, kid. I think you're a genius."

I practised every day, rushing home from school, singing the songs in my head before I went to sleep, dreaming to the rhythms. From the notebook, I learned "Red River Valley" and "Wildwood Flower" and "Bury Me Beneath the Willow." About once a week, Buzz came to the back porch. He would listen to me play, smiling when I had worked something out, correcting my hands if they strayed onto the wrong bars. Sometimes, he motioned for the harp, and I passed it over to him.

"Here's one I learned when I was about your age," he might say. Then he strummed, playing songs that weren't in the book.

Sometimes we talked about the broncs he had ridden on the rodeo circuit before he came back to the row.

"I got pretty busted up winning this buckle," he laughed. "The doggies and mounts kept getting younger and faster. Only thing wasn't getting better was me." Buzz looked down at his pale hands and lifted his legs, revealing how thin he had become during our weeks on the porch. He seemed almost transparent; I thought it was the winter light.

"Riding must be your special talent, huh, Buzz?"

"Might have been. Can't say right now. When you're young, seems like everything might be special for you. All you'd have to do is turn your attention to it and it would be yours. When you get older, you know it's the work that counts. In those days, the only thing that made me get out of bed was following rodeos around, waiting for the next draw, winning the prize money, driving on to the next town. Out in the arena, coming out of the chute on some mean-eyed bronc, smelling the dirt and manure, the crowd cheering like mad, I felt there was nothing in the world more important than me, that horse, that afternoon." As he spoke, his gnarled hands seemed to hold the reins of a bronc, and his heels rose up in a spurring motion.

"You going out again, Buzz?" I thought how I would miss these sessions, and wondered if he would be taking the harp.

"Nope. Don't think so. Think I'll just hang around here. Nice and slow, waitin' for the garden to grow." He reached down, picked up the notebook, and leafed through it. "Don't think I'll win the big ones now, anyway. This place reminds me that I did something right, even if it didn't start out that way."

It occurred to me on one of those long afternoons that I could tell my mother about the music, about the harp and Buzz. The harp was real, not like the paper piano. Once I had told her, I could play for her. She would see it wasn't just false hope. I was conscious that my hesitation had to do with the way Buzz's name wasn't mentioned around our house, though he was a neighbour of ours. Trying to penetrate the mystery, I quizzed my grandfather.

"Do you think Buzz ... Mr. Richardson, is a real rodeo star?" I kept my voice casual, and shuffled the cards vigorously.

He looked straight into my eyes. "People say there was none better. Only saw him ride once myself. Had the most beautiful calf-roping horse. Trained him himself, right here in the back of his ma's property, ridin' around in a split-rail ring. Sat bareback. By summer's end, he was brown as an Indian. Saw him ride the broncs, too. That horse could have bucked from noon to sundown before Buzz let go. Had a gift."

"Who's that you're talking about?" My mother had come to call me to bed. "What are you filling her head with now?" Her voice was edgy, tight. Neither my grandfather nor I answered, and her mouth stiffened, the tired lines registering her impatience.

"Just talkin' about a friend of mine. No harm done, Jo. We're finished here anyway. She's cleaned me out. You get on to bed now, short-stuff."

My mother stood silently until I left the room, then began to question my grandfather. I strained to hear, but the angry words were lost in the high-ceilinged house.

My reticence about the music lessons was vindicated soon after. Usually, I avoided Martha Swiss's visits, and fled to the sunporch when I saw her cross the field between our houses, carefully holding her Sunday maroon dress away from the damp weeds, her heavy brown shoes trampling the foxtail before her. All my life, she seemed to be waiting for me to slip up, to commit some offence worth repeating. My mother tolerated her visits, as far as I could see, from a sense of neighbourly duty. My grandfather nearly always found something to do in the barn.

"I've heard music ... hillbilly ... coming from the back stoop ... thought you'd want to know."

My mother called me into the room. Our neighbour patted the couch beside her. I crossed to the table and stood near the window.

"Has someone been coming by afternoons?" My mother twisted an embroidered handkerchief through her fingers. "Martha ... Mrs. Swiss, tells me she's been hearing music down here after school."

"Not that I can think of. Just the regulars. The egg man. Sometimes a pedlar." My palms warmed, and I felt my face redden. I gazed out the window, imagining myself and the house floating down the road, wanting my grandfather.

"I could have sworn I saw Buzz Richardson come out from 'round your stoop in his big hat. You sayin' he didn't?" Mrs. Swiss's voice challenged me, but I kept my eyes on the road.

"Not that I know of, ma'am." I noticed my mother relax into her chair. "Is something wrong?"

"Oh, no." The woman straightened her hat, dismissing me with a grown-up gesture. "I wouldn't want there to be no trouble, that's all," she said to my mother. "Can't see what reason that man has for stayin' on now his ma is gone. Sets his radio out in the garden at night. Says it's to keep the coons away from the tomatoes, but I know he wants to keep me awake. Better for him if he had stayed away. If a man's got to sow some oats, the piper should be paid."

My mother rose and smoothed her dress, fastening her apron tightly around her waist. Mrs. Swiss followed her into the kitchen, changing the subject, trying to stay on a little longer. They left me behind, forgetting my questions, as if they had been talking about something quite different.

At bedtime, my mother came to my room. It seemed like months since we had seen each other. She looked tired and her shoulders sagged as she settled on the edge of the bed. Her hands were gentle as she tugged the quilt up around my chin.

"You're not doing anything bad, are you?" She stroked the creases on my brow, as she did her own when she had headaches. The worriers, my grandfather called us.

"No, ma'am," I answered, hoping this would end it. I wanted not to lie any more. I wanted my mother to come sit on my bed every night and praise my maturity. That would be enough.

"There's nothing to be afraid of then. Mrs. Swiss thought she was helping, that's all." She rested her hand on my cheek and looked across the room. "Sometimes people are disappointed in life ..." She straightened the quilt again, running her finger along the appliquéd patchwork, then brushed my hair back. "Shall we leave it at that?"

Without waiting for an answer, she rose and turned the covers away from Darlene's face, revealing my sister's alert, curious expression. "Goodnight, you two."

Buzz didn't come to the porch any more. I missed his advice. I went on playing alone on the veranda, my fingers stiff in the winter air, keeping my circulation going by the motion of my arms and the rhythm of my feet. Only the rain interfered with my sessions, blowing horizontally under the gingerbread, drenching me, dampening the harp.

It was the finest winter of my life.

I decided to enter the spring talent show when I learned what the prizes were to be: two tickets to dinner at the Temple Hotel. I imagined my mother and me setting out, just the two of us, for supper in Pennington. I would be wearing my organdie Easter dress; she would have on the gabardine suit she saved for Christmas. We would ride to town in a taxi. I envisioned her face bending down to mine, the look of pleasure in her eyes as she thought about my talent.

I went to see Buzz, to ask him to help me choose something for the show. A scarecrow, clothes sodden and hat askew, stood guard over a few cabbages and leeks in his yard. The rest of the garden was blanketed with hay. He came to the door in jeans and a flannel pyjama top. I was shocked. I hadn't seen him in several weeks. His hat was cocked at the familiar angle, but his bleached skin was stretched tight over his face, and his limbs seemed barely strung together. His belt had been notched and adjusted again. It made me mad that no one had told me he was ill. The news must have been up and down the row.

"Hi, kiddo. What brings you here?" He leaned against the jamb, his breathing laboured as if even opening the door had been an effort. But his voice was strong and cheerful, and though he didn't move to let me in, he placed his hand against the screen, just where mine was. I felt his fever through the mesh. The smell of sickness hung inside the room and I was scared.

"What's wrong, Buzz?" I felt uncomfortable, and thought I must have been mad to think that the harp and my search for talent had been on his mind at all.

"Just a little hitch in my git-along. Come spring, when I can get back to my gardening, I'll put some meat on these bones." He drew his hand away from the screen. "How's the harp coming along? Get to the end of the book yet?" His face relaxed, his voice grew brighter, but I could see him slump as he tried to stand up straight for me.

"Going along fine, Buzz. I came to ask you to help me choose a song for the talent show." Then, hesitantly, "Maybe you don't feel like it right now ... maybe another day."

"No, no ..." He was smiling, knowing what I would do. "Think I'll have to hear you play first, though."

I raced home, yanked the case from beneath the bed, and ran back to his porch. He had pulled a folding chair up to the screen door and draped a blanket across his knees. As I took out my picks, he cracked the door and reached for the notebook.

"Let's see that old thing." He bent down a corner of a page without looking at any other, and handed the book back. A melody I knew by heart, one of my favourites. "That's the one for the contest. That's the one that'll really show off your talent." I began to play, concentrating on the harp so Buzz could see how far I'd come. When next I looked up, his head was bowed on his chest, hat crooked, his eyes closed. Most of his hair had fallen out. I stopped playing, and Buzz sat up, rearranging the Stetson.

"You do have a talent," he said. "Only a few own it. Sometimes it's music, sometimes something else—painting or talking. Brings people closer, reminds them they're a part of everyone else." The chill afternoon air had made him pull the blanket higher on his chest until he was swathed like an invalid. "Sure wish my ma could have heard you play that old harp. She loved it, you know. Said it reminded her of countries she'd never been to, foreign languages. She'd have liked it better if I had had a real calling for it, like you, instead of taking up with the rodeo. Your mother ..." He seemed confused, and drew the blanket closer around himself. "I think your mother will like it. Know your grandfather does."

He stood up, draping the cover around his shoulders. "Guess I'd better get some sleep now. Fresh air really tuckers me."

I smiled up at him as he folded his chair, then I knelt down to put the harp back in the box. "Must be some wild broncs you're riding in your dreams, Buzz."

"Yeah, I always stay on them, too." He was looking beyond me, down Hoecake Row. "In dreams, I always do the right thing."

I walked down the road, hurting all over.

I remember almost nothing of the week before the talent show, except that in my mind, even when the harp was not in my arms, I played over and over the song Buzz had chosen. I recalled the advice he had given me, "Bow your head at the end. Let the sound wash over you. You'll remember that long after the roast beef dinner you're planning has been forgotten."

The day of the contest, I smuggled the harp to school in a gunny sack. When my turn came that night, I carried the harp into the spotlight, placed it on the floor, and brought a stool to the centre of the stage. The smell of the waxed boards dizzied me, and I felt slightly nauseated, as if I were adrift in a small boat. I embraced the harp, clinging to those afternoons on the porch, and laid my chin on the maple bevel, praying I would remember the song. I didn't stand a chance against Sarah Calder, who had played the piano beautifully, or Steve Jenkins, who had cracked everyone up telling jokes, hand in his pocket like Jack Benny. Even Martha Atkins, prancing around the stage in a deer costume, was no bigger fool than I would be when my voice broke and the chords tangled. I didn't dare look up. I knew my mother and my grandfather were out there; I didn't want to face her disapproval of the harp. Not yet.

I arranged my skirt around my knees and said the words I'd rehearsed: "Ladies and gentlemen, tonight I'd like to sing for your pleasure, 'The Storms Are on the Ocean.'" I didn't try to sing at first. I just clutched the harp, changing chords, moving my fingers up and down the registers as I'd done all winter. I thought about the road back and forth to school and what Buzz had given me. The brilliant sounds flew over the audience like starlings.

When I started to sing, the drawl that belonged to the words came, too. First verse, then the chorus, the pure country notes Buzz had written in his book.

> I'm goin' to leave you love,
> I'm goin' for a while.
> Oh, who will shoe your pretty little foot?
> Oh, who will glove your hand?
> And who will kiss your rosy cheeks,
> When I'm in a far-off land?

I sang the second verse, then the chorus again. When I got to the musical break, I relaxed. I knew I could do it. My picks flew over the strings, I swayed with the song, my whole body moving to a rhythm somewhere far away, outside the spotlight and the auditorium. My foot beat time. I remembered Buzz saying, "Don't forget to step the time. It's your best friend, that beat. It'll take you there and back. That's what Mother Maybelle, best harp player in the world, would tell you."

At the end of the break, I lifted my head and peered out into the dim rows. Even if I didn't win, I wanted my mother to see how I felt about my talent. I spotted my grandfather in the fourth row, weathered cheeks gleaming in the reflected spotlight. Then my mother, her pale, tired face hovering above the dark mass of coats and kids and folding chairs.

In the instant before I began the final verse, I saw my mother before me, and in a moment so charged it arced the air between us, I realized what I was doing. The page Buzz had turned down: this was a love song; I was the messenger. My mother, Buzz, and I were part of something I would never understand. All I could do was sing, as I'd been taught, and play the harp.

> Oh, have you seen those mournful doves
> That fly from pine to pine?
> A-mournin' for their own true loves
> Just like I mourn for mine?

The storms are on the ocean,
The heavens may cease to be.
The world may lose its motion,
If I prove false to thee.

The grade six teacher pressed the dinner passes into my hand, but my mind was still on Buzz and I hardly noticed them. Backstage, my mother took the harp from my hand, where it had grown heavy. "Soon the porch won't be big enough to hold you. Nor all of Hoecake Row." As I clambered into the back of the truck, she lifted the case up, then climbed in beside me. We held the harp between us.

When we turned down Hoecake Row, the moon hung just over the switch line, illuminating the ocean of wheat and melons. Here and there in the ditches, I saw the eyes of jackrabbits waiting to lunge into the road, playing an old game of chance. I thought I heard my mother humming, but the sound was caught and carried back to town before I could stop it. The truck slowed on the dark road. We turned to look at Buzz Richardson's house.

THREE POEMS
FOR VIOLIN

BARBARA Nickel

PRACTICE

At five each day I watch sun ignite
air-dust in this corner to a swarm
of gnats the metronome's steel finger swats,
while giant flowered armchairs stalk the room.
My violin is a skinny girl.
I tap the measured belly, ribs, neck;
strings pulley me, cross-eyed, beyond the scroll.
Father shrugs his paper. Mother cooks.
My scales pinch the winter afternoon and slide
off-key, whine like children lost at fairs.
Mistake. I want to break cracker-thin wood
and see it burn, limbs turning blue in fire.
Instead I watch the dust gnats glint
and pick the hardened sore beneath my chin.

COMPETITION

I'm next. Fright spurts through me, threading
a way pricked by stares. The bow scuttles
across the strings. Music is a bead
inside my chest—it rises to my skull,
says, *Let me out*. I only feel a shaking,
new breasts that hurt like pinpoints underneath
the ruffle that my mother sewed. Bouquets
inflame the doors on every side. I breathe
and wait for judgement final as a knot.
You lost, the pencils blurt. I want a voice
unravelling, a spiral from my throat,
a curve unfurling, loose as silken floss.
Outside, the broken step, the smell of thaw;
a crocus like a bruise in muddy snow.

BUSKING

We play near aging cheese and scattered rice,
among the pumpkins, gulls and smell of fish,
breezes, clatter jesting on my face,
the jostles of the crowd and passing swish
of silk unseen. Our lines of music join
the cappuccino screams, juggle above
a pile of ripe tomatoes; seeds spill down,
and juice and music mash up in a sieve;
Mozart, the people shout. I laugh as doors
open, wind snatching notes and rumpling clothes.
Our cases on the wet and sticky floor,
the clinking coins on velvet, crumpled bills.
Beside my violin, a tiny boy
is moving to the shadow of my joy.

NORTH AND SOUTH

KRISTIN Andrychuk

THIS IS ABOUT NORTH AND SOUTH; a baby in a small house on Lake of the Woods; also a wicked witch, accidents, and secrets.

First, the baby in a small house on Lake of the Woods. (This part is a little like a Harlequin Romance—well, insofar as it contains a love story, but nobody's rich, and there are no jewels, furs, and fancy restaurants.) I, the mother of the baby in the small house, want to move to an abandoned farm with log buildings. I must see myself as a pioneer.

This brings us to North and South. I love The North, the miles of rocks and bush. This isn't surprising as I was raised on stories of the wonderful north. My parents lived in camps they built themselves on lakes outside mining towns and crossed the lake by canoe to get supplies. There was the story of the dog taking off with the baby (my older brother) on the toboggan to challenge an enemy (a dog at the end of the lake). In a later story, while my parents are bathing in the lake, their dog attacks another dog that's approached the sleeping baby in the crevice between the rocks. In the sad, yet somehow romantic story, at least it seemed that way to me, their dog, ill with pneumonia, licks my mother's hands, then pulls himself to his feet (for days too weak to stand), and gives his death howl. Far away, the wolves answer his call. *Life is so much more free in The North,* my parents' mantra.

I remember the corduroy roads, the bump, bump, of the old Ford driving to Rouyn, Quebec. Or have I dreamt this? I'm three when we move south. But I'm sure I remember the smoke from forest fires, the unpainted or tar-paper-covered houses and the solid wall of bush. And it's all beautiful and somehow superior to life in The South.

My parents' lives are neatly divided into North and South. Ten years in northern mining towns before the war, followed by the rest of their lives in Southern Ontario, in the small town where my mother was raised. Where what mattered were proper manners and behaviour. *Don't go downtown in that. What if Mrs. Sherk should see you?* Mrs. Sherk, my mother's foster mother; for me, Ridgeway's wicked witch.

In The North, all winter my mother wore old ski pants or her husband's long underwear. *Those cabins were so cold. But not the damp cold of around here. In March in The North the sun suddenly would get warm, and though there'd be six feet of snow in the bush, we could lie in our underwear on the rocks and get a tan.*

I can't imagine my mother lying anywhere in her underwear, or permitting me to lie in the sun in my underwear. (What if Mrs. Sherk saw me?) But then, as she said, The North is much more free.

Her daughters thought so. After university, both my sister and I headed north. My sister to Red Lake, as far north as the road went. I went north to fall in love, which of course was possible in The North, everything being so much more free there.

Hence, the new baby in the small house on Lake of the Woods. Hence, the young woman wanting to buy the abandoned farm with its log house. The young husband, a northerner, who no doubt would prefer a new split-level, must be so besotted with love as to think, *Well, if that's what she wants.* But not so besotted as not to ask, "But how will we know the house isn't about to collapse?"

"My father will know." (My father's an engineer.) "He can check it out when he comes on Saturday." (He's on a business trip in Northern Manitoba.)

"Okay, make an appointment to see the place. The price is right. Seven thousand dollars."

This brings us to accidents and secrets. My father is killed in a car accident. He falls asleep at the wheel. The secret is, he's been falling asleep at the wheel for years. Drove off the road coming back from Stratford when I was fourteen. It wasn't something the family discussed, though in high school I sometimes went along on business trips, sang to keep him awake, and helped with the driving. Other times, he drove long distances alone. Some secrets can be talked about: who hanged themselves and why, and how the woman, now a grandmother, once danced naked on a picnic table at Crystal Beach. But family secrets are best kept *under your hat*.

Instead of visiting the log house, we fly home for the funeral. Then we return to the small house on Lake of the Woods. I don't want to look at houses to buy. (I want to go home, but I don't tell him this.)

The lake freezes. The bush becomes a looming wall. The ravens attack when I hang out the diapers. Now, I go armed with the broom when I step out the door (which is seldom).

The baby cries and cries. Colic, the doctor says. Grief, I say. At night, I listen to the baby's breathing. Sometimes I'm certain he's stopped breathing. I wake him up and he cries and cries. Sometimes I listen to wolves howling. At least my husband says they're wolves. I doubt any animal could sound like the death cry of someone lost.

When I can't bear to listen to the wolves any longer, I walk back and forth, back and forth, my baby in my arms. I tell him stories of the other place where the forest floor is a brightly coloured carpet each fall and in the spring the trilliums are a mat of green and white. A place that's sometimes green in January and always green in April. Of an old house and a catalpa tree with its fan leaves and hanging branches, a leafy tent with a thousand orchid blooms each spring. Where there are no walls of dark prickly spruce. Catalpa limbs are wide enough to lie on. I tell him of a place where there are no wolves and the only sounds at night are the love songs of frogs and crickets.

The nights the wolves are quiet and the baby sleeps, I curl up against my husband's warm back, and sometimes sleep. But when the baby sleeps in the daytime and my husband's at work, the bush rises up around me and I'm caged. How can my mother's place of sun-warmed rocks be my prison? I want to say, *The North isn't anything like you said it was.* But my mother isn't here to accuse. What's more, for my sister The North is everything Mother claimed.

I'm stuck in a nightmare in which I'm at school, but all the stories are unreadable. There's this new dictionary. The meaning of North has changed from freedom and sunbathing in my underwear, to a cold prison with impenetrable bush walls. The meaning of South has changed from a damp place with a wicked witch to a green under-the-catalpa-tree place. The instruction manuals on how to deal with accidents and secrets are being rewritten.

I'm alone a lot. The baby sleeps most of the day when my husband's at work, and cries most of the night while my husband is sleeping. In the daytime, I spend a lot of time staring out the window at the frozen lake and bush, and think about North and South, a wicked witch, accidents, and secrets. There is no one to talk to. When my husband is home, what can I tell him? As nothing means what it's supposed to mean, what can I say? I think and think, begin to write it all down so I can see the words, and write out their different meanings.

Thirty years later, I'm still writing it down.

JOANNE Leah Gerber

LISTENING
TO THE
ANGELS

WHEN HE COMES BACK AT LAST—
his body simply unstrung and shivering with weakness—his eyes are the clue. Oh, they've always been blue, against all odds and theories of heredity, bluer than Lake Huron on the kindest of days, and brighter, so it isn't the extraordinary colour or even the light in them that tells me. No. It's the misleading absence of light. Stephen's been listening again.

He's listening now, the rattan settee creaking and groaning as he rocks himself. One hand grips his hair as though presenting it to someone for inspection, pale curls snagged like a fleece on his fingers. His other arm wraps his head, stopping both ears. His knees meet his brows. He's a curve, a bow, quivering with oblivious concentration. Within the circle of his bent form, within the silence of his muffled ears, whisper angels exclusive to Stephen. At least, that's what I think.

It's his knees that bother me most, drawn up like that. They hide his face. I want to see even his shuttered eyes, his intent chin, to read something there. Some tiny thing.

Our parents don't believe there's anything to be read. As always, Mother has fled the room, espadrilles flapping. Her exit was followed almost at once by the squeal and clatter of the drawer under the oven, where the pans are kept. She needs to bake. I can picture her out there, in her gingham apron, puzzling, running through the list of what's already on hand, what we could do with. She's stingy with goodies, preferring to serve up a pair of ginger cookies which have lost their snap, than to extravagantly give us three fresh at one sitting.

Wait, she's calling me.

"Ireeene, honey! What was that pie your father was asking about last night? Peach? Coconut cream?" A panicky edge to her voice. He does that to her.

"Lemon chiffon." She'll fuss and fret over the meringue, trying to get it perfect, even on an afternoon like this. First week of September, wilting weather; until the breeze quickens off the lake, I've abandoned my packing.

Packing—I fret over Stephen. Who will sit here with him when I'm back at Carleton? Who will make conversation—*milk* it out of thin air—at the dinner table? Mother and Father don't speak much to each other. To Stephen, either. Mother saves her comments for her wheezy Electrolux, for the cantankerous washing machine, for Alex Trebek on the television, and for me, when I'm here, because she thinks I need to master domestic dialect, being female. (She's wrong. I will never, never. Never. I will elope with a boyfriend and plant aspen on the Kamchatka Peninsula first. I will pitch a nylon dome tent on the blistering slopes of K-2. I will barter for goat's cheese and black bread with elaborate pantomimes in a Turkish bazaar. Anything.) But what about Stephen? He may suffocate, wither, become a mute, alone with the two of them in this house.

Technically, the angels are only conjecture. My own. I invented them in sixth grade, when one of my classmates came across Stephen in action. A cover story, created on the spot, without a moment's thought, launched into the shocked silence like a comet. But in its wake, seeing my little brother through my friend's awestruck eyes, I started to think that maybe I'd had a brush with Mystery. Ten years later, I'm a true believer. Though Mother is forever warning me that my overactive imagination will be my downfall. That, and my saying whatever comes into my head.

Stephen has never said a word about what's in his head when he leaves us like this. Everyone else assumes he's in limbo: unconscious, lights out, lost. But no. Definitely, no. It's to presence, not absence, that he relinquishes himself, his interest in the outer world suspended absolutely. You only have to watch him.

His body moves, there's a current in his limbs, you can feel it lift the hair on your arms, if you sit tight beside him. His head stirs ever so slightly as in answer to a delicate cadence. If he isn't trying to hear something, why that arm thrown up around his head, fiercely guarding his ears? He's listening for a voice in his inner ear.

And the squeezed eyelids? A screen that from the inside becomes a window for him. A well-lit window. Does he step through it? I can't say. But he *sees*.

My brother's eyes afterwards are opaque and sad in the way of clear water inadvertently muddied. He's reluctant to look through them. After whatever he's been seeing, we must present a bleak vista. I want to whisper, sorry. Sorry, Stephen. Because I'm part of the everyday world he has to deal with, a world diminished and diminishing. Diminishing in part because, at eleven years old, my brother doesn't write. He won't write. He could get all of them—a pretty substantial them—off his back with one paragraph. He's never written a paragraph, though. Has yet to produce a sentence. And he's not dyslexic.

Reading is nothing to Stephen, he's prodigious. Since I've been back here this summer, he's borrowed Chekhov, Dostoyevsky and Turgenev, Bulgakov and Zamyatin, and the twenty-odd novels *(Monsignor Quixote, Henderson the Rain King)* I picked up used along Bank Street. When he was just five, he worked his way through one of those children's series that torque reality to teach kids their place in the world. Mother couldn't help quizzing him afterwards about what he'd learned. Stephen told her, "Books are like yoghurt. You have to get through all this stuff that doesn't *taste* good before you get to the fruit at the bottom."

Intrigued, I asked, "What fruit?"

Stephen blinked at me and whispered, "Cantaloupe." Melon of any kind nauseates him. "*You* know, Renie—the message."

"Message?" He was a pre-schooler.

"Kids' stuff." He left the room.

School has been a crucible for him; he's hardly die-cast, reading like a wizard but not writing. They can't help speculating, wielding verdicts. "Hand-eye co-ordination," one theory went. (Had they ever seen him draw?) "Compromised linguistic connections." "Highly functioning autism." (Heard him talk?) "Repressed psychological trauma." That last one got my attention. But in a house where everything is *suppressed*, there'd be no trauma to *repress*. Would there?

The truth is, he confounds them. By grade five, they had him inscribing spirals and loops and uncrossed t's for a Hungarian tutor of penmanship who finally threw up his hands in melodramatic despair and consigned the child to a life of mock illiteracy. Officially, Stephen's an unclassified *Special Ed.* (On the school bus, a *Sped*.)

He must hate the label, for its vagueness as much as the stigma. He's dismayed by imprecision. That may be what prompted his conscientious objection to inscription in the first place. Grade one, those blunt ball-and-bat consonants and vowels. The pencils thicker than his thumb. The words themselves—the *at bat fat cat that sat* on a *mat* in a *hat*—between lines a *pat* inch apart. No wonder he resisted. And once he'd taken a stand ... He's stubborn. Implacably stubborn. Always has been.

Still, I say hats off to him. How dextrous does a kid have to be to spend years in directed doodling, in creative ciphering, without one lapse into a recognizable character? Pretty dextrous. He will write when he feels the need. I can just see him nonchalantly penning uncials, upper case and lower case, each letter round and satisfying and perfect. He did serve that time as a calligrapher's (albeit unco-operative) apprentice.

His stand-off is awfully hard on Mother and Father, who hunger for public proof that their boy's not stupid. Stephen recognizes their predicament with small kindnesses. A portion of breaded liver eaten without ketchup. Dandelions, bluebells, and cornflowers with Queen Anne's lace, for the breakfast table, after one of his sunrise rambles. (He wanders off regularly. At sunset too. Like Father when the fancy strikes, there's no keeping him.)

Then, his pictures.

He makes pictures with pastels. Not tawdry sidewalk portraits, enlarged eyes brightened by two starpoint dots of white. And not a child's ball on a stick tree, apple-studded, immobile under a tentacled smiling sun. No. No approximations. What Stephen draws is awesomely observed. He gets it right.

His landscapes are recognizable at once: As Lake Huron in certain weather from a particular gap in the screen of trees across the Bayfield bluff. As the hedgerow with blackberries on the way to the Rasmussens' run-down A-frame. As the spot on the breakwater where we're convinced one of the boulders, metallic and mysteriously scorched, is a meteorite.

Recognizable, that is, as minutely observed *strips* of Lake Huron, or the laneway or breakwater. Tantalizing slices, twelve-by-three-inch *vertical* strips, always. Why Stephen sets himself these boundaries, works within these parameters, I can't say. No one can. He lets me watch him, though. Like yesterday.

"Renie," he said quietly, standing just outside my bedroom door, "I need to work. Coming?"

Work. He's eleven. I was glad to go, though. My room a sweltering warehouse of heaped clothes and so-called essentials for off-campus housing.

"Where's—"

"She's out back," he said gravely. "Getting a zucchini and tomatoes for supper."

"Okay, give me five minutes." I had my hair on top of my head in a plastic banana clip. I'd stripped down to camisole and cut-offs against Mother's indignation. (Is it my freckles or exposed flesh she so objects to?)

Stephen nodded and retreated to wait as I dug for a T-shirt I wouldn't be taking back to school.

Quickly, I packed along something to read. I put almonds and raisins in a Ziploc and towel-wrapped two cans of (Father's) Pepsi. Threw sunscreen into my sisal tote in case Mother caught us. Hurried to join Stephen.

He was crouched out here, on the veranda, watching a pair of ants hoist a crouton. I tossed his Blue Jays cap at him like a Frisbee. "Ready?"

He grinned and ducked. "All set."

With his oversized sketchbook under one arm, and a fluorescent fanny pack full of pastels, he whistled a bit while we hiked to wherever it was he planned to draw. Good, towards the lake. Turning off the gummy road, through the bit of meadow, the woods, and scrub bush before the beach. Our beach, more rugged and breathtaking than the summer people's.

We had it to ourselves. How did he always seem to manage this?

The lake was spectacularly blue. I dropped to unbuckle my sandals. Winced and counted to ten. The sand was a kiln.

"Over here, Renie." Stephen had skipped ahead in his runners. Was halfway to the breakwater that girdled the curve to the point. "You know where we watched the meteor shower that night? Those rocks."

Bone numbing, they'd been. Ankle-wrenching (or jean-drenching) to get to. But the waves at two A.M. like glimmers of mother-of-pearl. The sky like glimpses into a vast Pandora's box, intermittent jewels, gemstones thrown across the velvet haphazardly, trailing stardust. It had been worth creeping away from the house like cat burglars. Worth limping home afterward in damp, wind-stiffened denim. Because Stephen was incandescent. Ecstatic.

"Sure, wherever," I told him, "but give me a second to get wet." I waded out thigh-deep to splash my face and arms, blessed cool, then followed.

Even in full daylight, the rocks were a challenge to negotiate with bare feet. No point arguing, though. Stephen never headed out randomly to sketch, never took my suggestions. He scouted, I guess, on his dawn and dusk rambles.

I stepped carefully into a tepid pool between boulders. Felt for a bit of roughness to give me purchase.

"I'll wait for you to catch up, Renie." His feet swinging over a four-foot granite drop.

We scrambled on together. Next week, I couldn't help thinking, he'd be doing this alone.

When we reached his spot, Stephen climbed up to the inner edge of the rocks, where they met the low bluff well back from the water. Then he sat for the longest time, just looking. Not a fixed gaze, but this horizon to horizon, earth to zenith sweep, dreamily intent. Next, he felt the wiry dune grass. Poked at the nubbled dirt, ran his thumbnail over the ridges of a clam shell. Baptized his hands and lips with sand, both white-hot and damp. He sniffed things, and got me sniffing, too, in spite of myself. A bit of purple crown vetch, the wind full-face from offshore, a licked stone with green indications of the lake bed in its cracked marble surface. (He always does this. What is it he's after?)

Then, propping his sketchbook on his knees, he unzipped his pastel pouch, sighed—and settled down to study the sky and landscape all over again. As though he were about to sketch a Grand Canyon of a scene. But, inevitably, a three-inch slice of what's out there.

I squinted, panned for an invisible seam, a strategic shimmer, even, in the atmosphere. Nothing. I scanned what he'd drawn in grids, casual about glancing from paper to panorama, so as not to alert him. Then I sat asking myself: Do his eyes have a frame I'm not seeing? Is this the most he can take in? Or is he trying to enlighten us about something with these fastidious cross-sections? Offering us an angel's-eye view?

I thought suddenly of the print I'd bought for my dorm room last fall. *Wounded Angel*, Scandinavian, turn of the century. It reminded me somehow of Stephen. Two boys carrying an angel: Young boys, one dressed like a sombre Lutheran pallbearer, black-hatted, plodding eyes-ahead-stoically, old before his time. The other taller, more graceful, a close-cropped blond farmer's or fisherman's son, but troubled, frowning inscrutably out from the tableau. Seated suspended between them on a wooden-poled litter, the wounded angel. Girlish, a few pale field flowers in one hand, her head and body bowed a little despite her radiance. And across her eyes, tied around her corn silk hair, a strip of dazzling cloth, a homemade bandage. One wing seems bent slightly, torn as though she'd snagged it. Beyond the little procession, tundra-coloured flats and water, a listless lake or river.

That enigmatic blindfold, about three inches wide. Stephen's luminous three-inch landscapes. Did he see the painting somewhere when he was small, before he took up pastels? Or was there another, more tangible, connection?

My brother was a boy full of secrets. I knew better than to trespass by asking. Leaving my book in my tote bag, I watched Lake Huron swell to vibrant life under his hands. Wondering when I would have the privilege again.

Nothing but nothing will tempt him to expand his vision. Teachers have tried laying in reams of good-sized manilla paper, Bristol board, even quality watercolour stock with the offer of a matte thrown in. Stephen says no thanks and negotiates access to the paper cutter.

At home, Mother has ventured roundabout remarks with Father or me in attendance. "Oh my, from the back, honey," she'll say to Stephen, "your pictures could almost be taken for flypaper! Who would guess they're so lovely?" (Flypaper—even Father snorted at that.)

"Just look at this little *bit* of the lake, Irene! Imagine if your brother drew the *whole scene!*"

At least she dutifully hangs them from the kitchen ceiling with thread. Like flypaper. (Or like tubular wind chimes, like parchment Haiku.) They rotate, slowly, shivering with the seismic pressure of our footfalls. Poor spick-and-span Mother. Her primrose kitchen's festooned with her son's anomalous impressions of the world, each proportioned like the satin Miss Huron County banner of her glory days, but infinitely more provocative. Earth and sky and water between them, stunningly rendered.

Adjusting his perspective is a dead issue with Stephen. Like the fixative. That was one of my blunders.

It isn't oil pastels he uses, but the other kind. The chalky, crumbling ones, which have a tendency to smudge. We drink a fair bit of tea in our house, and the warning whistle on the kettle isn't what it used to be. Those meticulous, multi-coloured fronds suspended from the ceiling. The surreptitious steam. Mother and Father's inattention. Stephen has suffered losses. So last Christmas morning he unwrapped what I'd thought would be a wonderful gift—a can of fixative.

As he sat dumbly holding it, rigid as a Lego chevalier, I sensed I'd gone over the line somehow. But how? I tried to dredge up enthusiasm.

"Stephen," I exclaimed, "you know how much we love your pictures. This will preserve them!"

Nothing. He set the can down on the neatly folded reindeer wrapping paper. Tucked his hands into the sleeves of his pyjamas (reindeers, too; Mother takes the festive season seriously).

I nodded at his most recent landscape. I'd hung it on the Christmas tree the night before, anticipating that he'd be eager to try out his present.

"Think of the kitchen, Stephen." Complicit noises from out there, where Mother was whipping up eggnog and waffles to justify waking Father before noon on a Holiday. Now I gestured at the blue and yellow aerosol cylinder. "The man at the store told me this will keep your colours from running even if moisture gets at them. Wouldn't that be great?"

Stephen heard me out, wide-eyed and silent. What was he thinking? Afraid of? I picked a strand of tinsel off his hair, felt him flinch and withdraw a bit.

Trespassing further, I reached for the fixative. "Just watch."

I uncapped and shook it. Then boldly sprayed his work of art where it hung: "Un, deux, trois. Voilà!"

With a flourish, I let him see how natural it still looked—snow still boot-deep against the Wilsons' rusted gate, ochre corn stubble bent under the white weight, sky opaque and placid as Wedgwood.

Still nothing from Stephen.

I demonstrated with my terry cloth cuff how not even rubbing would efface the pastel now. (Maybe it did look a little flat, though, on the paper.)

He cried. Covered his face and cried. Fiercely. His shoulders shaking, his legs pedalling against the floor. Maybe it was because the first gift he'd found under the tree earlier had been a five-year diary from Mother. Maybe it was because the spray smelled like death by ether. Maybe— Mother's guess—he had simply eaten too many Christmas candies before breakfast. He didn't say what upset him. Wouldn't say. Ever. Though I asked and asked him.

The can sat on his desk, unused, with the diary, for the rest of my Christmas break. It was still there when I got back in April. Victoria Day weekend, though, just in from a morning walkabout, Stephen announced that he had permanently—and conscientiously—disposed of the aerosol. Mother's hapless gift, more volatile even than fixative, evaporated about the same time.

He's long since absolved me. At least, he's never mentioned my mistake again. Nor have I. Even when a picture's been marred or rippled.

Well, this summer we're all suffering from humidity. Up away from the water, the heat can hang like a vapour, barely stirring. It saps you, you go around with your face and feet bloated, feeling pregnant with fever. The fields hum. The ditchwater stinks and disappears. The house smells of mildew. Father gets snappish and sarcastic. Stephen and I, lethargic. But Mother, in a haze, soldiers on.

Like this afternoon. It must be thirty-five in the kitchen, a steamy, sticky thirty-five, but she's got the oven pre-heating and the Osterizer whirling. To keep her mind off Stephen's spells. I think they terrify her.

"Aren't you worn ragged just watching? Where does he find the energy?" she asked guiltily from the doorway as she left me with him. We'd been sipping icy grape juice and trying to catch a breeze out here on the porch. It's all screens.

Where, indeed? He's still off. Head pulled down, quivering, oblivious.

I feel sorry for Mother. Her life hasn't worked out as she'd been led to expect, and she has no faith in Mystery. Here I am going into third-year Russian Literature, a choice unfathomable to her, but one she feels duty-bound to defend in the face of Father's hooting, and here is Stephen. Still inexplicably rocking.

For the longest time, she kept hoping some medical wizard would unravel the enigma of his silences and dispel them. Surely he'd be scribbling his alphabet in short order when his spells stopped. I think she's losing hope now. That pathetic diary.

But to satisfy her, poor Stephen still gets carted off periodically for testing. Over the years, he's been to University Hospital in London, to McMaster in Hamilton, even, after a seventeen-month wait, to Sick Kids in Toronto. They've done CAT scans and echograms, magnetic resonance imaging and electromyography. Monitored him waking, sleeping, talking, walking. Even half-heartedly sketching. Yet after all these years, sheer guesswork.

Because they've never caught him *listening*. Not even once. Which all the more convinces me.

No angel would be compromised like that, apprehended on electrodes or scanners. So of course they abandon Stephen when he's under scrutiny. He's a shell that doesn't whisper when held to the ear. A ship standing by on radio silence. He is unflaggingly present as long as the physicians observe him. No extinguishing himself, no reverberating arc, shuttered eyes and face. Poor doctors. (No summons to the holy mountain, no unseen afterglory. Poor Stephen.)

Last time (this past June) he came back from the hospital contrite, exhausted, and guileless, in clothes that smelled toxic. Still undiagnosed. Mother slumped on arrival, grey and frazzled from sleeping in armchairs, from facing incredulous specialists at yet another failed Mecca. She needed to slip, bathed, into Battenburg sheets for a good sixteen-hour sleep. I promised to take care of things if she did. She was too worn out to argue.

Father, mercurial, headed straight for the bluffs. But not before announcing (as he booted the overnight bags down the hall): "Told us nothing we didn't already know. Do they take us for morons? Does that kid?" He needed to stump, stew, smoke. I knew he'd slam his way back into the house late, to do some serious drinking. Understandable, I guess. Back when, he must have had visions of fishing trips and coaching his son's hockey team. Instead, humiliation and hospitals, extra billing. He gets more embittered and sullen every time he's dragged on one of these pilgrimages. (He often sleeps out here on the settee, homecoming nights, where, if the wind is up, you can hear the pounding of the lake against its moorings.) I checked to be sure the ice trays were full.

Stephen was on his rug dismantling a Lego castle. I closed the draw-bridge gently and sent him for a shower. Headed for the kitchen, tripping over one of the bags Father had unceremoniously left. From the look of things, the ride home had been as much an ordeal as the medical gauntlet. So when Stephen reappeared at last in fresh pyjamas, I fed him homemade French fries and two slabs of carrot cake with praline ice cream. He said, picking at crumbs with his finger, "Do you know they make cream of carrot soup? It's gross. And watermelon Jell-O?"

I made a face. "Sounds awful." I twisted my neck and began to study his delicate slices of life, one at a time, to keep from quizzing him. If he had anything he needed to tell, I'd hear it in due time.

All he said was, a few minutes later, in a small voice, "I think they're really mad at me this time, Renie. They wouldn't even stop to let me use the bathroom. All the way home." He had his head in his hands.

"It's not you, Stephen. It's the doctors."

"Then how come Dad asked Mom to sell tickets next time—ringside seats—" his face was tragic, "then maybe I'd perform."

"He's just blowing off steam." My hands shaking, I grabbed the ketchup. "Better put this in the fridge before I forget. Don't want to give Mother conniptions."

I sat beside Stephen on his bed, reading Tolkien, until he was asleep. Then I retreated to my own room. My own book.

Stephen seems to be slowing a bit now, his fingers loosening. Soon he'll be back, his face and body blearily tentative as on first waking. He'll look at me with these disappointed eyes and this mouth wavering like someone had smudged it.

"Ree-nie?" he'll murmur, and I'll ache. He may let me take his hand, then. Sometimes, he even lays his hot head in my lap. (His hair is dewed—smells sweet and sweaty as a toddler's, is just as fine and fair and tousled.)

We won't speak much. To soothe himself, he'll rock a bit, while the little tremors diminish. Weary as he is, he'll let me touch his cheek. And I'll do it, shyly, to feel his goodness. He has this goodness you can't get at. Sometimes, I think he wraps himself in it, it's that impervious. Other times, I'm impressed with the depth of it, the bottommost part of him, and the uppermost.

"Irene? Everything all right in there?" Mother. She's got the lemon simmering and the pastry shells in. The whole house shimmers with the fragrance and heat of the oven.

"We're fine." We are. Fine without her.

Yet I don't blame Mother for retreating, finding what passes for sanctuary in the mundane, in her baking and bustling. Her son's read more books than she'll ever read, but he's never signed his name to a Mother's Day card. She's had to face all those doctors and teachers. To appease Father. About his silences—what he's seeing, what he's feeling—Stephen's disclosed nothing. She's surrendered her faith in miracles. These things take their toll.

Almost time. When the angels are finished with my brother, he'll be turning shivery and wall-eyed towards me. If he's up to the walk later, if the sunlight is not too belligerent, a long float in the lake should cool him. Cool me, for another stint of packing.

THAT TIME OF MONTH

DEIRDRE Dwyer

It's like watching rain showering
a distance away: gentle,
but somehow ominous;
you don't know how close that rain
will come to you.
It's like whales adding new notes
to their elegies,
the sound of loons laughing
over the sky behind you,
like changing your clothes seven times
and none of them know
the mood you're in.
You don't know yourself.
Like when you're walking to work in the morning,
coming out of the graveyard
you discover the gold-green sunlight
of early September.
Summer's just gone and the leaves can't decide
what colour to turn.

Like walking home from work:
the sky's a mess: one part blue,
one large cloud above the trees
is the colour of the second layer
of wallpaper: a muted brownish grey.
Another cloud the colour of sour milk
has its edges covered in gold leaf
by undistinguished sunlight.

JANICE Kulyk Keefer

VIRGIN AND CHILD WITH SPOON — Gerard David

Home at last, just the two of us.
Let your father say what he likes,
there'll be no more jagged roads, and filthy inns,
and eating on the run for us.
No more haloes either—heavy, they were;
useless against sun or wind. No haloes,
just the fuzz of your baby head, and my veil,
mere breath clouding winter air.

Here we are, having a picnic indoors,
and nobody else is invited.
No donors, no patrons, no voyeur
saints, kneeling, snatching
your attention with their carnival tricks.
I have made things easy, pleasing
for the two of us: a book,
a jug of flowers on the windowsill
—not just lilies and roses, but lilac
to ripple the air. On a clean linen cloth

I've spread good things to eat: a round loaf,
an apple, that milky pudding you like so much—
two spoons for just one bowl.

Everything will be better from now on.
Here you may sit on my lap
naked as you please, my fingers warm
against your drowsy belly.
Soon you'll turn and burrow to my breast,
tugging your fill of heaven.

I haven't asked for heaven. I want
only this: to hold you for a while,
the way you hold your wooden spoon,
something that's yours
entirely, shaped to your hand.

Our window with its simple latch
looks out to a meadow,
a moat, an unimportant tower.
Then distance the colour of lavender,
dead lavender
squeezed of all scent.

My skin is butter and honey. I have loosed my hair;
it falls in small bursts, delicate as milkweed.
If my breasts ran dry, I would let you suck
the blue from my eyes.

Next to the apple on the linen cloth,
a paring knife. Men watch us from the tower.
Grip your spoon for all it's worth, my love,
your smooth, warm, wooden spoon.
We are home at last, eating
from the same bowl.

BERRY-PICKING POEM

JANICE Kulyk Keefer

This is not a poem from a husband to a wife,
a husband watching a wife
picking the fruit which reminds him
of the small, rosy nubs
which make her body
a cloud of juice.

Nor is this a poem from a wife
to a husband who reminds her
of swaggering stalks, or the deliciously
rough-haired leaves of raspberries.

This is a poem about a husband and wife
picking fruit in a field
between bouts of rain.
They are not thinking *sex*
but *sorbet.* The raspberries
are succulent: miniature pantheons
hung with small, yellow-spotted beetles.

All the way home, raspberry bushes
thrust out arms laden as Christmas trees,
but they walk right past, this husband and wife.
Only at the very end of the lane,
where thickets give way to back yards
do they stop

to fill each other's mouths with lush,
empurpled metaphors
for what isn't happening
at least, in this poem.

INDIAN
COOKERY

VEN Begamudré

Let the madness in. —RUSSELL HOBAN to CAROL SHIELDS

WHILE THE WORLD TURNS from west to east, from breakfast to lunch or dinner, let us consider how connected we are. Take Ramdas Gandhi (no relation to Indira or Rajiv). Ramdas lives in Oban, a town on the west coast of Scotland. Spring, summer, and fall, he dispenses medicines and advice to tourists, who often book passage on the *MV Columbia*. The vessel ferries them to the Isle of Mull, then a bus shuttles them across Mull to another, smaller dock. Here they wait for a motor launch that takes them, a dozen at a time, over to Iona. Ah, Iona, they wonder; how could we resist your call? They glance at the abbey, then photograph the Celtic crosses in the graveyard. Here they remark on the ages of the dead, most of whom succumbed in infancy or extreme old age. You'd have to be tough to live in such a place, the tourists agree, and sigh over what hardy people the Scots are. Sometimes, wandering into Gandhi Chemist's in search of cough drops or nasal spray, the few people who haven't made the crossing ask Ramdas whether Iona lives up to its billing. They look surprised when he admits he has never been there.

Just now, however, he's not in his pharmacy. It's late Sunday afternoon and he's making his evening meal. The main course will be spicy baked chicken, also known as *masaledar murghi*, accompanied by *tahiri*, a.k.a. rice with peas. The chicken needs to marinade for at least three hours (when he makes it on a weeknight, he skips this part).

The recipe serves six. Because Ramdas lives alone, he cuts it by two-thirds and the leftovers are enough for one more meal, usually lunch. Julie, his assistant, says he makes the best chicken salad this side of Loch Awe. Not that she takes a bite out of his sandwich. Heavens no. For one thing, she's married; for another, she's fifteen years younger than him. He cuts off a corner and she chews with a satisfied "Mmm!" Just once he would like to pop the offering into her mouth (and watch those peach-gloss lips close around his brown fingers), but it wouldn't stop here. Not that she would balk at having an affair with him, but Oban's too small a place to countenance pharmaceutical hanky-panky. Ramdas puts Julie out of his mind. For now.

To grind the spices, he uses a mortar and pestle identical to those in his pharmacy, only these have never come in contact with tablets or powders. The fact never reassured his former wife, and his skill in the kitchen became one more irritant she brought up during their divorce. Not in court, mind you. It would have made both of them sound ridiculous. Ramdas hopes she's happy now, snorting up the nightlife of Soho. She's an advertising executive, and her clients prefer the ethnic eateries of Soho to the roast beeferies of Westminster. Yes, he hopes she is happy. Ramdas isn't, but he is content. He supposes that's all a man can hope for at his age.

But back to the chicken. A third of the recipe calls for five hundred grams, just over one pound. First, he grinds a teaspoon of cumin seeds. Then, he measures and adds the remaining spices. The secret to Indian cooking, as he learned long ago, is to do things in a certain order. He would never pour tomato purée into a skillet, for instance, without browning the onions first. But just as one road to happiness lies in knowing when to break the rules, so the secret to Indian cooking is knowing the shortcuts. This is why he puts any spices that need grinding into the mortar first. For the chicken, he needs to grind only the cumin, so it's not much of a shortcut, but he likes to think he knows how to break the rules. Next, he adds a teaspoon of paprika followed by half a teaspoon each of cayenne pepper, salt, and black pepper. This last he grinds in a Perspex mill from a Scandinavian kitchen store. Then comes a teaspoon of turmeric, which he buys ground at McTavish Herb and Spice.

Now for the tricky part. He peels a clove of garlic, slices off the fibrous end, and places the clove in the mortar. If he's had a bad day at work, he pounds down with the pestle, which sends turmeric up into his nostrils. But today is Sunday, so he cradles the curve of the pestle in the curve of the clove and presses. Ever so gently. He's a gentle man at heart, and Julie likes gentle men. She also likes men who stay home, which her husband can't. He's a lighthouse outfitter for the Inner Hebrides. Three months out of four, he delivers supplies while Julie raises their children. But she never complains and Ramdas thinks he knows why: she doesn't want to give him false hopes. Besides, she's more than content; she is happy. The clove pops open, exposing its greenish flesh, which he carefully pulps. Then comes the juice. Lemon juice.

When he was married, he used bottled juice because he was always in a hurry. Now, he squeezes the lemons himself. A third of the recipe calls for two tablespoons, but this is too much because he won't be baking the chicken. Not at gas mark six, or four hundred Fahrenheit, or two hundred Celsius for forty-five minutes (turn over half-way and baste three to four times). He will use a microwave oven, and he long ago learned to reduce the amount of liquid. Julie says he could make a killing if he wrote an Indian cookbook, all the recipes converted for microwave, but Ramdas wags his head at this. He knows she thinks he doesn't have enough ambition (another thing his wife held against him—imagine settling for Oban when London beckoned), but he also knows Julie would disapprove if he developed an enterprising bent. He could never disappoint her, neither by making an advance nor by lusting after money. No, he could never disappoint his Julie, she of the peach-gloss lips and light brown hair. Ah, Julie. How can a man resist?

After stirring the marinade, Ramdas smears the gritty paste over the chicken. It's boneless breast. The pinkish grey flesh turns a deep yellow red. Before reaching for the plastic wrap, he licks his fingers, washes his hands, and dries them. He lays a length of wrap on the chicken, smooths the wrap over the edges of the platter, and puts it in the fridge. Before cooking the chicken, he will pull up one corner of the wrap and fold it back to make a vent.

When he first got the microwave, he would cook the chicken on high for five minutes, check it, and give it another three. Now that he's perfected the conversion from dry heat, the chicken takes exactly seven minutes on high. He could render the drippings into a sauce, but he doesn't bother. The chicken is juicy enough on its own.

And there we are. In two and one-half hours, Ramdas will start the rice with peas on the stove. Half an hour later, he'll settle in front of his television for the film on Channel Four. Out in the lamplit streets, tourists who've made the journey to Iona will troop into restaurants for their evening meal. The younger tourists will huddle in the warmth of fish and chip shops. Not that they'll order fish and chips. Most will try the deep-fried haggis with a side of neeps. Then the lovers among them will split one of the pineapple fritters for which Oban is renowned.

Ah, pineapple: a fine English word corrupted by Indian weavers of the Raj into *pinaphal* or *minaphal*. This is what such Indians call a certain silk they weave, thanks to its pattern of pineapples. So thinks Jasmin Bose (no relation to Subhas Chandra Bose of the Indian National Army). It's late Sunday morning here in the American city of Moorhead. Hardly a Mecca for tourists—it's in Outstate Minnesota—but Jasmin is comfortable here. She's an etymologist, so it's natural she should think about words while making *anaanaas sabjee* (pineapple curry) for two.

More to the point, Jasmin thinks of writing a popular book on English words of Indian origin. Not that this hasn't been done, but she wants to write the sort that will find acceptance by book clubs yet impress her colleagues with its scholarship. A coup like this would give her a one-way ticket from Moorhead State University to the Ivy League. How this might affect her relationship with her lover, Uma Natarajan, is something Jasmin doesn't want to consider. It's hard not to, because Uma has tenure and would like to stay at MSU. But, as she told Jasmin last night while they tried to read in bed, "Let's burn that bridge when we get there." It's the sort of glib remark Jasmin expects from Uma. Enough, Jasmin thinks. Curry won't make itself.

She lays the pineapple on its side and cuts off the top. The result looks like a cap studded with sharp leaves and she wonders what to do with it.

The cap looks too perfect to relegate to the compost bin. She supposes she could bury the cap in potting soil, but pineapples don't do well in Minnesota. If she had a child, mind you, she could sew the cap into yellow cloth and attach two green ribbons. "Look," the child would say at Hallowe'en. "Guess what I am."

Laughing off the fantasy, Jasmin stands the pineapple on end. She cuts away the skin and adds it to the cap for disposal. She lays the pineapple down again and cuts off the base. The pineapple lies naked on the cutting board. The flesh is still firm from lack of handling, and the juice hasn't yet risen to the surface. Or spread along the walnut and maple.

Uma once asked whether they shouldn't get one of those hard, white plastic boards from the Kitchen Shoppe in Fargo (Moorhead's twin city). Jasmin said she preferred wood. If a plastic board isn't washed properly, there's danger of bacteria growing in the nicks. True, a wooden cutting board has to be washed as conscientiously as a plastic one—though with little soap, then oiled—but wood can do something plastic can't. Wood kills bacteria. "Mother Nature knows best," Jasmin said, to which Uma retorted, "Mother Jasmin knows best." They never speak directly of this, but they both know Uma is the child Jasmin will never have. Sometimes, when Jasmin can't sleep, it occurs to her that, although she's only ten years older than Uma, their relationship is not without its hint of incest. Just enough to tantalize the emotional taste buds.

Fortunately, it's not the sort of thing that would occur to the good people of Moorhead. As Uma calls them. According to her, those who know Jasmin and Uma share more than a house fall into three camps. There are friends who are truly happy for them. There are acquaintances who consider themselves liberal-minded and say they understand. Then there are colleagues who exchange signals with their eyes and excuse the relationship on the grounds that foreign women are entitled to be different. Besides, what business is it of a true Christian? Not that people actually say as much, but even the true Christians Jasmin knows have such open minds she can read them like a book.

Now comes the hardest part. Jasmin puts her long knife aside and reaches for its smaller partner, good for close work. She begins cutting out the eyes. Some days, she cuts them out one at a time, but she wants to get started on her book, so, today, she takes the shortcut. She makes long incisions on either side of the rows of eyes and flicks them out. Once she's finished, diagonal grooves mark the flesh. It's growing softer now. Juice oozes into the grooves before trickling onto the board.

She stands the pineapple up again, reaches for the long knife, and cuts off the flesh in large chunks. She cuts them into strips, then cuts again until a pyramid of golden cubes glistens on the board. Lifting it carefully so the juice can't spill, she slides the cubes onto a platter. She licks her fingers, washes her hands, and dries them. Now for the onion.

One large white onion, though the recipe calls for yellow. This is the dangerous part, because Jasmin slices close to her fingertips. Still, she lets her mind wander—due east, across the Great Lakes into Canada, to the University of Waterloo Centre for the new *Oxford English Dictionary*. Here the historic work (*OED*2 for short) was computerized for its release by Oxford University Press. The very day she heard of the centre, she wrote to ask whether it could provide a list of all the words in *OED*2 that originate in Indian languages. She listed twenty, ranging from Hindi and Tamil to Dogri and Pahari. The reply came post-haste: a forty-four-page printout listing over eight hundred words. "This does not mean," the applications manager wrote, "that in every case the word originates in an Indian language, for it may be a cross-reference. However, since I am also sending you the etymologies, you will be able to figure this out." Now all Jasmin has to do is write her book. But the list has been in her files for over a year and she hasn't written a line. She hasn't bought her ticket out of MSU, let alone checked her *Bradshaw*. She's not even ready to write. Uma teases Jasmin about this, but Jasmin knows Uma hopes Jasmin will never get ready. Uma loves Jasmin, and Jasmin loves Uma, books and tenure be damned.

But back to the curry, which Jasmin will serve with plain basmati rice. Now she concentrates on roasting the spices. The recipe calls for using a thick-bottomed frying pan or even a wok, yet Jasmin uses a Pyrex casserole dish. It's easier to wash than a frying pan or wok and stays cooler on the stove. She pours two tablespoons of vegetable oil into the dish, turns the heat to medium, and plops the clear glass cover on the dish. While waiting, she thinks.

Most laypersons know many English words came to use from India: brahmin, rajah, and, of course, curry. The seventeenth century saw the addition of cheroot, bungalow, and chintz; the eighteenth century brought us jungle, jute, and toddy. Even Jasmin was unprepared for the extent of the printout because she doesn't specialize in Indian words (it would limit her chances for employment), but she knows she's found a gold-mine. Because if she was surprised by some of the words, her readers might be surprised as well. Take bandanna, from the Hindustani *bandhnu*, meaning a "mode of dyeing in which the cloth is tied in different places, to prevent parts from receiving the dye." Most readers would assume bandanna came to us via Spain. In fact, it was likely first adopted by the Portuguese. Or take cash, of all things, from the Tamil *kasu*, "or perhaps some Konkani form of it, name of a small coin or weight of money," from the Sanskrit *karsha*, "a weight of silver or gold equal to one-fourhundredth of a tula." Again, we can thank the Portuguese. And what about catamaran? It's from the Tamil *katta-maram*, *katta* meaning tie and *maram* meaning wood.

The oil is hot now—the glass cover is clouding—so in go the mustard seeds, half a teaspoon. This is the tricky part, so pay attention. (She hears herself saying this to the child she will never have.) Holding the lid onto the dish with one hand, she slides the dish back and forth across the burner to agitate the seeds. They start popping, turning dark, but not all of them. Mustard seeds are known to be difficult. Now comes the second trick: you lift the lid a few inches from the dish. As soon as the unpopped seeds start popping, she covers the dish and again slides it back and forth. She doesn't understand the physics involved, but thinks it has to do with replacing the moist air in the dish with drier air. This superheats the oil and causes the rest of the seeds to pop. When they're all done, in goes the onion.

She stirs with a spoon (a wooden spoon) while her mind returns to the book. Even some of the more common words we've adopted have interesting origins—so she'll tell her readers. Cheroot comes from the French *cheroute*, which came from the Tamil *shuruttu*, meaning roll, and became, in the English of the 1800s, *sharoot*. As for chintz, it's the plural of *chint*, from Hindi, also found as *chite* in French and *chita* in Portuguese but all coming somehow from the Sanskrit *chitra*, meaning variegated. Jasmin shakes her head over the onion, browning nicely now; over how everything fits if you look hard enough. As John Donne might just as well have said, "No word is an island, entire to itself."

It's finally safe to leave the onion, so she grinds one teaspoon of coriander seeds with two whole, dry chillies. She does her grinding with a mortar and pestle from the Kitchen Shoppe in Fargo. The recipe calls for four chillies, but she's not that Indian. She adds the spices to the onion and mustard seed; taps the mortar with the pestle to free those last, stubborn grains of coriander; and stirs. She adds the pineapple and stirs again. The recipe calls for half a teaspoon of salt, but she uses only a quarter teaspoon. The recipe also calls for two tablespoons of honey, but she leaves out the honey without telling Uma, because Uma has a sweet tooth. The secret to happiness, after all, is knowing when to break the rules. As for water, the recipe calls for one pint but Jasmin adds less than half, not quite one cup. The water sizzles in the hot dish.

Once the curry starts bubbling, she turns the heat to simmer. She leaves the cover off so some of the water can evaporate. Now for the rice.

Sometime in the next half hour, Uma will come home. She will slam the door, drop her briefcase, and exclaim, "Something smells good!"

"You're imagining things," Jasmin will call. She'll make a mental note to move the briefcase later.

When Uma enters the kitchen, Jasmin will hold out her arms and Uma will come to her. They'll exchange a brief kiss, a token of a morning spent apart—Jasmin in her kitchen, Uma at her office marking exams—while the good people of Moorhead were seen in church.

Jasmin will break away first because she doesn't want to seem maternal in case Uma asks, "Did you miss me?"

While Jasmin spoons pineapple curry onto rice, she'll say, "Cummerbund, from the Urdu and Persian *kamar-band*, meaning loinband. Dinghy, from the Hindi *dengi* or *dingi*, meaning a small boat, diminutive of *denga* or *donga*, meaning a larger boat, a sloop, a coasting vessel."

If Uma snorts now, Jasmin will stop, but today Uma won't snort. Jasmin will continue with, "Pariah, punch, pyjama. Saffron, sandal, shampoo. Tattoo, teapoy, thug, topi." She will end with, "Veranda, found throughout India in various languages as *varanda* in Hindi and *baranda* in Bengali, but they may simply have adopted it from the Portuguese or Spanish *varanda* or *baranda* meaning railing, balustrade, balcony." She'll turn with her own plate in one hand, Uma's in the other, and conclude: "What's really surprising, though it shouldn't be, is that the Indians adopted as many words from Europeans as the Europeans did from Indians."

Then Uma, who teaches geology (her specialty is tectonics), will recite: "No man is an Island, entire of itself; every man is a piece of the

Continent, a part of the main." But Uma being Uma, she will break the spell by demanding, "How come your plate's bigger?"

So there we are. Clearly it isn't money that makes the world go round. Nor is it love for another human, because this kind of love too often eludes us. No, my friends. Gandhi or Bose, what makes the world go round—what connects us if not into a continent then into an archipelago—is nothing less than our love of Indian food. Then again, perhaps not. And, if not, what is the point of this story if, indeed, it is a story? My dear, dear friends, allow me to tantalize you (one last time) with the following clue:

> *Won't be long now. These so-called writers of colour will start*
> *publishing recipes and call it art.* —ANONYMOUS

RONNA Bloom

BLUE RAFT

My sister's bed a blue raft
dim in streetlight. Cars drive past
carrying their own whispered news.
I've put the kids to sleep.
Snow moves over this family
of households. The Pluto nitelite
comforting the hall.
In my sleep, I hear the ring
of numberless telephones, hear
the hospital and the clocked breathing
of my niece. Tonight
I am the guardian of the ordinary. I wake
before the phone does, knowing her dead.

THE JOB OF
AN APPLE

RONNA Bloom

The job of an apple is to be hard,
to be soft, to be crisp, to be red,
yellow, and green. The job of an apple is to be pie,
to be given to the teacher, to be rotten.
The job of an apple is to be bad
and good, to be peeled, cored, cut,
bitten, and bruised. The job
of an apple is to pose for painters,
roll behind fridges, behind grocery aisles,
to be hidden, wrapped in paper,
stored for months, brought out in the dry heat
of India and eaten like a treasure.
The job of an apple is to be
handed over in orchards, to be wanted
and forbidden. The job of an apple is to be Golden
Delicious, Granny Smith, and crab. The job
of an apple is to be imported, banned, and confiscated
going through customs from Montreal to New York.
The job of an apple is to be round. Grow. Drop.

To go black in the middle when cut. To be thrown
at politicians. To be carried around for days. To change
hands, to change hands, to change hands.
The job of an apple is to be a different poem in the mouth
of every eater. The job of an apple is to be juice.

ICE

MARY Borsky

WHEN THE RUSSIANS SHOT A DOG UP into space, my father celebrated for three days. Later, when he got sober, he took us fishing, me and my brother Amel.

"B.B. Hunt and the other guys, when it's Russian, they think it's something bad," my dad said. He almost had to shout to be heard above the pounding of the tire chains on the winter road. Amel and I sat next to him on the front seat of the dark blue Dodge. I was wearing boys' clothes, the same as Amel, a parka, extra pants, tuque, winter boots.

"But you and me, we like that dog in space, don't we, Daddy?" I shouted back. "We think it's fine, right, Daddy?" Amel and I were drinking root beers. It pleased me to sit with a bottle in my hand and talk of grownup matters to my dad.

"The Russians," my father said, shifting down to go up a hill, "when they want to send a dog in space, do they ask The-Important-B.B.-Hunt, or do they just go ahead and do it?"

I took a moment to drain the last of my root beer. Sometimes, I didn't understand anything my father said—Power of the Proletariat, Science and Progress, the Emancipation of the Working Man. Still, I believed every word he said.

"They just go ahead, Daddy," I said. "They don't ask anybody." Then I checked my father's face, although I was pretty sure I'd answered right.

As we neared the crest of the hill, I could at last see the lake through the grey tops of trees. The ice, mostly blown clear of snow, was grey and flat as a cookie pan, so bright in a strip where the sun reflected, it was impossible to look at. The sky was as blue as the spark from an electric plug.

"Look," I said, pointing to the bay in the distance. "The fishing shacks."

My father watched the road ahead.

Then, to show whose side I was on, I added, "They look like outhouses on the ice."

"Some guys," my father said, "they got to have a shack to keep the wind off. They got to have a chair to sit on. They got to have a piece of paper to tell them what to catch."

He and Amel laughed out loud, and I tried to join in.

I'd heard about those new fishing shacks at school. I'd heard they weren't shacks at all, but almost a home away from home. Gwen Farris put up her hand for News and told us that inside there was a real stove, a little table to sit beside, a window to watch the road, even a calendar on the wall.

I put my hand up, too.

"Teacher," I said, pleased to contribute, "my dad doesn't do the same as every other Joe Blow. My dad catches more fish than anybody. My dad fishes with nets and catches as much as he feels like."

"Now, Irene Lychenko," the teacher said gravely, "is this *News?*" She paused while I tried to remember. "Remember, boys and girls, News is something you didn't already tell us the day before."

Beside me on the front seat of the car, I felt Amel turning and looking.

"Daddy!" he yelled. "It's The-Important-B.B.-Hunt!"

I turned to see a two-tone yellow Buick starting to pull up beside us.

Without moving his head, our dad looked into his side mirror, then stepped harder on the gas. The tire chains hammered faster on the snowy road, then slowly our car pulled ahead again.

"Here's the turn!" Amel called out, and Daddy made a sudden lurching left to the lake, exploded through a small snowdrift, then drove quickly down the trail to the fishing shacks.

I didn't like the look of B.B. Hunt following close behind in the blowing snow. He had a dark, definite look, the look someone following you home from school might have. But it was all right now, because we were with our dad, and it was fun, being first.

As we approached the shacks, I studied them quickly, taking in what I could. I saw brown walls, orange window frames, possibly the flash of green curtains. Our dad aimed the car between the shacks and shot through, chains hammering, right onto the lake.

The car fishtailed, once, then twice.

"Wheeee!" Daddy said, each time he straightened the wheel. "Wheeee!"

We laughed, then a minute later, laughed again.

Suddenly, there was a loud bang, like a gun going off, then smaller cracking noises. I felt the ice shift under us. I sat up straight and grabbed the door handle on my right, and Amel's arm on my left.

"Scared?" our dad laughed.

Amel looked at me and laughed too.

"Why be scared?" our dad said. "You got to use your head! You got to think! We're the same as flies walking across a piece of newspaper!" He took his hands off the steering wheel and criss-crossed his fingers to illustrate. "The Russians," he said, "they're scared of nothing!" And he continued to drive straight out onto the lake as if we were in a high, fast boat.

"That dog, Daddy," I said, "is it a real dog?"

"Real! What you talking about? You betcha it's real!" He pointed his finger through the windshield up towards the bright blue sky. "First, they send up a dog, and next! ... A man!"

Suddenly, he braked, turned off the ignition, got out, and unloaded the trunk.

Outside, in the stinging cold, I looked up where my father had pointed. There was nothing, only a blueness so intense I had to grab on to the car because it felt, for a moment, as though I would fall up into it.

Amel and I watched as our father started to chop a hole in the ice, but it took too long. We began to slide in our boots and to swing each other in circles with a rope from the car.

The ice was hard and clear, with tiny bubbles frozen into it, like the glass of marbles. Here and there the ice was buckled, as if the waves themselves had frozen. In other places, the ice was black and clouded over with white, as frightening to look into as Old Man Coons's bad eye.

When our father finished chopping the hole, the ice was as thick as the length of his arm, the water a black hole.

We watched as he dropped in his net, let it straighten in the current, spiked it to the ice, then walked off fifty yards to chop another hole.

From time to time, there was a rumble, like the sound of distant thunder.

"Listen," our dad yelled from where he was. "The ice!"

Sometimes, the rumble branched away before it reached us. Other times, it passed through the area where we were. I stood very still and listened.

Finally, when the cracking stopped, and I was sure I could hear nothing but the breathing of the wind on the ice, I grabbed Amel's hands and we spun in a circle.

"To Peace! To Progress!" Amel yelled, raising his imaginary glass to me. "To ... to ... porridge!"

I clinked back. "To pancakes!" I screamed, though not as well, because my teeth ached from laughing in the cold and I had to keep my lips pulled over them.

Then our dad pulled his nets out, and loaded the flopping fish into the trunk of the car.

"Fifty-seven!" he grinned, holding a pickerel up to show us.

But Amel and I were cold and went to wait in the car.

The sun had set, leaving a crayon-line of gold along the horizon. The ice was now blue-purple, the sky, violet. The first stars were out. Amel started to cry with cold.

Finally, our dad opened the door. His eyebrows were bushy with frost.

"The satellite!" he said. "Come and look-it!"

Amel wouldn't look. He was crying and kicking under the dash.

"You want to see that dog?" our father asked me. "Come and see that dog!"

I was cold, but I got out. Daddy stood behind me, positioning my head and pointing to something high up.

"There!" he said. "See it?" His hand was dark, and very large against the sky.

I looked. There was only sky, stars, and cold.

"Over my finger! It looks like a star, but it's moving!"

Then I saw it.

It was a regular yellow star, not the dog-shape I'd expected. And the star was moving, very slowly and evenly sideways. I squinted my eyes to see better. It didn't look like anything I'd ever seen before. It looked like a trick. It looked as if the star was being pulled sideways by a long invisible string.

"Where's the *dog*?" I asked, stamping my half-frozen feet. I was almost in tears. My face felt like wood. There were sharp shooting pains in my fingers.

"The dog's inside!" my dad said. "It's in a steel ball! Look! It's so high the sun is shining on it!" He sounded as if he was shivering.

I looked once more at the moving point of light.

"What *colour* of dog?" I demanded.

"Any colour! Colour's all the same!"

I hurried back to the car at the same moment that Amel started to pound on the horn.

Daddy got in behind the wheel, started the motor, switched the heat fan on full, and drove quickly back towards shore.

The car smelled of fish and cold exhaust.

My feet ached even more as they started to thaw out under the heater.

"You think it's *easy* to shoot a dog into space?" our dad asked as he drove. "You think it's something simple?"

I cried to myself and drained the pop bottles for stray drops. Amel whimpered, rocking back and forth over his folded arms.

Out of the dark, the fishing shack loomed up. Outside the shacks, there were two cars now, The-Important-B.B.-Hunt's, and another one. The other car had its headlights on and someone was loading the trunk. Several of the men were standing shoulder to shoulder, arms crossed, beside one of the shacks. Someone's cigarette glowed red in the dark.

Our father drove between the shacks and braked. Our car swung a little to the side. Daddy unrolled his partly frosted window and put his elbow out. He took off his cap, then put it back on.

"Nice night, boys!" he called through the swirling exhaust. "Seen the sky tonight, boys?"

I stopped crying to pay attention to what was happening.

Someone said his name.

"Get a look at that north sky, boys?" our dad asked, grinning.

"Fishing trip, Lychenko?" someone from the line-up said. It was B.B. Hunt.

"Why, sure," Daddy said. "You bet."

"Catch many?" B.B. Hunt asked, still from where he stood.

"One or two. Seen the sky tonight, B.B.?"

"One or two! You gotta be joking!" B.B. yelled. He came up to our window, bringing the smell of whisky and shaving lotion with him. He put his hands on the window ledge.

I looked at The-Important-B.B.-Hunt's Volunteer Fire Brigade crest on one side of his parka, the fuzzy Curling Championship crest on the other. On his pale puffy hand, I saw a gold ring with a square dark stone.

"One or two!" B.B. hollered again, looking back to check that his friends were listening. "Cripes, Lychenko, you're a pitiful excuse for a fisherman! You're a washout! We done better than that over here!"

None of us moved. Then I heard an odd wavery voice that took me a split second to recognize as my own.

"My dad got fifty-seven!"

B.B. Hunt's teeth were as even as if they'd been lined up against a ruler. They shone white even in the dark.

"Nice," B.B. said. "That's nice. A guy tends to get a good catch with a square hook, don't he? Open the trunk and let's have us a look-see, Lychenko."

"Ha-ha," my dad said. "Careful, B.B. … You gonna make me laugh."

"This son-of-a-bitch Communist is through disregardin' the laws of the land!" B.B. hollered. "This is a citizen's arrest and I got witnesses!"

He jerked the car door open, then our dad was on the ice and B.B. Hunt was on top of him.

Everything was happening too fast.

"Break it up, boys, break it up," one of the other men said.

The-Important-B.B.-Hunt was on his back on the ice, his mouth gasping like a pickerel's, a strip of white belly showing, and our dad was getting up, wiping his mouth, looking at his hand. He got into the car, started the stalled motor, and pulled away.

There was a commotion outside, yelling, then pounding on the trunk of the car. My dad rolled up his window and speeded up. Something hard—a bottle or a piece of ice—hit the top of the car, and Daddy speeded up again.

The car moved quickly down the side road, heaved itself up onto the highway, turned right, then sped down the road to town.

"She's not supposed to tell, is she, Daddy?" Amel said, crying. "How come she told?"

Our dad drove fast, sometimes checking in the rearview mirror.

Then, without warning, he skidded to a stop in his tracks. He got out, went to the trunk, and made several trips to the side of the road. I heard branches snap as he threw things into the bush. Then the trunk slammed and he was back, breathing hard, but behind the wheel.

"Will Daddy go to jail?" Amel cried, pulling at my arm. "I don't want Daddy to go to jail."

The sound of the chains pounding against the road roared in my ears. I held myself very still, as if to slow down what was happening.

We cut through the darkness in an almost straight line. I could see no light anywhere, except for our own yellow headlights, no familiar house or fence or sign.

There was the rapid hammering of chains, but the motor of the car itself seemed silent. Our dad was behind the wheel, but it seemed to me that he was not really driving. We were being pulled by some other thing. We were being pulled by the same trickery that had pulled the dog in its steel ball.

I turned to my father to warn him. I wanted to tell him what had happened. Or maybe to tell him I believed the things he said. "Daddy," I wanted to say, "I saw it, the dog, the star, the steel ball."

But in that half-moment before I spoke, I sensed some shift or lurch, some darkness in the air between us.

My father looked different as he hunched low behind the wheel. His face looked rumpled. His cap was gone, and I remembered now seeing the cap lying on the ice. Without it, and in the dark, he looked like someone else. He looked different than my dad.

I didn't say anything. Neither did he. From my place at the window, I watched and waited. White trees appeared from the blackness, flew past, and disappeared again.

Above, there were stars everywhere, in front of us and behind, but there were too many and we were moving too fast to see any one separate from another.

THE AIR WAS THE TEMPERATURE OF SKIN.

They walked in the zocalo, Gregory in cut-offs and short sleeves, Alicia in a woven Guatemalan shift she'd found at a roadside market.

With one hand on her hip, he steered her through the crowds of Mexicans and past the occasional clutch of sunburned tourists—forgetting, for the moment, that she hated being steered.

The waves were sounding on the distant beach.

They had come here for the sun but had switched allegiances after the first day.

Everything in daylight seemed overexposed, like photographs of snow.

They found the true beauty of the place in the warm chiaroscuro of lanternlight, the tantalizing sense of half-glimpsed things.

After sunset, vendors lined the sidewalks of the zocalo, offering silver and lapis lazuli and aquamarine jewellery, batiked cotton dresses, and lustrous black pottery.

The dark-muzzled mongrels that lurked in the daytime streets disappeared at nightfall, perhaps to stalk the *campesinos'* chickens.

It was the next best thing to nakedness, this air.

They turned in at the Hotel Cortez and walked through a stuccoed corridor to a beachfront terrace.

The rush and drag of waves on the muddy sand was louder here, though the water was not visible.

Out on the beach, before the boles of the palm trees, was a row of bamboo torches with pale writhing flames.

Alicia tucked her hair behind each ear.

She had nearly killed Gregory, and herself, two days ago.

But this was nothing like the surfing beach, where it had happened.

Here, the little cove, which ran the length of the zocalo, offered shelter from the deep-sea swells.

They walked past the bar and took a table close to the beach.

She thought she heard voices down there, children playing, laughing like cartoon characters.

The bartender brought red wine in earthenware goblets.

Perhaps these were the same kids they had seen fishing for mackerel from the gunwales of anchored boats, swinging tiny silver hooks above their heads and tossing them out.

The mackerel had moved like swarms of bees, breaking the surface in unison.

One boy had fished by himself from the buttress of volcanic rock that divided the cove from the surfing beach.

Twenty-foot breakers had curled into the rock face and exploded in geysers of spray, and as the water had cascaded down, the boy had scampered onto a jagged promontory and hurled his hook.

One slip on that treacherous surface and he would have been lost.

Alicia was crying again.

"Don't," Gregory said, reaching for her hand.

He had always thought this would be a dangerous place.

He'd read the guidebooks and knew what to expect: malaria, diarrhoea, sunburn, earthquakes.

Alicia had laughed at him, but now she brushed her teeth with bottled water.

The undertow was a danger he hadn't considered.

No matter how far the waves flung themselves onto the shore, the ocean always gathered them back in.

He hadn't seen her cry until recently and didn't know how to react.

The tears were barely visible, trailing down over her cheekbones and underneath her jaw.

"Sorry," she said, trying to laugh.

"You shouldn't be sorry for anything."

She turned to face the beach and inhaled sharply through her nose, then fumbled in her purse for cigarettes.

When Gregory saw that she had no matches, he walked to the bar and asked for some.

In mixed English and Spanish, the bartender tried to tell him about a two-hundred-pound sailfish an *Americano* had caught that afternoon.

"*Non quiendo*," Gregory said, though he had in fact understood.

Along with the matches, the bartender handed him the business card of a friend who would take *turistas* out fishing for only five thousand pesos an hour.

"*Gracias*," Gregory said.

When he handed the matches to Alicia, she avoided his gaze.

They were alone on the terrace, which was not surprising because locals never came to these places, and tourist season was already finished.

The summer rains would be here soon.

She dried her eyes on a tiny pink napkin, then rolled it into a wad, and dropped it in her purse.

According to her mother, her grandfather had died of cigarettes.

Cigarettes are not a disease, Alicia had told her.

The sounds on the beach came again, boys playing tag among the palm trees.

She wanted to have a child, but she hadn't told Gregory because she didn't want to scare him off.

They had only been seeing each other for three months.

She put the cigarettes back in her purse without taking one.

"I like how the people here smoke," she said, "as though they didn't know it was bad for them."

"They have no concept of safety," he said.

She wondered if he thought the same thing about her.

She had talked him into coming here in the first place, had discounted every one of his excuses.

She almost always got what she wanted.

That was what she'd told him the first time they went out, and he had laughed, thinking it was a come-on.

He was not at all like her ex-husband, who would have sat there on the beach drinking tequila while she drowned.

She would have almost preferred that.

Gregory took his sunglasses from his shirt pocket and cleaned them on the edge of the tablecloth.

In the lenses he saw reflections of himself.

The Mexicana DC-10 they had taken from San Francisco to Mexico City had shuddered during take-off, and the engines had wailed like huge saws.

The cars here had no seat-belts, no emission controls.

Every female dog in the place was either pregnant or nursing, the rows of shrivelled black teats swaying under their concave bellies as they loped from one piece of shade to the next.

Alicia touched her tongue against the glazed edge of the goblet.

She was thirty-two.

Gregory was only twenty-seven, and though they both said age didn't matter, she wondered if maybe it did.

Everyone said they made a beautiful couple.

She had almost killed him.

She remembered his hand gripping her wrist, the rip-tide sweeping them out towards a breaker that was lifting above them.

He could have swam back to shore on his own but refused to let go of her.

That was why she'd screamed for help.

She had never imagined herself needing a rescuer, but the screams had come easily, even with salt water in her throat.

Afterwards, she hadn't properly thanked the surfer who saved her, had instead collapsed on her beach blanket, coughing violently and shivering.

Gregory would have kept holding on to her.

Two beautiful young women had walked by, wearing thong bikinis and carrying expensive cameras.

She couldn't remember what the surfer looked like.

Gregory had thanked him for her, but that wasn't the same.

When she had climbed on the surfboard, she had spread her knees across it and paddled weakly with her feet.

The surfer had pushed the board from behind and could have looked right up between her legs.

The beach was quiet now, except for the waves.

The children here always went home at the same time, without being called.

When Alicia was a child and spent summers at Manitou Lake, she used to hide in the bushes near the public beach every warm evening, stealing a few more minutes of the night while her mother called out her name again and again.

Gregory leaned forwards on the table and looked into her empty goblet.

"Another?" he said.

"Please."

He waved to the bartender, who was leaning against the cash register, eyeing Alicia, like they all did.

"*Dos otros, por favor*," Gregory said.

Of course, he had eyed her himself when he first saw her.

It was at the welcoming reception for the new minister of justice, whom Gregory had supported in the election.

She was standing with her husband in the foyer of the minister's office, talking to a policy analyst.

She had a slender neck and large grey dissipated eyes, though she spoke with quick authority like all the other lawyers.

The husband stood sullenly beside her, staring into his glass of rye and water.

Gregory thought: this is the kind of man who could be violent.

After the separation, Alicia never once mentioned his name, as if she was afraid of invoking him.

She looked at Gregory now, over the rim of her goblet.

"What are you thinking?" she said.

"I don't know. That we're still here."

"A miracle, is it? We've survived four days."

He took a short breath and exhaled through his teeth, a washing sound.

"Time is going slower than I thought."

She had a crack in her lower lip from sunburn or salt water, and the wine had seeped in, so it looked like she was bleeding.

He would rather taste his own blood than salt water.

He had gone into the ocean before her, diving beneath the cresting breakers and drifting out with the backflow.

The water was as warm as the air.

It was surprisingly shallow for a long way out.

They had watched the surfers slide down those glistening walls all morning.

Some of the Mexican children were playing in the surf, running just ahead of the upwashing waves.

When he turned back towards shore, he felt the undertow dragging him farther away.

It quickened to the strength of gravity.

Then the next breaker extinguished it, tumbling him shoreward.

He recovered in time to body-surf on the next wave, windmilling his arms to stay on top of the water as long as possible.

The salt made his tongue swell up like a blowfish.

He rode several more waves, until his foot brushed against the bottom and he stood up in waist-deep water.

Alicia was lounging in the surf only a few yards away.

"Go back," he said. "Go in!"

She smiled and splashed frothy water in his direction as the rip-tide pulled her farther out.

"This isn't funny," he said.

He was already swimming out to her when she felt another surge of undertow.

It swept her out thirty feet before a huge wave broke over her head and rolled her under.

She couldn't find the surface.

She inhaled anyway, found air mixed with foam that caught in her windpipe like gravel.

When she opened her eyes, she saw Gregory standing on a sand bar in front of her, the water only chest-deep.

She stretched out her hand and he grabbed it as the undertow started again.

He pulled against it, but the sand sifted out from under his feet and in a second he was floating with her, rushing out towards the next wave.

"Swim!" he said, but already he felt her sinking.

The sand had dissolved like a pillar of salt.

They were lost in the surge and heave of the ocean, casting pieces of itself on the shore and gathering them back in.

She knew he wouldn't let go.

The ocean always gathered them back in.

Gregory sipped the last drop of his wine and felt it evaporate from his tongue.

There was a hint of rust in the after-taste.

Alicia looked past him and saw the bartender leaning on the stump of a straw broom, watching her.

"He must think I'm a goddess or something," she said.

"Finish your drink, and we'll go," Gregory answered.

She stared back at the bartender and lifted her wine towards him in an extravagant toast.

"If only he knew," she said.

She drank quickly, then placed her goblet back on the table.

They stood up and Gregory led the way to the south end of the terrace and down a concrete staircase to the beach.

The wind was picking up, bending the palm trees like reeds.

They took off their sandals and walked towards the water.

When they reached the wet sand at the water's edge, they turned down the coast towards the string of orange patio lanterns that marked their hotel's poolside bar.

Shaggy whitecaps bore down on them out of the darkness, and the spray flew with the wind.

Gregory wondered what would have happened if the surfer hadn't been there.

He put his arm around Alicia's waist and she leaned against him.

He should have known he couldn't save her by himself.

At some point, he would have had to decide: either let go and watch her drown, or keep holding on and join her.

When they reached the rock where the boy had been fishing, they turned towards the road.

The surfing beach was unlit, and bandits were said to wait there for tourists.

It was safer to walk near the lights of the private cottages.

The only things Alicia remembered about the surfer were his suntanned arms, his California accent, and the word "Pipefitter," which was scrawled across the front of his surfboard in hot pink lettering.

They passed a tiny rust-pitted sign they hadn't noticed until the day after the incident: *Playa Peligrosa.*

Dangerous beach.

The waves were a few hundred yards away, but they seemed to travel through the sand like tiny earthquakes.

At the edge of the hotel grounds, bougainvillaeas and birds of paradise shuddered in the wind.

A group of young couples sat near the pool, sipping colourful drinks and talking lazily.

Perhaps the surfer was among them.

Alicia found the key in her purse and walked ahead of Gregory to unlock the door.

It was cooler in the room than on previous nights.

She flipped off her sandals and padded across the concrete floor to the bathroom.

Gregory chained the door behind himself, then he lay down on the bed.

He would have let go of her.

Whether he'd wanted to or not, he would have let go.

The fan above him wobbled, as if one of the blades was about to fly off.

Alicia came out of the bathroom carrying her shift, which she draped over a chair.

The tan lines on her shoulders and along her neckline gave the impression that she was still clothed.

She lay down beside Gregory and kissed his temple.

The sand sifted out from under his feet and he was swept out with her.

She switched off the bedside lamp.

She unfastened the buttons of his shirt, then opened it and kissed his chest, circling his nipples with her tongue.

Pipefitter.

She pulled his shorts and underwear down to his knees, and he kicked them off.

The fan whirled like a child's fishing line.

She moved onto him and they made love slowly, eyes closed, listening to the muted concussions of the waves.

The ocean always gathered them back in.

SALLY *Ito*

HONEYMOON

"WOULD CANADA BE ALL RIGHT?" He looks at her. On Shizuko's lap lie travel pamphlets of blue lakes and snow-topped mountains. Bright *katakana* and *kanji* lettering flashes across the top "KANADA—DAI SHIZEN." CANADA—BIG NATURE.

Shizuko nods shyly. Years ago, she would have preferred Europe for a honeymoon, but now she does not care where they go.

"I shall make the reservations tomorrow."

"Yes, that will be fine." She scoops up the pamphlets and carefully arranges them into a pile on the coffee table.

The two sit in silence. Shizuko folds her hands in her lap. Kosuke Tanaka, her fiancé, shifts positions, parting his legs slightly. He takes out a handkerchief and wipes his forehead.

"And so what have you decided?" Shizuko's mother appears with the tea tray.

"Canada," they reply in unison. They look at one another and laugh nervously.

They arrive at the Calgary airport in the late afternoon and are put on a bus headed towards the mountains. Shizuko has chosen to wear a suit, cream-coloured with gold trim and buttons. She carries a square black handbag. Kosuke also wears a suit—the exact same suit he wore the day they met. Theirs was an arranged meeting, an *omiai*.

Shizuko notices that all the couples around them are younger. They wear jeans and matching sweatshirts. Some are holding hands. Shizuko thinks how old she must look. Kosuke looks his age, forty-seven. Black tendrils of hair scraped up from the side cover a shiny bald spot. His stomach protrudes over his belt. *Not a handsome man*, Shizuko thinks, *but I'm no beauty either*. The years had passed by, steady as the march of ants. There was no flowering of looks or poise, just the accumulating of age—twenty, twenty-five, thirty, thirty-five. The *omiai* opportunities became fewer.

Kosuke Tanaka was introduced as something late—a last effort by her now elderly parents. Shizuko had never told them she would not marry. When her mother heard through a relative that an older bachelor working in Asakusa was looking for a wife, Shizuko did not decline the offer to meet him.

They met in a small café in Asakusa on a rainy day. "I'm a *shitamachi* boy," he said, somewhat proudly. "I've worked all my life in this part of town." He patted the table-top. He told her he lived with his widowed mother, who was old. "She is eighty-two. I look after her," he said plainly. Though soft-spoken, the man displayed an earnestness Shizuko found vaguely appealing. There seemed to be no airs. That was what was considered noble in *shitamachi* people—their earnestness.

In past *omiai*, Shizuko had easily determined "yes" or "no," but as she sat across from Kosuke Tanaka, she could not tell. All she could think of was herself. She looked at her hands and thought of them as old and wrinkled, absorbed by her lap. When would they touch a man? Would they ever?

The man was looking out the window, his hand propped against the ashtray with a cigarette between his fingers. Shizuko loosened her hands in her lap. They would yet touch a man. Maybe even this man, Kosuke Tanaka.

That was six months ago. Now they are married and on their honeymoon. On the plane, they sat in silence. The brave but mindless chatter that marked their brief courtship had disappeared. Shizuko was secretly glad. What was their courtship anyway but an endless series of politenesses exchanged? Long and unimaginative conversations endured for the sake of that unspoken goal, marriage?

"We'll be in Banff in approximately an hour and a half," the tour guide says. The honeymoon tour has begun.

Shizuko shifts her attention to the window. The scenery is vast. Broad fields roll into the distance, the sky hanging above, pale and impenetrably blue. No living creature can be seen, except for the occasional clump of cows clustered in a protective circle.

"Why do you think they're doing that?" Shizuko says to Kosuke, pointing to the cows.

"Hm?" Kosuke looks out the window. "It's probably to keep away the flies."

Flies? *Dai Shizen.* That was Canada. Big Nature. Shizuko looks around the bus again at the other couples. Most have fallen asleep, heads against each other's shoulders, arms entwined. They are all wearing casual and comfortable clothing. Shizuko feels overdressed. Has she even brought a pair of pants? It looks windy outside and the mountain air will surely be cold.

"You know," Shizuko leans over. "I think we should phone your mother when we get to the hotel. Tell her we've arrived safely."

"I've already done that," Kosuke says. "I phoned Mother from the airport."

"You did?"

"I knew she would worry, so I called her right away. You know, we must call your parents, too."

Shizuko nods. She does not particularly care to call her parents. It is just a duty. But perhaps with Kosuke it is different.

While they were courting, she visited his mother only a few times. On the first visit, she brought the customary gift and spent an hour politely listening to the old woman talk about her son.

He's loyal, he's devoted, he's faithful. Over and over again the mother repeated herself—how good Kosuke was, how much she as a mother did not deserve her son's love or attention.

The mother was old and frail. She walked slowly, putting her hand on the wall or on the furniture to steady herself. Kosuke was always at her side, scooping his arm around her to help her sit down, clasping her trembling hand firmly in his grip.

Shizuko thought it would be hard for such an elderly woman to do things around the house, but as she looked around, she noticed how immaculately clean everything was. The *butsudan* had fresh fruit in it and incense had recently been burnt there. A faded picture of a uniformed man was propped in the right corner. Kosuke's father. He had served in the army. Kosuke told her he had been born shortly after the war when his father returned. His mother was in her mid-thirties then and had been barren. Kosuke's father died of tuberculosis soon after his birth.

Shizuko knew if she married Kosuke she would be obliged to live with and look after his mother. Married friends told her what an onerous task this was, but Shizuko had not found the idea particularly daunting. She was tired of living for herself. She wanted to live for others. For her husband. Her children. The family.

The bus pulls up to the Banff Springs Hotel. Everyone clambers over to the left side of the vehicle to look at the famous hotel while Kosuke and Shizuko quietly gather their things. They get off the bus and go to the lobby, following the others.

"The Tanakas. Room 506." The tour guide hands Shizuko the key. "Very nice room—faces the mountains," he adds. Shizuko feels the dull weight of the heavy golden key in her hand. She will guard it carefully, put it near her person, in her pocket or purse.

When they get to the room, Shizuko notices the bed. It is spacious and wide, covered with a white bedspread. There is much light in the room. The curtains are drawn wide open. Kosuke moves to the window.

Shizuko goes to the bathroom to change. She pulls in her suitcase and closes the door. She worries about what to wear. They will soon be having dinner.

She comes out wearing a navy skirt and a fresh blouse. Kosuke is staring out the window. She goes to him.

"Wonderful view, isn't it?" Kosuke says. The setting sun casts a pale yellow glow onto his face. He looks old. Sad. Shizuko feels a trembling of pity for him. She wants to touch him, satisfy him. She will be what he has longed for all his life.

"Kosuke-san." She says his name softly, gently.

"Yes?" He turns to her.

"Oh, nothing." Shizuko looks down.

"That's a different skirt you're wearing."

"Do you like it?" Shizuko unfolds her hands and runs them down the front of her skirt. She looks at him.

"Yes, it's very nice."

"Are you going to wear that suit to dinner?"

"I was thinking of it. Why?"

"You should change. Relax a little more."

"Yes, you're right. I'll change."

Kosuke brushes past Shizuko as he moves towards his suitcase. Shizuko can feel the rustle of his shirt against her, can smell his cologne.

"Which one?" Kosuke says, pulling out two shirts.

"The yellow one."

Kosuke begins taking off his shirt. Shizuko turns to the window. The sun is beginning to set behind the mountains. She can faintly see in the darkest corner of the window a reflection of Kosuke changing, his hands slowly unbuttoning one by one the buttons, opening the shirt, exposing his chest. Shizuko looks up. She notices movement on the lawn. Two elk. The large one with the antlers, mounting the smaller one. Shizuko stares, her eyes glued to the rumbling mass of brown fur openly mating on the manicured lawn.

"Shizuko-san," Kosuke calls. "Should I wear a tie?"

"Yes, of course," Shizuko replies. The elk have moved away.

"Here, let me help you."

She goes to Kosuke. The light in the room has grown dusky, casting shadows. Kosuke leans back his head, darkness enveloping his face. Only his neck is exposed, thick and warm, the Adam's apple bobbing, almost imperceptibly, up and down as Shizuko knots the tie below his collar. *He's letting me do it*, Shizuko thinks, *knot his tie for him*. She feels her cheeks grow warm.

They are the first couple down to dinner. The other couples come later, dressed up in suits and bright coloured dresses. Shizuko realizes she has again misjudged the situation. At least Kosuke is wearing a tie. Her skirt looks dull compared to the dresses of the other young women.

The tour guide seats them beside two couples from Kansai. They are young, in their twenties. They smile shyly at Kosuke and Shizuko, bowing their heads. Shizuko asks all the polite questions like an older sister. *Where are you from? What do your parents do? How long have you been married? What are your future plans?*

After dinner, Kosuke and Shizuko take a walk around the hotel. It is dark, the mountains invisible. For the first time, they hold hands.

When they return, Shizuko goes to the bathroom. She looks at herself in the mirror. The warm, red flush in her cheeks is still there. She closes her eyes. Slowly, she brings her hands to her shoulders, onto her neck. Her skin feels smooth. She knows that her delicate white skin is a mark of beauty. She opens her suitcase and pulls out a lavender silk nightgown. She had bought it on the Ginza at Mitsukoshi two days before the wedding. A quiet, private purchase. She slips it on. It feels cool on her body, releasing a shudder of goosebumps on her skin. She breathes deeply, turns herself around, and looks once more in the mirror. *I look fine*, she thinks.

She enters the bedroom. Kosuke is sitting straight up in bed in his pyjamas, his back against the headboard, hands folded in his lap.

As Shizuko turns off the lights and slips into bed, Kosuke turns and looks at her. When he doesn't move towards her, Shizuko reaches for his hand and gently places it on her breast. His hand feels like a damp, warm cloth, and for a moment it lingers on the curve of her skin before slipping off.

Kosuke swallows visibly. His brow shines with sweat. He cautiously raises his hand again and places it on her breast. Shizuko arches her back to encourage him. Again, his hand falls off.

Shizuko moves closer, pushing her body against him. She slips her arm around his waist and brings his arm up to her shoulder. The arm is heavy, leaden. Kosuke swallows again. His arm slips off her shoulder. He looks away. Shizuko looks at his groin. It is lifeless, limp. A wrinkle of cotton pyjama.

"What is the matter?" she finally says in a high, tremulous voice.

"I ... I c–can't ... I'm n–not normal," Kosuke wheezes out. He pushes himself down and turns the other way. His whole body trembles.

Shizuko cannot speak. She is dumbfounded.

The dark ceiling hovers like a dead weight over Shizuko. She lies still, a corpse, her hands resting on her breasts as she breathes in and out, pretending to be asleep. Kosuke has gotten up and left the room.

What's the matter with him? How can this be? All night, questions dog Shizuko, the words spinning around her in the darkness. *Why? Why is this happening?*

She tries recalling their dates to see if there was a sign then. *The French restaurant in Aoyama, cherry blossom-viewing in Ueno Park, visiting Sensoji temple, seeing that Austrian symphony*—nothing there to indicate that lack. He was always so polite on their dates, running ahead to pay for tickets, buying small things like keychains, postcards, souvenir charms.

What is it? What is wrong?

Keychains, postcards, souvenir charms. Shizuko closes her eyes. Something forms in the back of her mind—a memory, an image. *Postcards, souvenir charms.* Shizuko stops. Souvenir charms for who?

Why, for the mother, of course. Kosuke's mother. Everywhere Shizuko and Kosuke went, he bought something for his mother, discreetly purchasing it and putting it into his pocket.

The memory comes back. A warm afternoon, sitting in the Tanaka living room, Mrs. Tanaka kneeling on the tatami, bowing deeply, her forehead pressed to the ground, her hand clasping Shizuko's. Over and over again, saying, "Thank you, thank you so much for agreeing to marry Kosuke. He's not much, I know, for a woman like yourself, but he's been good to me, such a worthless mother I've been, keeping him all these years. Thank you, thank you so much."

Shizuko had not known what to say. She remembered looking up. Kosuke stood in the hallway, partially hidden, his eyes dark and wet.

His mother. That's what it is. His mother.

Sunlight streams through the window. Shizuko gets up and opens the curtain. The lawn is bare, the sun harsh on the green surface. No trace of wildlife outside. The elks of the evening before seem an illusion.

"Shizuko-san."

Startled, Shizuko turns around to face Kosuke, standing behind her, his head hanging low. He falls to his knees.

"Shizuko-san, I'm sorry," he says, unable to lift his head.

Shizuko begins trembling. "You brute," she wants to say but controls herself. She clenches her hands and turns back to the window. The grim curl of her lips is reflected in the glass. Something in her is about to snap.

"Please, please forgive me. I, I wanted to be, to be m–married."

His voice is a whimper. Shizuko feels like kicking him.

"I have never been with a woman. I have lived all my life with my mother. She has no one but me. I am afraid of what I am doing to her by marrying."

"What is wrong with you?" Shizuko turns to look at Kosuke. Her voice is clear, cold. "We are not children. Everything we have done is proper and natural. How can you say that?"

"Natural?" Kosuke says. "Please forgive me then. I am not a natural man. I discovered this long ago. I am unnatural. That is why I have been unmarried so long."

"It's your mother, isn't it?" Shizuko says, her voice rising. "Poisoning you. Mother complex—that's what you have, isn't it?" The word "complex" fills Shizuko with a superiority of loathing. She has seen that word some-where in a magazine and it suddenly unleashes her anger, "You're afraid of women, aren't you? Aren't you? You're afraid that they'll control you like your mother, that they will suck you up, that they will drown you with their demands, aren't you? Admit it—you're afraid of women! Aren't you? Aren't you?"

Kosuke stands stone-faced. The pitch of Shizuko's voice has risen higher and higher until it sounds like the shrill whine of a siren. Kosuke grabs her by the arms.

"Stop it!" he says. Alarmed by his own aggression, he lets go.

Shizuko is weeping.

"Listen," Kosuke says. "It is probably as you say. I have a mother complex. Yes, I am afraid of women. They ask me to be things I cannot be. Look at yourself. What did you marry me for? Certainly not for love. We are neither doing this for love, are we? Then what are we doing it for?"

"Because it is a natural thing for men and women to do." Shizuko sniffed, "and it is also natural that I should expect of you at least—at least, this which you cannot do."

"Yes, it is a natural expectation. But I have told you already, I am not a natural man."

"Too late. It's just too late."

Kosuke sits down. He pulls out a handkerchief and wipes away the sweat on his forehead.

"I know that. I, I was just hoping things would be different. I thought you could help me. You seemed so kind, understanding. But I see that I am too much a problem. I am not a man. You may leave me if you want."

"That's it?? Go?? After all this embarrassment, this shame upon our names?"

Kosuke shrugs his shoulders. "I am not unaccustomed to shame," he says bluntly.

Shizuko stops. She feels sheepish though she doesn't know why.

They go down to breakfast together and eat in silence. The chatter of voices, the tinkling of silverware, the bustling of the hotel staff are a dull buzz in Shizuko's ears. She is tired and has little appetite. She eats a slice of toast and drinks a glass of orange juice. Kosuke does not eat.

"Please meet at the bus in ten minutes!" the guide announces to the group.

Shizuko looks at Kosuke. He is fiddling for his bag.

"What are you looking for?" she asks.

"The camera."

"Then we're going?"

"I would like to," he says. "Please, we should go together."

Shizuko does not answer. She folds the napkin in her lap. What would she do all day alone in the hotel? She decides she will go with Kosuke.

They board the bus with the others. The guide begins talking at once. Shizuko shifts her attention to the window. Slowly, the hotel—a ruddy brown colour—moves away. The bellman waves. Shizuko's hands tighten in her lap. *I will not wave.* She turns to Kosuke. He sits stiff and upright, his face thrust forward. Shizuko turns back to the window. *He won't see a thing, sitting like that.* She notices an elk grazing on the lawn of a house. *Look, an elk!*—the words rise in Shizuko's throat but do not emerge. She swallows them.

They do not speak, until the first picture stop.

"This is Castle Mountain," announces the guide. "We'll stop here for photos. Five minutes."

Shizuko and Kosuke step off the bus. Castle Mountain, tiered and pinnacled, stands in the distance, a picturesque block of stone. Shizuko closes her eyes before she speaks. *Civil, I must be civil.* "Did you bring the camera?"

"Oh—" Kosuke begins checking his pockets. "N–no, I forgot. I'll go and get it." He starts back to the bus.

"No, never mind. Forget it."

"I'm sorry." Kosuke hangs his head.

"You're sorry about everything, aren't you?" Shizuko's voice rises without warning. She is amazed at her own cutting quickness, the sharpness of her words.

Kosuke takes out his handkerchief and wipes his brow. They go back onto the bus. The guide picks up the mike. "See how thin the trees out there are? They're called lodgepole pines and were used by the Indians to build teepees. I hear Canadian log houses are very popular in Japan right now, but these trees can't be used for house building. They're too thin."

Houses. House building. Trees too thin, too fragile, too brittle. The row of matchstick trees shudders and topples in front of Shizuko's eyes. *House. No house. That's what marriage is for. Children. A family. It's my right.*

As the bus nears Lake Louise, Shizuko notices Kosuke shoving his camera into his pocket. They get off the bus. Shizuko lags behind, unconnected to the others.

In front of the hotel is a signboard. CHATEAU LAKE LOUISE. Couples are having their pictures taken together there by the guide.

"Mr. and Mrs. Tanaka! How about a picture?" the guide calls out.

Kosuke begins pulling out the camera. Shizuko stops. *No,* she thinks, and gives a harsh, quick glance at Kosuke. But it is too late, the guide has the camera in his hand.

"Now stand together."

Shizuko freezes. She will not move from her position, left of the sign. Kosuke is standing on the right. He inches towards Shizuko. She puts out her hand. *No. Stay there.* She clasps her hands in front of her and looks straight at the guide.

After the shot, the guide hands the camera back to Kosuke. He puts it in his pocket.

"Shizuko-san," he says slowly. "Perhaps we should not take any more pictures?"

Shizuko does not answer and looks away at the mountains.

Kosuke begins to shuffle off. Quickly, Shizuko puts out her hand. *Stop. Take pictures of the mountains. So beautiful you can't ignore them.* The words linger in Shizuko's mouth, but she cannot say them.

Kosuke is looking at her, his eyes searching hers. *I've been sarcastic to him,* Shizuko thinks. *So unlike me, indulging his earnestness.* Earnestness. *Shitamachi* people are earnest. Shizuko remembers that thought from long ago—the day of their *omiai.*

Shizuko looks at the mountain. Slowly, Kosuke takes out the camera, aims it at the spot she is looking at—a glacier gleaming in the sunlight, a white wall of ice.

When Shizuko gets back onto the bus, she thinks of all the other *omiai* she had. Names, faces flash through her mind—Miura, Honda, Kadota. She remembers odd things. The way Miura-san held his cup, what colour tie Honda-san wore, the first words Kadota-san spoke. All the *omiais* of that time were half-hearted attempts, something Shizuko did to please her parents. They were forever setting her up with somebody—her father going through his business connections, her mother asking all the relatives. Shizuko wasn't really interested in any of the men. All she could do was compare them to Makimoto-bucho, her boss.

For seven years, she had nurtured a crush on Makimoto-bucho, a married man with two children. He was several years older than her. But Shizuko could not help it. She was so close to him, the most senior of his office secretaries. She served him tea, filed his documents, arranged his appointments. Day in, day out, seeing him always.

One night, he took the staff to his favourite bar. He was being promoted, moved to a higher department. In a moment of drunken gruffness, he turned to Shizuko and spoke the words she had longed to hear. *"You want me, don't you?"*

Shizuko paled. She was paralyzed by his words. How had he known? Was she that obvious? Makimoto-bucho's hand moved into her lap. He was drunk. Repulsed, Shizuko stood up and fled.

Seven years mooning over a married man. Seven years of wasted infatuation.

Shizuko closes her eyes. What did Makimoto-bucho look like? She can barely remember now. He was tall, taller than Kosuke. He had some grey hair. He wore blue suits ... or were they black? It was Kosuke who wore blue suits. Shizuko opens her eyes to check.

Kosuke is searching in his pocket. Slyly, covertly, he brings some small thing to his lips and pops it into his mouth. He puts his hand back into his pocket. A few seconds later, he puts another one into his mouth. Shizuko looks down at his bag. There is packet of *umeboshi*—tart, red plums pickled into wrinkled balls. The kind of snack old people take on trips, the ones who believe *umeboshi* to be a cure-all, a daily vitamin. Kosuke notices Shizuko looking at him and smiles sheepishly, offering her one. Shizuko declines and turns her head to the window. Embarrassed, Kosuke offers some to the couple across the aisle. Shizuko cringes. *How silly—offering* umeboshi *to that young couple.*

The sky outside draws Shizuko's attention back to the window. *How blue it is.* Impenetrable. Day after day, the same blueness. Indifferent to change, the perfect frame for mountains.

The guide is talking about glaciers now—how they were formed by the packing of snow, the pressing of snowflakes into heavy layers of ice that began to move down the mountain, grinding the stone behind it. *Powerful.* Shizuko looks at the glacier. She feels small, suddenly impoverished.

The sound of heavy breathing comes from Shizuko's side. Kosuke has fallen asleep and leans precariously against her shoulder. Shizuko shrinks back against the window. The land has grown suddenly flat. There are no trees except a few small, stunted firs.

"We'll be reaching the highest part of the road here soon," the guide says. "This is alpine meadow. You'll notice the lack of trees. Cold winds constantly sweep down from the ice field, making it hard for things to grow here."

Where are the buildings? Why so empty? Shizuko looks again at the flat expanse. *Where are the people? The children?* She thinks of the lakes, the open fields, the mountain air. *For the children. Land for the children.*

The bus toils up the hill, the sound of the engine rumbling louder. The driver shifts gears, making a low, cracking sound. The bus slows down.

Children, Shizuko thinks. *Whose children? Not mine.* The land that has flowed across her eye now seems to creep and crawl to a standstill. Shizuko looks out the window. The reality is barren-ness.

It will be an hour before they reach the ice-field. Shizuko is tired but cannot sleep. She thinks she will look for wildlife, fixing her eyes on the spaces between the trees in the forests, on rock ledges and shelves on the mountainsides. Miles, minutes creep by. Still nothing. The land rolls out before her like a scroll of painted scenery.

Shizuko's mind begins drifting. *Maybe I should look at this more practically. Kosuke's deficient. Such husbands are to be divorced. That would only be right. Divorce. But who would divorce who? How do you divorce, anyway?* Shizuko frowns. *Who would make the announcement? Kosuke? Would he be man enough?* Man enough—*ironic.*

What if I announce it? How can I do it without sounding bitter? Harsh? They would all think I was over-demanding, unsatisfied. They would think I have no gaman. *"Oh, she's a selfish type, can't endure hardship"*—*that's what they would say. "Kosuke Tanaka is such a good man. It must be her fault. Ruining him like that."*

Shizuko looks out. They are fast approaching a cliff wall. *If I divorce, where would I go?* The wall towers, sheer and upright, a mass of limestone. *A thirty-five-year-old woman, now divorced?* Dark stains run down the front of the wall where water has seeped into the stone. *Same old routine again, every day. The way it was before.* The wall grows closer, tighter to the window. Shizuko can no longer see the sky.

Then she spots it. A small cream-coloured speck. Moving. Shizuko squints her eyes. It's an animal! A mountain goat, standing on a ledge no bigger than itself. It stands isolated, suspended, a small white blotch that looks almost like snow.

"Kosuke, look!" Shizuko cannot help but nudge Kosuke. "A goat!"

"Where?" He strains over to see.

"There!" Shizuko points.

"Where? Where?"

But it is too late. They have passed it. Shizuko falls back onto her seat. *He didn't see it. Of course, he didn't see it. He couldn't see it if he tried. Or maybe it's just me wanting him to see. See things only I can see. Maybe it was just a patch of snow.*

They stop at a gorge. People clamber out of the bus to view the small canyon. Kosuke convinces Shizuko to come.

This gorge is small, deep. Water gushes down the sides, churning and foaming against the rock. Shizuko peers over the rail. The sight is mesmerizing.

"So beautiful, so beautiful," someone mutters. An old Japanese man from another tour group stands beside her.

"Makes you want to jump?" he says. *"Neh?"*

He looks at her. His eyes are small, milky.

Shizuko feels the cold spray on her hands and feet. The white water churns, leaps up from the stone, gushes and roars into her ear. The rock walls recede, stretched back as if elastic, the gorge widening like a mouth.

"Shizuko-san," Kosuke's voice interrupts. "We must go back to the bus."

Shizuko looks up. Her hands are trembling. She has been gripping the rail too tightly.

Back on the bus, Shizuko stares sullenly out the window. Words creep into her throat, seal themselves under her tongue. The sound of water even now thrums in her ear, vibrating against every nerve, every muscle in her body.

"Over there is Bridal Veil Falls." The guide points to a long column of water pouring down the mountainside. "An old Indian legend tells us these are the tears of a weeping warrior's wife. A woman who lost her husband in battle the eve of their wedding night."

Shizuko looks away from the falls to her lap. Her cheeks feel warm. Tears well up in her eyes, slowly trickle down her face.

Kosuke has been watching. Without looking at her, he exte. handkerchief. Shizuko notices how damp and dirty it is. He has using it all day.

"We'll be at the ice-field very soon now!" the guide says excite "Please get ready!"

Shizuko's feet crunch the grainy surface of the ice as she walks on top of the glacier, farther and farther beyond the others. For a fleeting second, she takes a look behind her. The sno-coaches, the special buses they boarded for glacier travel, look like small larvae in the distance. She turns forwards and heads towards the mountainside. Peaks rise up around her, their bald rock surfaces exposed to the sky. The glacier, an opaque ocean, throws up waves of hardened ice, fixed like stone monuments. Above her, monstrous cracks and fissures of blue ice gleam like cavernous mouths waiting to swallow up the living. Shizuko squints at the glacier. The thoughts in her head grow thick with dull purpose. *I cannot go back there. I cannot go back to a life I do not want to live. I want to disappear. I want to stop wanting. Become white-ness, pure and indifferent. Become snow.*

Shizuko has come close to the mountainside. She sees ahead a broad tumble of ice. Beyond, Shizuko knows, is the ice-field, the source of the glacier. She will walk and walk towards it, her feet moving her body forward, mapping out the ice, hoping for the moment when hard surface will give way, become air.

The sound of her feet is loud. Louder than she expects. Crunching. Grinding. Crushing.

Shizuko stops. The crunching noise continues. It is not just her feet making the sound. She hears voices, faintly, and turns to look behind her. Clambering down an icy ledge are a middle-aged couple, dressed in climbing gear and roped together. As they reach the ground, they are chatting amicably to one another. The man is tall, silver-haired, wearing dark breeches, a red jacket, and hiking boots. A coil of rope hangs from his shoulders. The woman is about the same age, white hair gathered loosely in a bun. She too is wearing breeches and a red jacket. They notice Shizuko.

"Well, hullo there!" the man says in a startlingly loud voice. "What are you doing here?"

Shizuko does not reply. She remains standing frozen.

"I don't think she understands, dear," the woman says. "She looks Japanese."

"Where do you think she came from?" The man turns to his wife.

"I don't know. I suspect she's from one of those sno-coach tours."

They look at her together. The woman's eyes are kindly, concerned. She extends her hand to Shizuko.

"My dear, you must go back to your group. They'll be waiting for you."

Shizuko nods, though she does not understand. They are speaking English far too quickly for her. She wonders where this couple has come from. Roped together. Friendly. Unafraid. The glacier suddenly recedes from her mind, the blue crack closing up its mouth, the ice growing flat and dull. The sky is now a dazzling blue, the sun shining brightly.

Just then, a shout.

"Mrs. Tanaka!" the guide waves his hand, running towards her. Kosuke is a few steps behind.

"Mrs. Tanaka! Here you are!" the guide says. "We've been looking all over for you! You made us all worried. The sno-coach has been waiting for fifteen minutes!"

Kosuke approaches Shizuko. Briefly, his eyes meet hers. They are filled with something that makes Shizuko look away. Not anger, but something else. Suddenly, he embraces her, the force of his arms jerking Shizuko's back. The guide turns away, embarrassed.

Kosuke breathes hard into Shizuko's ear, the hot rasping sound tingling her skin. Shizuko's lower lip begins to shudder. She wants to push him away, but his grip is strong like an animal's, his body pressed against her, the frantic heartbeat slowing down, the breaths now coming evenly, one after the other. Shizuko closes her eyes. Soon his breath will match hers and for a moment they will be one.

BILL *Gaston*

TRY A
YOUNGER
MAN

Lately woman's way
is to younger lovers. It is natural
you have your revenge.
So go ahead, try the
turbine howling love of juveniles. Do so, but recall
my love is a morning's woods,
sap sensate but still.
Moss hums close to earth while head high
a red bird calls in flat-minor, simple.

Go, forget me,
try a tango with Ramone, follow
his cashier's wink and testosteronic bagging of cukes.
Just know that, when we touch, you remember yourself.
Mine is the seduction of empty space, warm brandy, talk.
A dusty history, opened along a strong spine.
When we touch, we hear Ramone's roar in the alley.
When we touch, the stars are cleaned of irony.
When we touch, we make a playground.
At the fence, the Ramones buck and lurch and cry.

Or try Vince. He will finger your confusion
with a maxim, binding time and mystery
as you grope your cheapest route out of
hard and shiny clothing.
Recall my love is a heron's walk, poise on ancient stilts,
and your love is the flashing of minnows.

Unlike young Jon, I hate *I Ching*, cards, and dice games
unless they are played upon an altar.
I still have this love of pencils. So, go.
Take with you, facts.
When we touch, we kindle not the flame
but the growing space around it.
When we touch, children wake once quickly
and settle back.
When we touch, the howlings are made mute,
in the shapelessness
of our loving.

JEAN *Rysstad*

CONTIGUOUS

It is six o'clock and Candace is waiting five more minutes just in case Hank comes home. She has the kind of supper in the oven—chicken, potatoes—that she makes when he is home, but she realizes, this second time the kids come in from the yard asking, "Isn't it time to eat yet?" that she forgot to ask Hank if he will be home. What time?

Early this morning, she drove him to the dock. Half asleep, all of them. There were no words spoken. Just the code. Candace catching Hank's eyes and, with her eyes and shoulder, directing him to look at their kids. The two of them, still in pyjamas, each fingering their satin-edged blankets, unquestioning. They knew they were driving their father to the dock. She and Hank had exchanged a look after he glanced at them. That was all. He had gotten out of the car and taken his long steps to the ramp.

It is June. Hank and Candace have talked about his fishing season less than usual, less than last year, less than the year before. They both know the possibilities. There is not much to be said. It could be a good season or a bad season or a fair season. If it is a poor season, Hank will have to figure out what to do in the winter to pay the bills. UI will not begin to cover them. Recently, they bought a house, and the mortgage on Hank's boat is always there. A constant.

Their house is an old one, one of the oldest in town, and it is very much like the childhood houses they both grew up in. The house makes them feel, sometimes, that they are home, free, on a course that has been set. Automatic pilot, as when the men take wheel turns, when they are travelling to the fishing grounds, running all night at the same speed. All they have to do is check occasionally, pay a little attention that they are on course.

Candace half-expects to hear Hank's voice, "Hallo *you*," at the front door at any minute. She half-anticipates him throwing his cap on the table like a skipped stone, the sideways, easy toss, the wipe of his hand across his forehead. He will have a drink and take a smoke to the can and she will start to set the table. But she half-expects the phone to ring, Hank saying that he will not be home. She is sorry she did not remember to ask him what time he would be home. And yet, she thinks, it's good, in a way. It means she is accepting, after ten years of this life as a fisherman's wife, that he does not know. It is a different kind of time. Working until you are finished.

Just as the kids come in again, hungry, hot, flushed, asking, "When's supper?" the phone rings and she says into the phone, "Now, supper's now." She hears Hank's voice and she has to shake her head to clear the channels. He will be home in a bit, he says. He is giving Willis a hand.

Willis has just invested fifty thousand dollars in crab traps and has rented storage sheds at the dock for the traps until salmon fishing is over. Hank is helping him move the traps into the shed. Carson White is there, too, and they are going to go and have a drink on Carson's boat after they finish, Carson having something to say about crab-fishing that Willis wants to hear. Carson is one of the few men who makes good on crab. Hank doesn't say that he wants to hear this for himself, to think about it for himself, but Candace knows that is what he wants to do. She does not feel annoyed or hurt as she might have a few years ago, when she was just getting used to being alone, setting her own course.

When Hank and Candace first met, Hank would have said, from the phone booth at the dock, "Grab a cab. Come on down." Candace would have sat in the galley with them after Hank met her at the top of the dock and paid the driver. Later, she and Hank would have gone for the last set at the Surf Club.

She helps the kids get washed and seated, and she fixes their plates. Thinks of how she might call a sitter now and join the men. She might. It is possible to do that, but he has not asked her to. She has a reserve of things to do now that please her. A separate sanity that carries over year round, growing from something she worked at only sporadically when she met him first.

Her painting. In this house, the house with all the space, she has a room on the third storey overlooking the harbour, the glassed-in sunporch.

She'd taken watercolours on one of their first trips together. And one night, the two of them in the wheelhouse on cushioned swivel-stools, he'd shown her how to read the charts. He'd shown her how to cup her hands around the rubber scanning mask. The water flat calm, running down the coast. She'd put a little water in one mug and a little rum in the other. A paintbrush and a tube of sepia. She'd put him down quickly on the rag paper, captured his ease, his pleasure at the wheel that night. Hank Olsen, his chair tipped on hind legs, one foot beating the rung as the bow slapped the waves, the other braced on the instrument panel. One hand loose on the wheel. He liked what she'd caught of him, and the water-colour hung in the galley all that trip for the crew to see.

Now, as she sits on the step-stool his father made for the kids to brush their teeth at the high pedestal sink, the kids in the tub, she thinks of her painting; it has improved because she works by feel, instinct, memory.

She doesn't mind his trips away, she thinks, as the kids dump water on themselves and threaten to invade each other's territorial half of the tub with their plastic cups. She sees her son teasing, flicking, snicking the surface with his thumb and index finger at his sister, who laughs and imitates the gesture. "Time to get out," Candace says, and though both children complain they are not ready, they climb out, relieved, she thinks, to avoid the tears that would have followed as the game built. They waddle like ducks to their own rooms, happy to go to bed.

Hank wants Candace to stay with the children. Be home with them and for them. He does not take Candace very seriously when she offers to go back to work to help out in the wintertime. He asks her what she could do that would be worth the disruption to the family. What she could do that would be worth handing over their kids to someone else, into some-one else's routine. Candace is relieved that he sees it that way, because she cannot imagine going back to work. She likes what her life is.

Now, especially, with the new, old house that seems so perfect for them, she goes to her studio whenever she can, as often as she can. She can see the children in the back yard from that room, and when there is trouble, she yells down from the window that is not painted shut.

Candace goes downstairs when the children are settled, and she thinks she has an hour or so before Hank comes home. She took a temporary job, telephone interviews, last month, to counteract some of her guilt about Hank working so hard. She has a chance to make calls, follow up, without interruption. She gets started immediately, without any sighing or wishing she hadn't taken the job. She thinks this is one of the things that marriage and children have done for her; put time into perspective. There is not much of it. Fishing, the time is endless, without time. Fishing is motion. She used to take two days to rid herself of the hollow feeling after he left. Now, it takes her only several hours. She has a sense of her own pace, and the kids switch into her rhythm easily. They breathe with her. They accept the canned soup at supper, the brown bread—he likes white, sliced—tomatoes, cheddar. When they were first together, she never knew when she would look out her apartment window and see the boats coming in the harbour, two and three abreast. She would watch, and it seemed to take forever for the boats to be any closer. She knows now, to the hour, when they will come back in. She knows which boat is his from quite a distance. Wives make calls back and forth to each other all week; news of a good trip, nothing, a few, known long before the men are home.

Candace works for several hours, talking on the telephone, smoking, drinking coffee as she works. But all the time she is working, she is anticipating his coming home. She is thinking sometimes, between calls, between deciding who to call next, that it has been a long time since they really talked and that she and he will sit tonight, at least, and talk. She anticipates he will be relaxed, with stories of Willis and Carson. How, probably Willis didn't hear, really hear, a word Carson had to say. Or if he did, and it made sense, Willis would argue that it was wrong. They will have a drink together this harbour night, and he will tell her some of the things he has been thinking during the day and during his time away. Things she is familiar with but they haven't talked of for such a long time. How he takes pleasure in men's company, even the company of men he doesn't naturally like, takes pleasure in telling her, she thinks, or used to think, in telling her what he has understood of men and how they fish. She is going to ask him questions like she used to. She will say, "I didn't quite understand. Was he smiling when he said that or did he spit?" Or he will tell her those details without her having to ask, because he knows she likes those details especially. He will tell her something technical about the traps or the live tanks, and he will take her pen from her hand and begin to sketch the thing he is explaining on her survey work. She will hurry to get a blank piece of paper before he loses the urge to explain it.

It will be that kind of a night, she thinks, the kind they need to have. To come together after days of travelling separately. After a few drinks, they will start to talk about love, what it is after a few years, a few kids, mortgages; how they still love each other. How they both worry sometimes about living too separately.

She will tell him how she walked with the kids a few days ago along the waterfront after supper. That is the hardest time, she'll tell him, after supper and before bedtime, when you are gone, to pass the time. She will tell him how they had lain down on the wharf and watched the jellyfish swim. Expand, contract, expand, contract. Moving that way. Not very fast but moving towards somewhere. She will tell him that she feels like that sometimes, that she expands somehow when he is gone, becomes someone who takes all things in, in order to move at all, to push forward instead of being hollow, dry, waiting. Or no, how will she put it? That she does not know whether she expands or contracts when he is gone or when he is home. She is getting confused. She wants to tell him all this.

But, he does not come, and Willis's wife, Lee, phones with the drag of tiredness in her voice, a disappointment that is always there, it seems to Candace. Lee wants to know if Candace has heard from Hank, or is Willis there, at their house. Candace tells Lee that Hank phoned at supper to say he would be home soon.

"Well, I'm going to bed," Lee says. "There's no sense waiting up for Willis now. If he's this late, he'll be later." Candace hangs up the phone and starts to put away her telephone survey work. She feels nauseated by the scraps of information she gleaned. How can she put these bits together to make a picture? She sees Lee's baking for Willis on their kitchen counter. When the cookies are stale, after a few days on the boat, he will throw them to the seagulls.

Candace goes to bed knowing she will not sleep. She picks several novels from the bookshelf, thinking that if one does not draw her in, the other will. She switches from book to book. She cannot decide whether to try to stay awake or to try to sleep. The bedside light can be seen from the street, and when she hears Hank's voice, the two other voices, feet coming up the front steps, it is too late to turn off the lamp and pretend she is asleep.

She takes a book and props her pillow, fusses with her hair, listens as they mumble, then laugh. Words, then laughter. Her heart beats slow and fast, sorry he is not alone, excited for company. She is angry, then glad as she hears him coming upstairs.

"Candace," Hank says softly, as he enters the bedroom, "Candace. Come down and have a drink with us, will you? They're just going to stay for one drink. I want you to be with me." His voice is slurred thick as she has never heard it slurred, uncontrolled somehow, loose and tight at the same time. This movement. Contracting when he realizes how it sounds: too loose, too stretched, extended, needing. Hearing how it sounds, he is then boisterous, hearty. All slurred and jelly-like, feeling for the right approach, for attitude, stance; trying to stand straight, sit straight on the bed, slipping, losing position, fumbling for a cigarette.

She is feeling her way in it, this liquid, the pool around them, inching along, wondering how to move. Finally, she tells him she will be down in a minute. "I love you," he says in this slurred, funny voice, and she cannot answer. She cannot find her voice.

They are sitting, the three men, at the kitchen table with a bottle of rum. Ice-cube trays on the table. The back door open for air. They are sitting in the bright light and Candace turns the dimmer switch low, without saying a word. Hank looks up, stunned for a moment to see her. He has forgotten he invited her to come down.

She leans in the back door-frame, waiting.

"We should get home," Carson says, nudging Willis. "Hank's old lady looks like she's mad."

"She's not mad," Hank says in a voice that dismisses the idea of her anger, replacing it with his own. "Have another drink," Hank says. He pours himself a drink and tilts the bottle towards the men, setting it down before they have a chance to decide on the offer. "Me," says Candace, holding a glass out to Hank.

Hank turns. It is as if he is alone with her. Appraising her from bare feet to eyes. He grins until his eyes can no longer focus. He cannot remember why he is smiling. "Me," she reminds him, raising her glass. He splashes a shot into it.

Carson and Willis finish their drinks in one gulp, the ice chinking as it tips towards their lips. There is no mistaking the time to go, the sound of the empty glass set down hard on the table. Carson's, then Willis's. Hank is sleeping with his chin resting on his cupped hands, his elbows spread wide on the table.

"Lights out," she says to the men as she begins to clear the table. She thinks she might smile, but she retracts the expression before it forms, hardens her face. "Lights out. Go home."

After they leave, Hank makes it to the couch: three steps forwards, one to the side; inner ear bringing him to the place where he will sleep.

In the morning, the kids wake her. She is not in any motion at all today, cannot expand or contract. There is a stillness in her. She talks to her kids patiently at breakfast, asking what they would like best: cereal? yoghurt? toast? She hears him, the water running in the bathroom upstairs. By the time he comes down, her face is puffy. He will have to leave again at noon. There is an hour, two at most, to make the next few days go right at all.

He does not feel well. He feels worse in his stomach and heart than he felt the night before, but he cannot name it, start to say it. He feels worse, even though he thought he might feel better. It bothers him that he will have to leave in an hour. It bothers him to think that he will have to be bothered about it all week.

They pass each other in the long, narrow kitchen many, many times in that hour or so before he has to leave. Many more times than they need to. Each of them restless, pacing almost, back and forth the length of the house, swerving if they come too close, travelling on a course they hope will come close, as if by accident, swerving, a dive almost, to the centre of a course. Sometimes they touch, brush a sleeve. Close, but not really touching. They do not want to leave each other this way, say goodbye this way, only close, but not touching.

MARGO

 *GP* | *Greenwood*

Margo drank champagne from a Mouseketeer's hat on her fortieth birthday. She still likes cotton candy; she still looks hot in fish-net stockings. She names her cars after sexy film stars, and when she plants her sequinned sneaker on Marilyn's gas pedal, a wind from a Saturday summer night in 1962 puts its tongue in your ear. Two cups of her amazing coffee have been known to cause marriage proposals, astral travel, the purchase of impractical shoes.

Her soul is both durable and fanciful, a gold lamé bag stuffed with bargains. Her friendship, for instance, costs ninety-nine cents and lasts a century.

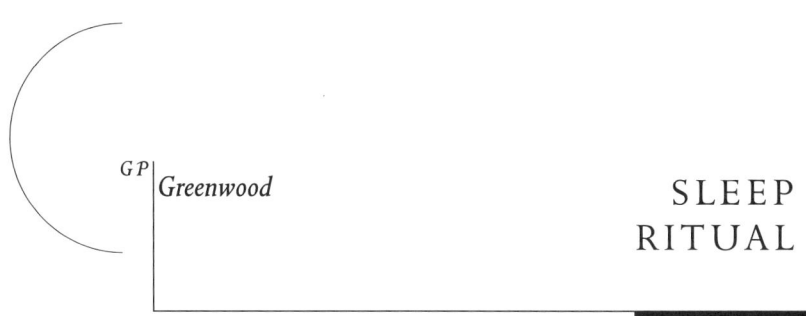

GP Greenwood

SLEEP RITUAL

1. Do not think of raccoons.
2. Embroider your pillowcase with the deepest initials you can find.
3. Leave a plate of silver biscuits for the sky.
4. Bind the day with yellow thread. Set the bundle gently in a corner for the eternal Ragpicker.
5. Put your consonants in a glass on the nightstand. Then walk twice around the bed, holding up a vowel cut from the middle of a long roll of paper.
6. Paint a river on your forehead. Make it slow.
7. Close your eyes and use your eyebrows as oars.

BLUFFING

GAIL |*Helgason*

SHE REACHES FOR HER double-faced pile jacket in the hallway, opens the front door, and runs down the sidewalk as fast as she dares. It's only three blocks to the Jasper hospital. Wind-driven rivers of ice have formed on the hospital steps and Gabriella almost loses her footing. She grips the railing. She wonders what her grade ten students would think if they could see her, clutching the rail, as if the slightest breeze could blow her down.

Inside the hospital, equilibrium returns. The tiled floor feels cold, even through her vibram soles. The hospital is modern and all on one level. The corridors are eggshell white, full of promise, Gabriella thinks. She would have preferred vomit green. Even the reassuring medicinal smell seems diluted. The scent reminds her of the homemade cleaning solution she prepared at Liam's insistence. She used the mixture for a week, until she noticed that it took twice as long to remove grime as the concentrate she bought at the janitorial supply store. Liam hadn't noticed that she'd stopped using it.

The nurse at the station nods to Gabriella. "It will just be a few minutes," she says. "Won't you have a seat?" She can't be more than twenty-two, thinks Gabriella, three years younger than she is. She sinks into the vinyl couch. Only three weeks since the accident, and it seems as if she's been waiting forever.

On that morning three weeks ago, a light frost had silvered the clubmoss along the trail. Ahead, the plum-coloured peaks of the Maligne Range cut razor-sharp silhouettes against the sky. Gabriella noticed how Liam's thick black hair was cut as fashionably as ever, unusual for a climber, although his face appeared lined and travel-worn.

Gabriella hadn't proposed the hike until the night before. She'd called it "one last outing before the snow comes." She didn't want to let on that it might mean anything much to her. At the lake, she planned to bring up the subject of the lease. The landlord said he'd have to know by October 31 if they would sign for a year. Housing was so tight in Jasper; he had at least three people who would take the house sight unseen. Would they sign the lease or not? He always speaks to her about these matters, not Liam.

The morning sky began to cream with cumulus clouds. Below, in the valley, the dark greens of white spruce and tarnished golds of the poplars wove an intricate montane tartan.

Liam stayed in the lead. At times, Gabriella had to run, the way her students sometimes did to keep up with her on field trips to nearby bogs and meadows. But she didn't mind Liam's pace. She sensed a special energy to the day. They'd be able to firm things up at the lake, the way they never could in town, knocking elbows, rushing about. She couldn't take the uncertainty much longer, now that Liam was talking about going off again for the winter, and she couldn't afford to keep the house herself. She thought that signing a one-year lease demanded a certain courage, a certain faith that the earth will keep holding them up, a certain commitment. She planned to introduce the subject in this way, as a challenge.

"Should get the lake all to ourselves," Liam said.

His boots left the partial prints of an expensive trademark on the soft loamy trail. His jacket was new, too. He spent most of his money on outdoor gear—the little he made guiding American and German tourists up easy climbs in the Rockies. Liam liked to joke that one day he would have his photo in glossy magazines for high-tech outdoor gear. Prestigious companies would seek his endorsement. He always laughed when he said this, but there was a steel edge to his voice. He really believed it. She thought he was getting a little long in the tooth for this kind of fantasy.

When they were half-way to the lake, they stopped for a short break on a fallen log. They heard a man's laughter from somewhere below. Liam turned to Gabriella, his eyes vigilant. She had seen that expression once before, when Clive, one of the other mountain guides in the town, asked Liam if the rumours were true. Had he almost lost his nerve on Mt. Robson last year, when he realized the American climber he was guiding couldn't set up a belay that gave Liam adequate protection? Liam told Clive to go to hell. But Liam was secretly jealous of Clive. Liam has never been asked to join a big expedition; Clive was invited to Mt. McKinley last year.

"I'll handle it," Liam whispered.

Two young men approached. They looked to be in their late teens or early twenties. They took big elastic steps, as if springs were attached to the soles of their boots. Grey jays emitted staccato cries into the spruce air.

"Planning on going up to the lake?" Liam asked.

"You bet," one of them replied.

"Might not be such a good idea," Liam said, his voice thick with sympathy. "We're turning back ourselves. Came across an elk carcass by the lake. Some grizzly had himself a dandy breakfast."

"Grizzly, eh?" said the hiker. "Sure it was a grizzly?"

"Can't mistake those long front claws," Liam said. "They usually come back to the kill, you know."

"Guess you're right. Doesn't sound like a great place to be."

The pair turned around on the trail; the spring was missing from their step. When they were out of sight, Liam and Gabriella continued on to the lake. The grey jays had stopped shrieking.

Gabriella hears footsteps in the hospital corridor and looks up from a *Canadian Living* magazine to see the young nurse coming out of Liam's room.

"He's sleeping but I'll wake him in a minute," she says. Gabriella thinks she catches a quizzical look on her face. The nurse seems to be weighing whether to say anything more, then shows her straight teeth in a smile. "He really wants you to be here today, doesn't he?"

Gabriella nods. She doesn't know what to say. The nurse leaves her and pads down the corridor. Gabriella draws her legs under her. Her feet still feel icy.

Tell us what happened, the strangers said, pressing in on her with their uniforms, badges, khaki jackets, and pressed pants. All of them urged her to tell. "To aid in our understanding of how these attacks occur," said one warden, a safety specialist, with a smooth chin and a particularly insistent manner.

In the end, Gabriella felt she'd fooled them all. Oh, she'd answered all the questions, but that wasn't the same as telling the whole story. How could she, when it still wasn't clear?

Gabriella watches as a merlin alights on a bare branch outside the window. Odd that he'd get so close. Then she sees the streaky yellow plumage. Just a baby. He thinks the world is a nurturing place.

Where is that nurse?

Gabriella looks again at the merlin and remembers how she taught Liam to spot wildlife. He said he hadn't really taken much notice up till then, his eyes were always on the peaks. But he wanted to know more. This was after they'd moved in together, before he'd gone off to Leavenworth with Clive for two weeks' climbing that turned into six weeks.

She and Liam had been looking for wildlife up on the Pyramid Bench. Liam couldn't see anything. Gabriella said the problem was that he was trying to focus on a single object. Instead, he should try to soften his eyes and take in the entire horizon. Liam tried this. He wasn't always willing to learn from people who might know more than he did, but she hoped he'd recognize her authority here. After all, she was the biology teacher.

They crouched behind a stand of young spruce. In a few minutes, they observed movement at the edge of the forest: a cow moose, holding her head high, ears up instead of out.

"Means she senses danger," Gabriella said. "She probably has a calf around here. Better freeze. The worst thing to do would be to run."

They both froze. Afterwards, Liam said he'd learned a lot being out with her. It opened his eyes, he said.

At noon, Gabriella and Liam reached the lake. She found a rock of flat limestone along the shore and they spread their foam pads to sit on. Liam dug into his pack and pulled out a small bottle of Remy Martin, French bread, a wedge of Camembert, and chocolate-covered almonds.

She felt a small rush of pleasure. He never lost the ability to surprise her, sometimes through astonishing small deceits, sometimes through extravagant gestures. In a way he reminded her of the plants and animals she so loved teaching her students about: organized, coded, identifiable as a type, but ultimately unknowable. Gabriella decided not to mention the foil-wrapped egg sandwiches in her day pack; she wouldn't dream of spoiling his surprise.

"To celebrate," Liam said. He didn't say right away what they would be celebrating, but Gabriella took this as an encouraging sign. She planned to mention the lease after lunch. She imagined winter nights with Liam hunkered over topographical maps at the yellow kitchen table. Only this time, she saw him studying places they could explore together, high meadows and alpine lakes. She smiled up at him.

"Clive and I worked it out last week," Liam said. He shook his crop of black hair and his voice pranced. "If we pool our resources, live in his old van, we've got just enough to get by for three months over the winter. So we're gonna head down south."

The words hit Gabriella like small, sharp rocks.

"I've had enough of this limestone shit," Liam continued. "Three months of good, technical rock—I'm talking Yosemite, maybe New Mexico—is gonna make all the difference for me."

Gabriella grabbed for her pack and pushed herself off the rock. She strode as fast as she could without running. She didn't care where. Once she looked back. Liam was following her. Let him hoof it a little, she thought. She willed herself to walk fast and stay angry, because she didn't want to think about what might happen to her if she relented one more time. Maybe there would be nothing left of her except endurance, maybe all her other strengths would be sucked away. She'd seen it happen.

The sandy shore of the lake ended and Gabriella crashed through a thick stand of dwarf birch and rock willows. A twig snapped and cut into her cheek. She hauled herself through one last bush to the end of the lake, where the willows gave way to huckleberries.

The grizzly sow stood twenty paces ahead. The bear's hump and dished-in face were unmistakable. There was not a climbing tree within reach.

In that instant, every cell in Gabriella's body yearned to turn and flee. But some inner force held her, a force she'd never before sensed.

Gabriella dropped her eyes from the bear's stare and slumped her body forwards. She noticed how scuffed her boots were. She knew that if she retreated too quickly, the bear could be on her like a cat on a wounded bumblebee. She tried moving one foot back. The bear stepped forwards a foot or two. Gabriella froze. The bear stopped.

Behind her, she heard rustling in the shrubbery, and then Liam's voice. "Jesus," he said.

"I don't dare move," Gabriella told Liam. It took all her willpower to stay where she was. "Try backing off slowly," she said. "Bluff him, remember?"

And now, as Gabriella sits on the hospital couch, the part that was missing comes back. How she waited to hear Liam take one or two cautious steps backwards. How instead, after one long minute, she heard the rustle of footsteps through shrubbery. Liam wasn't just stepping back. He was running away as fast as he could.

Gabriella hit the ground as the bear lunged forwards. She intertwined her fingers behind her neck, legs drawn up over her vitals. But even as her forehead pressed against the gravelly earth, she felt the powerful sweep of the bear hurtling past. It was giving full chase.

The nurse is back. She bends down to Gabriella.

"He'll be counting on your reaction," she says. "Are you sure you feel up to it?"

Gabriella nods, but as she is ushered into Liam's private room, she is no longer so sure. He sits propped up in bed beside a table brimming with gladioli, carnations, cards from the climbing team. He looks a bit like pictures she has seen of mummified Egyptian princes. Bandages wind round his scalp, over his cheeks and forehead and chin. Only his blue eyes, nostrils, and mouth are visible.

What was it the doctor had told her after they airlifted him to the hospital? "No damage to the vital organs, that's the main thing." Then he'd listed the injuries. Gabriella had to bite down on her fist to keep from screaming.

"Gabriella," Liam whispers. She goes to his side. Broad beams of light penetrate the room from the west window and hurt her eyes.

"I'm here," she says. She places her palm lightly over one of his bandaged hands.

"Christ, I'm glad." Liam stares at her unflinchingly. "I thought you'd be here before this."

"I've been here every day for the last three weeks," Gabriella says. "You've been sleeping most of the time. It's just hard for you to remember."

"You know I wasn't trying to run away up there," Liam says. "You know that?"

"Of course."

"I meant the bear to come after me instead of you," he says.

Gabriella's mouth feels dry. She looks at her outstretched fingers, the irregular roof her knuckles and joints form over Liam's bandaged hand. She wonders if she could move her hand if she tries. For a moment, she hears Clive's accusing voice and the bear's low grunt.

The doctor sweeps into the room and the nurse announces that they are ready to begin. The nurse starts to snip at the facial bandage. Liam's forehead emerges, what is left of his eyebrows, just shadowy lines really, then his cheeks and chin. Beneath the bandages, the skin is all puffed up, mottled, with ridges of shiny, rubbery scar tissue criss-crossing like tributaries on a map. Gabriella's eyes linger on her feet.

When the last bandage is removed, she pulls her chair closer to the bed and stretches her lips into a smile. She knows in her bones that she can manage this way, for the rest of the afternoon, at least. She still has that much bluffing left in her.

ASTRID *Blodgett*

LEARNING TO
SPEAK

O N   A   M O N D A Y   N I G H T, I went for dinner at Earl's Restaurant, where parrots perch overhead and luscious green palms surround the tables, creating the illusion of intimacy. Mr. Richards asked for a spinach salad, with extra almonds. I ordered a BLT sandwich. Mr. Richards and I ate quickly. We hurried. We were late. It was nearly seven o'clock and at seven I would begin telephoning Red Cross blood donors: I was a telephone volunteer.

Every Monday night at seven, I sat in a spiderleg network of phone tables encased in sound-proof glass and spoke into a piece of cream-coloured plastic, asking strangers for their blood. I sat with three other volunteers from Mr. Richards' high school chemistry class. The telephone was jammed tightly between my ear and my shoulder. My hands were free to book appointments and leaf through pages of blood donors' telephone numbers and draw spindly trees and wide-petalled flowers in the margins. The next day, the next week, though I held my head upright and stood tall, I felt that hard plastic squeezed unnaturally against my ear.

The first evening we began volunteering, Mr. Richards drove all of us to the Red Cross in his dark green Buick. He unlocked the back door and took us on a tour of the building.

"The donors," he explained, smiling, "go in the main door and check in *here.*" He gestured towards a brown book. Except for this first evening, Mr. Richards said very little. Usually, he pointed, gestured with his hands, moved his head or eyes. "Always identify yourself when you come here during the day. Always let people know who you are. And what your intentions are." He paused. "If you drive a Porsche, for instance, make sure you let people know so you get faster service." He waited for us to get his joke. I looked at the others and we giggled. We were in the eleventh grade. None of us had a car.

Mr. Richards was a tall man. He was nearly fifty, I guessed, and starting to lose the hair from the top of his head. He spoke quietly, so that we had to stand close and strain to listen. He listened with similar intensity when his students had something to say. We all talked to him. About every-thing. He smiled warmly. His blue eyes were bright. He was a happy man.

We followed Mr. Richards past the donor beds, the rest area, and the plasmapheresis beds with their tiny television sets attached to long robot-like arms. We stopped at the donor-volunteer coffee corner, where cookies and soft drinks had been left for us. At this time of night, the blood machines had been shut down and the beds were empty. Not a soul was in sight.

"Help yourself," Mr. Richards said with his usual generosity. He nodded towards the Voortman's cookies and poured himself coffee in a Styrofoam cup.

I never liked the taste of Voortman's cookies.

"Always be polite," Mr. Richards reminded us the first night. "Never push. Joke if you're comfortable. Tell them"—he paused, letting the words come slowly—"you're a vampire. You want to suck their blood. That usually relaxes them." His lips widened into a big smile, and we laughed.

Mr. Richards didn't telephone donors. He sat, ready to answer our questions and to deal with difficult calls, at his desk outside the phone tables and watched us through the glass window. I didn't like this arrange-ment. I told myself, each week, that he didn't like it either. He couldn't possibly. He told me, when I asked, that the glass was there because there were too many distractions during the day. The daytime telephone volun-teers couldn't do their job. I could picture the daytime women, before the glass was there, sitting with their backs to the room and feeling unidenti-fiable flutterings against their ears and necks.

We knew from the tour where people gave blood, where we could have a cookie break, and where we worked. Everything had a place.

But the building is very large. There are other rooms.

Six o'clock one Monday night, Mr. Richards took Lisa and me for dinner at Earl's, where blue and red parrots hang from the ceiling and monstrous green palms surround the tables.

Lisa and I had done some extra volunteer work on the weekend. We'd been hostesses at a satellite clinic at Castledowns Mall. And now, Mr. Richards was taking us out for dinner. The two of us. A treat, because we didn't go out to dinner with our families. My kid brother still threw food off his plate when he didn't like it. He screamed in public places. He hadn't learned how to sit still until the adults were finished. Lisa and I ordered Earl Burgers with fries and talked about telephoning. My fingers reached up to my neck.

Lisa and I liked talking to Mr. Richards. We told him what we wanted to do on the weekend. We told him what we wanted to be when we grew up.

"You never know," Mr. Richards said, smiling. "One day, one of you might be a nurse and take people's blood."

"Yuck!" Lisa and I said in one breath.

The parrots squawked. The palms swayed gently in the breezes. We were quite sure, later, Lisa and I, that we were somewhere warm. Somewhere exotic. Somewhere *else*.

"So, how do you like being vampires?" Mr. Richards asked.

Lisa laughed and said, "It's kinda fun."

No. She didn't come, that time. Mr. Richards and I sat down at a table for two.

There is a room at the back where the cookies are stored.

Six o'clock one Monday night, Mr. Richards and I went for dinner at Earl's, where colourful parrots mimic curious words, where a breeze from a fan brushes a frond against a bruised neck.

I ordered a BLT sandwich. Mr. Richards ordered a spinach salad with extra almonds. We talked about math class, about English essays, about my younger brother. Was I getting anything out of volunteering? Yes, I said, yes, and moved my fingers self-consciously to my neck. I thought the bruise was so red and large now that everybody could see.

And will my summer job interfere with my volunteering? he wanted to know. His voice was gentle, but the words came like padded bullets, little black staccato notes, hard and quick. I stopped chewing and looked over at him. I shook my head. His blue eyes wandered lazily across my face. They looked sad. It was a strange sadness, because he was so happy. "There's something you're not telling me," he said. My mouth opened to speak, but he was quicker. "You've always told me everything," he said, and I knew, by the way he said it, that I hadn't, of course I hadn't. "Talk to me," he begged in a whisper. The space was silent now except for his breathing, his slow and forceful breathing. His eyes were deep and sunken, as if he hadn't slept for days. His eyes seemed to say, if you just talk to me, everything will be all right again.

Voortman's cookies are hard and dry.

My BLT sandwich was so thick a toothpick held it together.

"What do you mean?" I said. I was exasperated more by his apparent sadness than anything else.

"Just anything. Tell me anything," he invited. His voice was so soft I almost didn't hear it.

I started to laugh, then choked on a piece of bacon. I looked at his soft, quiet face to see if he was joking. He was smiling again. His eyes had a light in them. But he wasn't joking.

"You know I take an active interest in my students," he went on. "In young people." His voice was almost inaudible now, but it seemed to me that the couple at the next table could hear him through the palms, that even the couple beyond them could hear. I stared at the farther couple, wondering what sounds were coming from the vague, animated movements of their lips. What was he saying, way over there, and was she so far away that it wouldn't come to her till later, much later?

"Go on then," Mr. Richards continued.

The room at the back is not a huge room, more like a closet. On the far wall are six shelves of cookies, from the floor to the ceiling. There are boxes and boxes of Voortman's cookies. Chocolate chip. Oatmeal. Raisin. Sugar. Shortbread. Peanut butter. They are packed loosely in big boxes, so that as soon as you open the box, you can reach in and take a cookie.

A BLT sandwich is a sandwich that's toasted and at Earl's that Monday night the toaster made toast so crisp and dry it grated at the inside of my mouth and the bacon was practically raw.

"Well?" He breathed deeply as he waited.

"Bastard," I thought. The thought was so far in the back of my head I didn't hear it, not then. But the parrots heard it. They picked it up and tossed it from one to the other, croaking it again and again, their hoarse cries sliding down the broad leaves of the palms and gliding up again. They repeated it in different ways, louder and softer, faster and slower, like small children who have just learned a new word and need to announce it to everyone they see. I sat unable to move, watching for the waitress to arrive with the bill, watching Mr. Richards eat his salad, staring down at the mess of bacon and lettuce and tomato and crumbs on my plate; everywhere there were crumbs. How would the waitress ever clean this mess? I waited to go, to return to my seat behind the sound-proof glass, and to begin to breathe again, my own breath, unheard.

Voortman's cookies leave a vile after-taste on your tongue.

Six o'clock one Monday night, Mr. Richards and I went for dinner where parrots hang from the ceiling and palm trees surround the diners from all sides. We ate quickly so we wouldn't be late for telephoning. We ate so quickly we didn't have a chance to speak at all, which was just as well as I could hardly breathe. Mr. Richards wrapped his hands around his clubhouse sandwich, large heavy hands that burned the skin, and we had so little time he didn't say anything at all, but his lips didn't stop moving. Not once.

That wasn't true of course. Even the parrots will tell you he ate a spinach salad that day.

One night we ran out of cookies, chocolate chip, and the new packages were on the highest shelf. I stood on the top of the step ladder and he stood behind, to steady the ladder, he said. It wobbled, sometimes. When I felt the wings against my legs, heavy, fluttering wings, the sound leapt out on its own, a parrot's hoarse squawk, an involuntary cry from my throat, with nowhere to go in that small space. First flapping wings, then beaks nestling, claws snatching. I leapt upwards and grabbed the boxes. They fell, first one, then another, still more, breaking open, the cookies tumbling out over my head. Hands flew up to stop them. Reaching for the cookies, he said later. Such a confusion. The wings sent a shiver along my back while cookies continued to fall like maimed birds, dry, mute things, unable to save themselves as they plunged.

That night we went to Earl's, Mr. Richards moved too slowly, his mouth forming words I almost couldn't hear.

"Come now," he prodded. "What, don't you trust me?"

The dinner was intended to make up for spilling all the cookies. So I wouldn't feel bad about breaking so many cookies, he said. Because it was an accident.

"You *are* enjoying yourself at any rate." His eyes narrowed slightly as he waited for me to respond. I looked away and saw the farther couple again. The man's mouth continued to form words, an endless stream of words I could not make out, while the woman rose up and floated away between the swaying palms.

"You are getting something out of volunteering," he continued.

When bacon is half raw, it gets stuck in your throat and on your tongue and sits there so you can barely speak. Mayonnaise, when it is soft, runs down your hands and sometimes you don't have a napkin to wipe it. You think about wiping your hands on your jeans, but that would leave a stain.

"Aren't you?" he asked.

"These things," he went on, "are important."

When bacon turns cold and the toast crumbles, a BLT is not an appealing dinner.

"Aren't they?" he asked.

I moved my head to one side and felt a throbbing in my neck. When you are having trouble breathing, you want to save your breath, so you don't speak at all.

"We have to hurry," he reminded me. Then, glancing down at the mess of bacon and lettuce and tomato and toast, he added, "My treat."

AN EXCERPT
FROM
...*BECAUSE*

If MISS CLARKE WAS SURPRISED to see him, she recovered smoothly, waving him into her apartment with a warming enthusiasm.

"I'm glad somebody's here," she said, backing down the short hall towards the kitchen. "I guess everyone else decided to be fashionably late."

"I'm pretty punctual," Phil said. He tried to correct for the too-fussy, schoolish sound of "punctual" by adding, "It was the bus, really, that was on time. All I had to do with it was be there when it came."

She turned to look at him, the wall sconces of the kitchen nook reflecting off her glasses, so he couldn't read her expression. Hearing himself, he thought he sounded demented. He shut up.

Despite her statement that Phil was the first to arrive, there was a man in the kitchen. He was wearing a white shirt with the sleeves rolled up to his elbows, and was using a small knife with a serrated blade to cut up some lemons. He was wearing a tie, grey slacks with a leather belt, and—Phil peeked down—black shoes. With a swirly design of perforations. Narc shoes. Waving the knife at Phil, the man said, "We'll have to skip the shake thing. My hands are all sticky. Hi."

"Hello," Phil said, the Union Jack cape rippling over his upper body as he returned the wave. The man looked expectant, but Phil couldn't think of anything to add.

"It's hi," the man repeated.

Phil merely nodded, not wanting to get into an endless loop, like responding to the letter his grandmother sends him acknowledging receipt of his thank-you note for his birthday present. The three of them were very close in the tiny room, almost touching. The two men had to stand back a bit from the counter, to keep from bumping their heads on the cabinets. Phil could hear his own breathing and he looked over at Miss Clarke, helpless to break the impasse.

"My manners," she said, twisting a corkscrew into a bottle of red wine. "Hy, this is Phil. He was my top student this year. Phil, this is my, uh, Hy. And," she passed him a glass of wine, about a quarter full, "I'm Wendy."

"Oh, *Hy*," Phil said. "*Hy*. Hi." He took a sip of the wine and felt his gums contract, but he thought he managed to maintain a neutral expression. When Hy finished making the sangria and passed him a replacement drink, Phil tasted it cautiously, then, grateful, said, "Wendy, this is fabulous."

Everything was fabulous. For years afterwards, Phil would consider the small apartment his Platonic ideal and spend weeks at lease's end climbing badly lit stairwells behind property managers, unable to articulate his desire beyond, "You know, a *pad*." What he got shown, instead, was a series of dives, cramped rooms with no emotional resonance at all. With his time running out, he'd end up, desperately, settling on places that felt temporary from the time he took possession until the time he started searching again. One year, he lived with a bedroom closet that opened to reveal the back of the refrigerator. He started freelancing for a couple of agencies then, and spent most of his time in the studio.

Wendy's own paintings, some familiar to him from school, covered most of the wall space. The canvases were stretched but not framed, looking somehow more sincere as a result, but Phil was especially taken by the wall under the one double-hung window with its view of a similar window eight or ten feet away. Beneath that, the surface around the column radiator was lifted away in thick sheets, layers and layers of paint almost *authoritatively* cracked, like the bed of a dry lake. The impression was of a great force having thrust the matte-finish metal coils into the room from the outside. Bracketing the image were the first bean-bag chairs Phil had ever seen; shapeless, squooshy lumps covered with red, wet-look vinyl. Across from them, in the same fabric, a long, snake-like tube was folded back on itself twice, creating a deep, low-backed sofa.

Hy put the pitcher of sangria on a card table set with glasses, large plates of cut vegetables, and bowls of what appeared to be wet plaster of Paris.

Phil pointed to the furniture, about to comment that he'd seen bean-bags in a magazine, but never in person. There was a knock at the door—*meat-on-the-hambone*—which took both Wendy and Hy from the room, so he was abandoned before indulging an impulse he later decided was unattractive: calling attention to details for which he has no responsibility. It's a passive way of calling attention to himself. It's a habit almost impossible for him to break, so instead he'll learn to be grateful for interruptions.

One of the first guests that Wendy introduces him to squeals, "Phil Peddles! I don't believe it. I just finished a year at *Cosmo*-girl school with your sister."

"Yes?" He didn't recognize her name. "I'll tell her we met."

"Oh, we weren't friends or anything. But I remember her. Everybody does and will forever. Right at the beginning of the year she got a hall pass. To go to the john?" She rolls her eyes. "The way secretaries have to do in offices, you know?" With one hand raised so her palm faces Phil, she says, 'Mr. Johnson, can I go pee-pee?'

"Anyway, Alison wasn't gone for very long, and all of a sudden she bangs back into the room, holding up a tuna fish sandwich, and yells, 'This is my *brother's* lunch!'

"It was really surreal, almost *conceptual*. Do you have any idea what it meant?"

"Not a clue," Phil says quickly, starting to back away. "How could I? I wasn't there."

He intercepts Wendy as she's going to place another pitcher of sangria on the card table.

"I'm about due," he says.

A slice of lemon dams the spout as Wendy pours and she lifts it out, drops it into his glass.

"Don't count that as food," she says, putting down the pitcher and pointing to a tray where there's hacked-up broccoli ringed around a small bowl of dip. "You'd better eat something."

"I'm fine." Phil holds up his drink, the way the actors do in black-and-white movies. There's something he's supposed to add, a witty catch-phrase delivered with one eyebrow raised, but he can't think of anything.

"Men never eat vegetables, do they?" she asks. "Just meat and potatoes, right? It's all meat and potatoes with you Georges. At least try the hummus."

Before Phil can respond, she's pulled the tips of two fingers through the bowl and is holding a rosette of dip up to his mouth.

Phil's scalp tightens. His skin is so taut over his skull that when he pulls his lips over his teeth, so they don't scrape Wendy's fingers, he thinks his head will burst. His forehead will split open in a line above his eyebrows and his entire blood supply will shoot out, all at once, like paint from a punctured spray can.

With his mouth slightly open, he nods and goes, "Uhmm, *humn*," the sound mostly nasal, in the token noise meaning "hot but delicious." He doesn't wave his hand in front of his mouth, however, the dip being room temperature.

Hy leans into the space between them and says, "Donald wants to know where your guitar is."

"Tell him I gave it to my sister to take to camp," Wendy says and, when Hy goes to relay the message, she whispers to Phil, "It's really in the closet, but I don't want to hear 'Kumbaya' again for the rest of my days. I'd better go make sure he has something else to do with his hands." She points back at the table. "Eat."

Phil looks down at the bowl of dip. He has no idea what it tasted like. He takes a deep swallow of his drink, on the chance that the new flavour will trigger a memory of the old. It doesn't seem to, so he tries again, then refills his glass.

At the party's maximum intensity, about a dozen people have the place heated up and Phil feels feverish. Nobody has expressed any surprise at his being there, or given any indication that he's only in on a pass. With some satisfaction, he notices that he's not the shortest man in the room. In the candlelight, he might even look as old as everyone else. He moves from one pocket of conversation to the next, adeptly shifting gears, matching comments to topics. He's amazed at how helpful having read his mother's magazines proves to be; he always has something to contribute.

He knows that plush carpets tend to shed, and that shag needs to be raked. And he's able to suggest "Microfauna?" when a man loses his train of thought during a discussion of yoghurt's beneficial qualities. "But IUDs are not *contraception*," he corrects one woman, his statement followed by a silence that sounds appreciative.

As the party winds down, he's standing with a cigarette in one hand, sangria in the other, and his back to the window.

"Far-out threads," a man tells him.

"Thanks."

"Where would you get something like that?"

"I sort of made it myself." Phil looks down at his chest. He can feel the radiator behind his calves, the cool metal coils. "I mean, it was a flag first, and then I made it."

"It's very ..." The man puts his hand up to the vee of the neckline, taking the fabric between his fingers and thumb. His knuckles graze Phil's sternum. He extends his pinkie. "Very smooth," he says.

"Oh, well." Phil waves his cigarette in front of him, almost under the man's nose. *"This,"* he says, by way of explanation or apology and twists away to stub it out. There's not quite enough room for the manoeuvre, not enough distance between them for Phil to keep both arms under control, although he's acutely aware of them. They're covered with goose-bumps, the fine hairs standing on end. His drink tips and splashes over the bottom of the cape.

"Phil, come with me." Wendy appears at his side. "A little club soda will keep that from setting." She starts to pull him from the room, calling back, "Franklin, I think you'd better call me tomorrow. As soon as you get up, okay?"

Phil lets himself be drawn into the kitchen, where it's much brighter.

"It's all right," he says, watching her twist the cap off a bottle of club soda. The trapped carbon dioxide is released with a hiss. "I'm still having a good time."

"I'm glad." Wendy wrings out a sponge and pours soda over it. "Here," she says, and starts to blot at the flag, holding the fabric away from his waist. Her nails are cut short and straight across. "I'm a little surprised you're not at the dance."

"That's tonight?" Even to his own ears, his voice sounds false and evasive. "Yeah, it is," he admits. "I don't know, I didn't really want to go by myself."

"There wasn't anyone you wanted to ask?" She soaks the sponge and continues scrubbing at him, with more energy now. The dangling end of the chain belt jingles. "What about Margaret? I thought you two were pretty close."

"Oh, no," Phil says. By slow degrees, he pulls his hips back, so he's pressed against the cabinet behind him. His palms are flat over the edge of the counter. "I mean, we're friends, but not like that."

"Yeah, I guess that's how it works. Girls that age never like the nice guys. Luckily, at least some of us grow out of it."

Phil's hands grip the counter edge. He runs what she's said through his mind. There's no ambiguity in the words, not that he can detect. She thinks he's a nice guy. She *likes* nice guys. And "like" is, obviously, a euphemism.

"Damn!" Wendy abruptly pulls away from him. "Look what I've done. I'm really, really sorry."

"What?" Phil says. He glances down to where he can feel the damp cloth against his skin. The blue and red of the Union Jack have run into the white, creating a swirl of purple. He flaps the material up and down. "This is actually really cool. It's like tie-dye or batik or something."

"I just assumed it would be colour-fast." She drops the sponge into the sink. "Aren't they out in the wind and rain?"

"I guess this one's an indoor flag. Maybe that's why it was on sale in the first place. But I like it like this. Really, I do. I'm going to soak the whole thing, get it all to go like this."

"Well, thanks for reassuring me. Still, I ruined it, and I should make it up to you somehow."

"Hey, Wendy. Have you put down roots in there?" Hy sticks his head into the kitchen. "Peter and Carol are leaving."

"I'll be right there. Really," she adds, to Phil, "let me know what I can do."

"Okay," he says. "Could I use your, uh ..."

"Sure. Right through the bedroom." She points to the left, then goes to join Hy in the hall.

Phil listens to the social noises for a few seconds before he enters the next room, stopping just inside the door to get his bearings in the dimmer light. To take in the details. To gawk.

Wendy sleeps in a double bed. The mattress and box spring are right on the floor, covered with a paisley spread. Instead of a night table, there's a row of large art books, banded together and held upright by a man's leather belt, serving as a base for a sheet of glass, circular with a bevelled edge. The glass supports an old-fashioned black telephone and a clock-radio. In the glow of the lighted clock face, Phil can see that the radio is tuned to an FM station.

He walks lightly along the width of the bed to the bathroom, closing and locking the door behind him.

There's a lot of flapping and tugging before he gets things worked out. He slides the flag under the belt and bunches it up, keeps it out of the way by clamping it between his chin and his chest. The chain belt is warm against his naked belly. Done, he checks to make sure someone else has used one of the towels before he runs water over his hands, presses them into the already damp cloth.

On the back of the door is a full-length mirror in a painted frame, ivy vines against a white background. Phil stands in front of it and tries to re-drape the flag. He can't get the blousing quite the way it was, gives up, and puts the belt around his neck. He takes a step back to examine the effect. The patch where the colour has run is low down, close to the hem, a smudge of purple against the clean, hard-edged lines of red, white, and blue. He can't get a complete picture of himself. His eyes keep returning to the patch. It's like a too-large signature painted on the lower, right-hand corner of a landscape. The material is the same, but the information is different.

He has his hand on the doorknob and is giving the room a quick, checking glance, when he spots a detail that had escaped him. In front of the tub—a deep, yellowing, enamelled thing on clawed feet—there is a small mat. Where a normal person might have a fluffy, rubber-backed square, where an *average* person would have a length of absorbent cotton, Wendy steps from the tub onto a white rabbit skin.

Phil bends down from the waist, keeping his legs straight, and examines the fur. He's not thinking of bunnies, how they change colour to camouflage themselves against the snow, not the shocking retort of gunshot on a clear and silent winter day. He's not thinking of the snapping jaws of a sprung trap, not the terrible squeal of helpless prey. He stretches out one hand and, lightly, puts the tips of his fingers into the depressions left by Wendy's toes. Warm and pink. Fresh from her bath.

In the bedroom, Phil looks closely at the table made of books, so he can pass on the information to his mother. He doesn't imagine she'll act on the tip—those big art books probably cost ten or fifteen dollars apiece—but she may be pleased to file it away with her other decorating "ideas."

The clock-radio makes a low, humming noise. Phil looks at the time, looks at the phone, weighing the possibility of his sister, Alison, answering if he calls home.

Back in the living room, Wendy is tearing off plastic wrap, covering the bowl and trays left on the card table. Hy is leaning against the wall beside her, with his arms crossed over his chest. Most of the candles have been snuffed. The overhead fixture is on.

"I haven't tried these yet," Phil says, flinging himself into one of the shiny red bean-bags. The polystyrene pellets compact under his weight; there's a sound like a sigh. He lies on his side, pulls his knees up.

"A frog on a lily pad," Wendy says.

"Wait, wait." Phil is inspired. He stretches his legs out and hooks the other chair with his feet, slides it towards him. Then he half-pulls, half-lifts it on top of his body. "They're lips," he explains, although he thinks this must be obvious. "It's a mouth."

"And what are you supposed to be?" Hy asks. "The tongue?"

Phil and Wendy exchange a look. Her glasses catch the ceiling light. Even the plastic wrap stretched over the bowl in her hands glows with reflected light like a tiny moon.

"Of course not," Phil says, curbing the archness that threatens his civil tone: not everyone appreciates Art. He flings out one arm. "I'm *lunch*."

"Well, gosh," Hy says. "Look at the time. So, how are you planning to get home?"

"Oh, I missed the last bus half an hour ago." Phil has a small struggle, getting the top bean-bag off, and sort of claws himself into a sitting position. "But it's all right. I don't have to get home." He looks in Wendy's direction, without looking at her face. "I borrowed your phone. They're not expecting me."

"I—Hy, give me a hand with these, okay?" Wendy starts passing him trays and bowls, the lot precariously stacked to clear the table in one trip, making what Phil's mother would call "a lazy man's load."

"Right back," she says, giving Phil a broad smile. He dips his head, managing not to wink. Not while Hy's in the room. He's not insensitive.

Alone, he stands and fluffs up the bean-bags, enjoying the way they resist a bit before giving under his hands. The sensation is like smoothing a place in the sand to stretch out on the beach. He can hear Wendy and Hy in the kitchen, their voices low and overlapping. Phil imagines she's giving Hy his walking papers. He hopes there's not going to be a scene.

He's relieved at how amicable they appear when they come back into the room.

"I was going to make coffee," Wendy says. "But I'm all out, not even instant. So I thought we could go to Harvey's."

In the back seat of Hy's Vauxhall, leaning forwards with his elbows on the tops of the driver's and passenger's seats, Phil watches the city come at him through the windshield. He wonders if he should have pointed out, back at the apartment, that they were only three or four blocks from the Party Palace. It wasn't really necessary to get in the car and drive clear across town. They're practically in his neighbourhood now, going down Baseline Road, past the car dealerships, the GEM store, a skeleton of a garden-home row, the expansive fields of the Experimental Farm, knee-high in corn.

There's a fresh-scrubbed look to the street at this hour, a reflective cast. Everything is hard-edged and clear under the streetlights. Phil has never been here at this hour before. It's as new and strange to him as Addis Ababa would be. He can't think of anything to say, and doesn't disturb the silence in the car.

"Here we are," Hy says, pulling into the Harvey's parking lot. He turns his head and says, "Why don't you get the coffee?"

"We're not going in?" Phil climbs out of the car, bends to lean into Wendy's window. "Okay, I'll do it. What do we want?"

"Just black for us," Wendy says. "Hy, give him the money."

"Forget it," Phil says. "I've got money." He takes out his wallet to prove this, and he has it in his hand when he steps up to the counter. He's the only customer and, for some reason, he almost whispers his order.

"Two black, one double-double."

"You sure?" The girl points over his shoulder.

Phil stares at her hand for a moment, the way a dog does when it's told, "Look!" Her skin looks blue in the fluorescent light, waxy and unreal.

He has to tug his attention back, then he turns to see what she means. The Vauxhall is pulling out of the parking lot. Neither Wendy nor Hy looks back. They might be test-crash dummies, the way they're sitting, rigidly upright, staring straight ahead.

"I drink a *lot* of coffee," Phil says, turning back to the girl.

He carries the three paper cups out to the parking lot and sits at the picnic table there, instead of sitting at a booth inside. By taking a large mouthful of each of the burnt-tasting, harsh black coffees, he makes enough room to dilute the rest with his own. His last six cigarettes are crushed from being carried tucked into the waistband of his jeans, but only one has the paper split. He straightens out the rest and smokes slowly, sipping at his coffee, until the orange-and-white Harvey's sign goes out with an electric crackle. This is his cue to leave, before the girl comes out. He pulls himself to his feet, dropping the last butt-end into a half-full cup. He's emptied two; she won't think he was lying about his appetite, if she checks.

Once he leaves the road, cutting diagonally across fields that were once farms, he might be the only man in the world. Behind him, the streetlights recede to a thin line on the horizon, a faint glow like sunrise. And then there are lights ahead of him, as his neighbourhood nears.

His shoes and the cuffs of his jeans are soaked with dew. He stands inside the door of his building. He can't go upstairs. He never did call to tell his mother he was staying out. It's too late to explain anything now.

He doesn't have a key. Even if he could somehow pick the lock and let himself in, he'd have to turn on the lights, in case she's moved the furniture. He could break a leg, trying to navigate by memory.

He goes downstairs. The laundry room is unlocked. There's a piece of folded linoleum, used to hold the door open in the daytime, that he wedges under the door from the inside. He stands in front of the stationary tub and empties his bladder, faster than the drain can take it away, creating a swirling whirlpool, flowing counter-clockwise. His knees twitch with relief. In seven weeks, he'll turn sixteen and, a few months after that, he'll get his driver's licence. For a time, he'll be feverish with possibility, the feeling that he can go *anywhere*, pack up and split. This will be followed by a jolt of crushing reality. Without a car, he's as grounded as he ever was. The licence was only a formality, a ticket rather than transportation.

He gets down on the floor and crawls under the stationary tub. There's not enough room to stretch out, but it seems important that he be tucked in, not out in the open. He hooks his feet around the metal struts supporting the tub, anchoring him in place, so he doesn't roll away. The poured concrete over his head has an odour like disinfectant. He puts his hand up, above his face, but the tub hasn't been at all warmed by the hot stream from his body. The floor is also cool, and as hard. Only because he's exhausted is he able to fall asleep, wrapped in the flag of another country.

SOUTH ISLAND

MARLENE Cookshaw

I want
just the flash of its
spirit.
　　—CONSTANTIN BRANCUSI on *Fish,*
　　　one of his animal sculptures

After sunrise over Gowland Point,
I lie on the carpet listening
to Steve Reich's *Tehillim*, whose fragments
lured me onto rocks when the seal

swam near. Now sun

lights up the fishline which,
last spring, suspended the hummers' feeder
outside the east window
　　　　　　　　　　so the fishline glimmers
not like some forgotten hook but with

its own sinewy fire. It comes to me I'm afraid
to want what I want. Brancusi. *The Seal*, also called
Miracle. Yesterday I learned

"confidence" means "with faith"

and the word has swum with me since, rising
up out of everyone's speech. It leaps again—
flight, what bliss!—after a perfect
poached egg on toast, after my friend Barbara calls,

setting "denial" end to end with
"mystification," wanting

a recipe for trifle.

IT CROSSES
MY MIND

MARILYN | *Dumont*

It crosses my mind to wonder where we fit in this "vertical mosaic," this colour colony; the urban pariah, the displaced and surrendered to apartment blocks, shopping malls, superstores, and giant screens, are we distinct "survivors of white noise," or merely hostages in the enemy camp and the job application asks if I am a Canadian citizen and am I expected to mindlessly check "yes," indifferent to skin colour and the deaths of 1885, or am I actually free to check "no," like *the true north strong and free* and what will I know of my own kin in my old age, will they still welcome me, share their stew and tea, pass me the bannock like it's mine, will they continue to greet me in the old way, hand me their babies as my own, and send me away with gifts when I leave and what name will I know them by in these multi-cultural intentions, how will I know other than by shape of nose and cheekbone, colour of eyes and hair, and will it matter that we call ourselves Métis, Metisse, mixed blood, or aboriginal, will sovereignty matter or will we just slide off the level playing field turned on its side while the provincial flags slap confidently before me, echoing their self-absorbed anthem in the wind, and what is this game we've played long enough, *finders keepers/losers weepers*, so how loud and how long can the losers weep and the white noise infiltrates my day as easily as the alarm, headlines, and *Morningside* but "Are you a Canadian citizen?"   I sometimes think to answer, *yes, by coercion,   yes, but no ... there's more,* but no space provided   to write my historical interpretation here, that *yes but no,* really only means *yes* because there are no lines for the stories between *yes and no* and what of the future of my eight-year-old niece,   whose mother is Métis but only half as Métis as her grandmother, what will she name herself and will there come a time and can it be measured or predicted when she will stop naming herself and crossing her own mind.

A HARD BED
TO LIE IN

MARILYN Dumont

a hard night, slept up against a rock face on the side where my mortality
  looms like a mountain, leaving my life where it is   on an edge
  looking down.

tempted to jump, sprout wings as fantastic as the married arms that would
  catch me if I leapt

I could have easily been a doe on a highway, (you a driver, your wife
  beside you sleeping)

me grazing, ruminating the coarse clover, wet blades a mixture of green
  desire and

regret that I didn't accept the offer even though

a gold band shone like a beacon, to ward off prey
  —not to be mistaken for a jacklight,

just a doe, a stretch of road, high beams

headlights, your eyes,

legs petrified at the speed of light, a flash burn, flare

transfixed by the jacklight and the daylight of the woman who moves
    touching you
with her mouth of the moist night,

the night of my turning, aching, having you disclose your desire for me,
    turning to yet
another confession in my bed, another crease,

the safe imagined hand crosses my breast to my waist, pubic bone, and
    thigh, turns to
another imagined and perfect clean slice of a meeting, the one where I
    would have met you years ago when you were an open space, a
    meadow to be walked through at high altitudes

and the night's turning

down, wears out

trust in my age, that

flat sheets and a hard bed will not forgive.

TYMPANIC
MEMBRANE

CATHERINE Kidd

There are three things which are
stately in their march,
Even four which are stately when they
*   walk:*
The lion which is mighty among beasts
And does not retreat before any,
The strutting cock, the male goat also,
And a king when his army is with him.

—PROVERBS 30:29-31

THE LOCKED ROOM was tucked beneath the basement stairs like a small gland, oyster-like self-contained. No one held a key to it except my father.

Just as I knew the words to certain hymns without remembering how and when I had learned them, I knew that there was a mat inside the room, and many stacks of paper things, notebooks and magazines and binders and books. I must have been inside the room at least once, unless a person can inherit knowledge of a room she's never seen, the way young cuckoos inherit the song of the genetic parents they've never met.

I knew there was a rowing machine in the room as well. Not the kind that plugged into the wall and had a digital screen to monitor how many strokes and their rate, but an older type with only a seat on an alumin-ium rack, and a set of handlebars. Under the seat were four grooved wheels that rolled back and forth along the parallel bars of the rack like a boxcar. The handle came at the end of a long lever, which was held in tension by two thick springs. The machine creaked when in use, back and forth, back and forth like a swing-set in a playground. *Pull, release. Pull, release.* Until I found out what the machine was and what it was used for, I imagined the source of the sound as a torture device or some other unspeakable thing only grown-ups could use behind locked doors.

The basement room was where my father went instead of going fishing or out to pubs, instead of working in a parish or an office or a factory, instead of sitting in an armchair in front of the fireplace and cleaning his pipe or his rifle or his boots. Sometimes he would stay down there for days, surfacing only for meals, which he would spoon into margarine containers and take back downstairs with him. *What is Dad doing down there?* my brother would ask. And my mother would say, *Why don't you ask him yourself?* because she knew that neither of us was going to do that. Without knowing the reasons why not, we knew that my father didn't want to be asked. I became accustomed to envisioning him as the sound of creaking wheels running back and forth along a track, red hands with white knuckles curled round a set of handlebars like the hands of Euphemia's father on the handlebars of his motorcycles, only different.

My father only seemed to appear in shifting parts. It was impossible to ever imagine him fully and accurately, as though to do so would have been unbearable to him. Sometimes, he would come upstairs half-dressed in knee-shorts and an undershirt like a man sleepwalking, but I would see only the elastic brace on his knee or the hair under his arms. Other times, I would steal a glance at his face, and could tell by the hollow of his cheeks whether or not he had his teeth in. Or I would notice only his hair, floating in wild dark wisps about his head like a blizzard of gnats.

It is possible to figure out the missing features of a thing by imagining the shape of the space it takes up. The mass of a thing has a correlative shadow described in space, like that red-and-blue hollow sphere I'd once had with the yellow blocks fitting into different holes. The shape of my father would have to have some negative correlation to the objects surrounding him; he would be the hole that was left if I shaded in every other feature of the locked room.

I drew a dark room in my mind and tried to place him inside it, which was a fair task, not being certain what the space around him looked like, not knowing how much I had to shade in to be left with an accurate profile of him. If I didn't shade in enough, then I would envision him larger than he actually was. If I shaded in too much, his image would be too small, like the time I'd tried to draw a crescent moon by colouring in the sky around it with black felt pen. The black had flowed so easily from the pen that I went too far with it, until there was not enough blank page left even to make a moon.

Envisioning the space that my father displaced seemed as impossible as hitting the carnival target that sent a seated bather plunging into a pool. I would have liked to be able to submerge him in water, as my mother did with her slices of butter, to read his mass by the red line the water level reached inside the measuring cup.

Instead, I envisioned the rowing machine. Once, I had seen the seat of it without the rack, when my father had brought the seat out of the locked room to fasten a square cushion of yellow foam to it with silver duct tape. I could envision the buttocks described by the two concave hemispheres of the seat, and extrapolate from there. My father's back would be bent, reaching forwards to grasp the handles at the end of the lever. His head would be bowed, maybe his face would be scrunched like the faces of Olympic rowers or the galley-slaves in *Spartacus*. I had seen his face like that at least once before. It was on an aeroplane, when we went to Winnipeg.

As the pilot's voice announced the beginning of our descent, the stewardess came down the aisle with a tray of hard candies. She said the candies would help stop the earache I was getting from the change of air pressure, and were safer than plugging my nose and blowing until my ears popped, as I had been doing. The stewardess had winked at me, I liked her. *You go ahead and take a couple, sweetheart, if it's okay with your mom*, she said. *Well, they're your teeth*, my mother said. The stewardess laughed and I took two red candies.

My brother had the window-seat and my mother was sitting beside him, in the middle, with me on the end. My father's seat was next to mine across the aisle. I was sucking one of the red candies, which turned out not to be cherry, only red-coloured, but still it seemed to help. I sucked and swallowed and sucked and swallowed as the stewardess had told me, then looked across the aisle to ask my father which colour he had chosen and whether it had a flavour, and whether it was helping. It seemed not to be helping. My father was bent-backed and red-faced, doubled over with his head practically between his knees. His large red hands were held over his ears as though holding the plates of his skull together so that his head would not explode, implode.

My mother said that this was the reason we so seldom went on trips. My father found landings extremely painful, because of the punctured eardrum in his right ear. The hole in his eardrum was responsible for his canine habit of tilting his head to one side like the RCA dog in order to hear things clearly. The hole also meant that sucking hard candies was not enough to counter the pressure pushing in on his unprotected ear canal. I imagined the air pressure needling into his skull, wheezing around in there and creating bubbles of air inside his head, air pockets holding the scent of aeroplane food and aeroplane carpets, the swirling blue chemicals of aeroplane toilets.

There wasn't anything I could do. I couldn't do anything to help him and I couldn't even pretend I hadn't seen him, bent over like that, though I wished with all my heart that I had not. The *Please fasten your seat-belts* sign had been lit up, so I couldn't escape to the bathroom, and I'd been forbidden to go sit someplace else. The only other options were the exit doors indicated in red, located two at the front and two at the rear of the aircraft. But these were several rows away, and I was belted in. And airlines tended not to consult people my age about what might constitute an emergency, though the odds are good that more harm would be done to us if we suffered one. The emergency of witnessing one's father unable to take pressure does not formally constitute an emergency, although damaging side-effects have been shown.

A picture absorbed by the eyes is a strong intoxicant. It can remain in the bloodstream for years, changing its composition in trace but significant ways. The picture of my father bent-backed with his head between his knees, his hands held over his ears like the painting of a figure on a bridge, was such a picture. It would burn its shape onto my retina and it would seek out its own likeness in other men, men in stories, men I would meet. Men with curved spines, men who couldn't fly, men who covered their ears when outside pressure became great. It must be common knowledge that pictures can have this effect, or television stations wouldn't bother warning grown-ups that certain programming might be inappropriate for family viewing. But no PG warning ever appears in the upper-left corner of a retina, to protect people my age from things they might not want to see their parents doing. And anyway, the whole suggestion of parental guidance becomes moot in this case.

It is for good reason that the unmasking of heroes often occurs without forewarning, the impact of unmasking somewhat depends on not being prepared to see it happen. Masks have been snatched away by curious lovers, riotous rivals, virtuous rebels, envious writers. Sometimes, they are vindicated seeing what they see; other times, they're devastated just as easily. There are risks involved in the desire to unmask things. *I'm telling you this, Rose,* on the off chance that you may need to know it someday, if ever you're faced with a choice to know or not know something. I shouldn't call it advice, because advice should only be given out by the very strong, but it has seemed to me that some illusions are vital. Without them, a person's head may explode, implode. Illusions are a membrane between pressure without, pressure within.

Also, there is a difference between not needing to know and needing not to know. I didn't need to know about the man from the riding stable, my mother's lover, probably because on some level I already knew about him, his necessity, his inevitability. His appearance is unsurprising. But I needed not to know of the bowed slope of a spine, the puncture of an eardrum, the possibility that emperors may have their clothes stolen while they're splashing around in the bathtub. I had needed not to know of the soft pale face of Darth Vader beneath the mask, so much depended on the illusion of his mask and cloak, which mirrored poreless space, the thunderous voice and massive hands of faceless space.

I don't know how it happens that illusions of this type inherit such weight, I don't think I came up with the idea myself. But the model being in place, what is a body to do? I had needed not to know that in the final reel, *my god,* the mask and cloak would fall away to reveal nothing more than a face like any other, only paler, softer, more vulnerable than most to the tiny violences of invisible rays. In the theatre-dark, my eyes had sought longingly the red exit signs to the left and right of the screen, but there was no point in leaving my seat, it was too late to un-see what I had seen. There was no way of undoing the damage once I'd seen it.

There is no way of repairing disillusionment despite so much depending on illusions. The illusion of time travelling in a straight line is one of these, and the illusion of being understood by people, and the illusion of any one thing seen as separate from the rest of the universe without which it has no meaning whatsoever. The meaning of things in general is probably an illusion, but people do insist that things have meaning, for reasons of simple faith. If there had been any way of un-seeing my father bent over like that, I would have done it, I would have followed it out onto the narrowest ledge of faith, and severed completely the suspension bridge of disbelief. So there was no way of crossing back.

The air pressure in this cabin is controlled for your comfort. Perhaps this is what should have been written above the door to the locked room. It seemed that my father had to be very careful of outside pressure. It seemed that the pressure of things went directly into his brain and gave him headaches and made him unable to do much. Perhaps his ears were too open, just as my eyes were too open. They took in more than they were able to contain. Perhaps it was right that he learn to cover his ears, just as I had to learn to cover my eyes.

There had to be a balance between what pushed in from outside and what pushed out from inside. There was either not enough pressure in my father's head to counteract the weight of the world, or too much. I had hoped that it was the latter. I had hoped that there was so much force inside my father's skull that the world was simply too thin and insubstantial for him. *Sometimes, I think my head is so big because it's so full of thoughts,* said the Elephant Man. *What happens when thoughts can't get out?* I had hoped that it was this way with my father, rather than the other way round. That his head might explode implied a certain degree of inner strength, force, even a certain amount of dignity. Explosions are things difficult to contain. But that it might implode was unbearable to consider, as though his head were a shrinking balloon, or a Styrofoam cup in the oven.

If my father had been more like Darth Vader, the *real* Darth Vader before the unmasking, he might have worn a black helmet to hold the plates of his skull intact, to balance the pressure within and without. To hold himself together. Instead, he locked himself inside a room and rowed back and forth, back and forth, perhaps in the faith that simple exertion would strengthen the force inside his body, the force pushing back when the world pushed in. *What is Daddy doing down there?* my brother would ask, and I would tell him that our father was only protecting us from the enormous weight and force of his brain. That our father's brain could lift a body into the air by sheer force of will and asphyxiate it without even touching the person. That his thoughts alone could fill a room and swallow the air like a black hole. I wasn't sure any more that this was true, but I thought I should do everything I could to believe it.

Other times, I told Gavin that our father locked himself up for the same reason that a compassionate werewolf might chain up his human body during the day, so that at night his lupine form couldn't cause regrettable harm to other humans he cared about. He was only protecting us from the powerful creature he sometimes became. It didn't occur to me that this could have any negative effect on my brother's perception of our father, because most children were more impressed by Mr. Hyde than by Dr. Jekyll anyway, and would eagerly trade all their Luke Skywalker bubble-gum cards for even a single Darth Vader.

My, what a big strong man my daddy is, I once had said. *My, what a big strong man.* It had been at a Greyhound bus station, several years earlier, when Gavin still had to be carried about in a pack like an overdue library book. But stations and airports are like distilleries where years of words spoken or left unspoken may be condensed into a few parting words, or words of greeting, or oblique general reminders on how to go about having a safe journey. *Don't take any wooden nickels,* my father would say. *Keep your neck covered and don't catch any bad germs,* would be my mother's advice. This particular occasion was one of those trips to my Aunt Hilda's place, which was less of a visit and more of an attempted escape from the invisible elephant in the house. My father would stay at home to battle it alone while the rest of us got out of the way for a few days.

Neither of my parents spoke during the whole drive to the Greyhound station. As soon as the green Torino pulled into the parking lot, my father got out and hauled both big suitcases out of the trunk, then went striding over the black-top like a colossus. It looked that way to me, at least. All he was doing was carrying our bags into the station, to deposit them there before driving back the same way he came and arriving home to an empty house, outside my vision. I was only about three, and couldn't have lifted even one suitcase. One of my father's footsteps covered more ground than three of mine, his legs seemed longer than ski-poles compared to the chunky little limbs toddling after him. Striding over the black-top like that, he looked like a man going somewhere.

My mother had got out of the car more gradually, like a woman determined to take her time. She had pulled endless green chiffon scarves from her purse, carefully draped one over her head and tied it under her chin, watching herself calmly in the rear-view before splashing out into the brisk, bright air. The scarf held her jaw closed, I decided. She sometimes reminded me to hold my jaw, to prevent saying imprudent things.

Now, she was pacing coolly across the black-top several yards behind my father with my brother screaming and struggling in her arms. My stumpy legs in pink tights hurried as quickly as they could after him, then doubled back to catch my mother by her camel coat-tails, to help move things along. *My what a big strong man my daddy is,* I babbled breathlessly, receiving in response a sharp cuff to the ear that rang hot like the hum of a space-heater for quite a while afterwards. I wasn't sure at the time what I'd done wrong, or wasn't sure why it was wrong.

It had been very chilly in Winnipeg. During the flight home, I created as many distractions for myself as possible to avoid noticing my father. Luckily, it was my turn to sit by the window while my brother had to sit across the aisle from him, but I thought it best to borrow my mother's blue gelatinous eye-mask, which obscured peripheral vision entirely. I took three cherry candies from the tray this time and put them all in my mouth. This covered the possibility of speech. I kept my head-set on even after the in-flight audio entertainment went dead, muffling my hearing as much as possible. From my mother's perspective, I was making a scene when a different stewardess than the first one came to collect the head-sets and I wouldn't let go of mine.

I suppose it would be too much to ask you to wait until we got home before you started making scenes, she whispered shortly, but what I was doing was trying to prevent a scene more than make one. It would have been a scene to see my father curl up in a ball again like something unborn. It would have been a bad scene. Seeing it twice might have exceeded the limit of pressure my own skull could withstand, and I might have exploded, imploded. Everyone had things they preferred not to see. Surely, my mother of all people would have to appreciate that.

JAY *Ruzesky* SNEAKING INTO THE
STEPHEN HAWKING LECTURE,
THEN SNEAKING BACK OUT AGAIN

Why don't we notice all these extra dimensions,
if they are really there? —STEPHEN HAWKING

Show me the room full of electric minds
shuffling papers. It's true, they all
wear tweed jackets.

I'm with a handful of idiots at the door
who think uncertainty is when we don't know
for sure.

Still, when all the scientists have filled
their Styrofoam cups from the silver urn of
attentiveness,

the usher lets us sneak into the creaky chairs
at the back of the room.
God knows

why anyone would want to hear this so badly.
God knows. Someone with a beard wheels Hawking
to the front of the room.

Let the congregation rise, then sit,
let even the introductory remarks glide over my head.
The scientist's neck

attaches but does not hold up the head full of stars.
He seems to sleep through his own explanation of
sigma minus infinity.

A brilliant computer delivers his lecture
with the eloquence of a new American car demanding
the seat-belt buckled.

Every now and then, his eyes open. He is
one of those paintings that look straight at
everything at once.

Teach me that time is a box we put things into.
Things are not what they seem. When numbers appear
overhead,

my mind creeps out the back way, touching ground with
the world of fear and control I've been living in.
Enlighten me. I've fallen

in love with my best friend's wife.
I understand only that we walked by the river
Lassie once swam to rescue someone.

We heard trains: mourning some kind of loss, I thought,
but she said they were just wishing they were
somewhere else.

We sat in a wild place, tall grass by a glacier-fed stream,
thinking of fish we couldn't see, thinking of
the animals

moving in the forest's imagination across the water.
Maybe a river otter, anything more wild than
a cat with collar and bell.

Tell me all about anti-particles. I want to believe in
a parallel universe where three or four people can love
one another without flying apart.

A final phrase and the lecture's over, the voice
a bulletin saying if you didn't get it, too bad:
"That is all."

We sat together until the sun shifted off the edge of the planet.
I couldn't remember
the name of a single constellation

but we made up the stars we couldn't quite
make out. Ah yes.
So that is how you fill yourself with light.

ROLLER COASTER

JAY | *Ruzesky*

My father laughed and it was
the first and only time so far
I've heard him do it; a real
laugh deep from inside
climbing like an artillery shell
up his throat and pushing out of
his Edvard Munch mouth.
We were commuters aimed at heaven,
riding a steep, open train towards
the sun-god at the end
of the line, padded straps
reefing our shoulders against
plastic seats. This was
the last place I wanted to be,
locked in like an astronaut,
someone else driving,
lunch rising in my chest.
My eyes were open to
the whine of pulleys as we
ascended a slope snow wouldn't

hold to if snow fell through the
ridiculous summer air. There was
a moment as we reached
the first peak and crested
when I smiled too at weightlessness,
the feeling as you float
from a swell in a fast highway until
most of me dropped. I felt
my stomach's desire
to stay behind up there where it could see
half-way to Saskatchewan and
to bail out again at
the bottom as we were
caught like eggs by a
giant hand and sent up again
over a short rise only to
plunge face-first at the ground
continuing as we rolled
through a giant loop, swooped
with the energy of descent and
twisted through a series
of corkscrew turns, our
brains in startled mobius,
my father wide with giddy terror.
Somewhere along the way he
reached over and squeezed my hand
and our astounded spirits
or some other part of us
that it seemed we could do without
for a while raced behind
like after-images as we rolled on
through the inverted morning,
clutching each other,
wearing death-masks of happiness.

THE MARY DUNBAR LETTER

GREG Hollingshead

TWENTY YEARS AGO, the British Library was still called the British Museum, and I was visiting the Students' Room of the Department of Manuscripts, reading through a stack of volumes of documents and autograph letters relating to Jonathan Swift's tenure as Vicar of Laracor. After three or four hours, I found myself—as I always seem to be doing in the British Library—looking through a volume that had been delivered to my desk by mistake. This was a collection of mainly legal papers (d. 1703–11) from the office of a County Antrim puisne Justice of the Queen's Bench (and later, very briefly, of Common Pleas) named Anthony Upton. Dry-as-dust stuff, except for a series of depositions relating to a witchcraft trial that Upton and another judge presided over at Carrickfergus on March 31, 1711. But more interesting to me than the depositions was a letter of six close-written pages that had been mounted, in error, in the volume along with the depositions, which at first glance it resembled. It was not, however, a deposition but a letter written—and apparently sent (it is dated the day after the trial)—to Judge Upton by Mary Dunbar, the woman whose experiences were the occasion of the trial.

I present the letter here as a sort of "found narrative," exactly as I copied it out in the Students' Room in November 1969, with only the spelling and, here and there, the punctuation regularized. In square brackets, I provide information gleaned from the depositions, as well as from various published accounts of these events and of the trial,

*and have inserted occasional words and affixes (also in square brackets) when I thought
I could make the sense less obscure.*

ALL FOOLS' DAY

Sir:—

I entered service at the house of Reverend John Haltridge
[Presbyterian minister in the parish of Island Magee, near Carrickfergus,
County Antrim] on my fifteenth birthday nine years come May. Reverend
Haltridge dying of a cancer, Mrs. Haltridge [i.e., his widow, Anne] and
myself went in the last week of September to stay at the house of her son,
James Haltridge, also of Island Magee. There my mistress suffered griev-
ance in the night for many nights from some thing, that threw clods and
stones at her bed while she slept though the casement was not open.
Many times the curtains [of her bed] was forced [open] by blows and three
times they [? the blows] drew them all round. With my own eye I saw it,
though invisible, snatch pillows from under her head and pull off her
bedclothes entire. These it made to storm in the room until my mistress
cried out. When the servants come in they [the bedclothes] fell down of a
heap. But we seen it both. Mr. Haltridge made a close search but found
naught. Two days after[wards] my mistress moved to another room and
all annoyance ceased.

On 11th December my mistress was a-sitting in the evening by the
kitchen fire when a small boy strut boldly in and squat on the hearth-
stone. As my mistress told me, he was twelve or eleven years, with black-
cropped hair, wearing a black bonnet on his head, a dirty vest, and a worn-
out blanket. My mistress asked him questions: "Where he [had] come
from? Where he was going? Was he cold or hungry? Would he have rest
by the fire?" He did not answer but frisked round the kitchen then ran
out [of] the house and disappeared in the cow-shed. I was fetched from
my room and give chase with the servants by request of my mistress. We
looked all about, [but] he was not to be seen. Yet Bess [the upstairs maid]
returned to the kitchen and he was there. He had snatched a bit of
mutton out of the fire and eat it snapping and snarling like a ravening

beast. When she tried to catch him he run off. We looked again and he was nowhere to be found. At last Bess, spying the master's old dog trot in, cried out that Mr. Haltridge was come home and *he* would soon catch this vexsome creature (or some such words), whereupon he puffed into smoke before her eyes, or so she swore after. And indeed we were not much plagued by his company till February this year.

On the 11th, which was Sunday, my mistress was alone in the sitting room abovestairs reading Dr. Wedderburn's Sermons on the Covenant. When she lay the book to one side a short time it was suddenly took away. She looked for it all round her chair but could not discover it. On the day following he [the boy] thrust his hand through the windowpane of the scullery with the volume in it, telling Margaret [Spear, the kitchen maid] that this book my mistress would never see more. Margaret, seeking to detain him, asked if he could read it. To this he replied that he could, the Devil had taught him that wee trick and a hundred others beside. Hearing this, Margaret cried out, "The Lord bless me from thee! Thou hast got ill lear [learning]!" He then let fly an oath and, drawing a sword, swore further that he would kill every Christian in the house. Margaret ran into the parlour and fastened the door, but the boy laughed at her and told her that the Devil had taught him to crawl through the smallest holes like a toad or mouse. Saying this, he took up a large stone and heave[d] it through the [parlour] window.

Somewhat after, we looked out and saw him seize the turkey-cock by the tail. He then threw it over his shoulder, the bird making great fuss with his feet so that the book was shook out of a knot in the blanket. Directly he leaped on the wall with the bird over his back he would draw his sword for to kill it but the bird escaped. Missing the book then, he ran nimbly up and down in the yard in search and then come with a club and broke seven panes in the kitchen. We looked out and saw him in the yard, mining [i.e., digging] with his sword. Seeing us watching he said, "I am making a grave for a corpse which will soon come out of this house." He then flew over the wall as if he was a bird. When Mr. Haltridge, who had been away the while, come in, he examined the book, which pages was all bedaubed with dung.

For three days nothing. On the morning of the 15th the clothes was pulled of Mrs. Haltridge['s] bed and stuffed in a bundle behind. New being put on by me they was again took off, folded up and placed under a table that was in that room. A third time I made up the bed and this time they was put in the middle of the floor, shaped in the form of a corpse.

Now several gentlemen, believing a trick, come to inquire. Reverend [Robert] Sinclair [Presbyterian minister at Island Magee, successor to John Haltridge], with Mr. [John] Man and Mr. [Reynold] Leaths [church elders], stayed the next day and night, passing many hours in prayer. The night following [their departure], my mistress went to bed, but at midnight she cried out. Upon [my] going to her, she told me that a knife had been stuck in her neck. On the next day Mr. Haltridge put her in his room (for he and his wife kept separate chambers), himself moving into the room where she was first troubled. But the pain never left and at the end of that week, the 22nd [of] February, she died. All the time she lay ill I stayed at her bedside, and when I went out [of] the room (as from time to time I must) the clothes was took off her bed and shaped in the middle [? of the floor] like a corpse. Once I tied them to the [bed]posts with stout cord, but upon my return the knots was all undone and the clothes laid out like a corpse. The morning before my mistress died they was took off and folded with great care in an upstairs chest.

I was pleased then to be engaged by the daughter[-in-law] of my late mistress. When preparing her room on the 27th [of] February, I saw her new mantle, bodice, vest, stockings, and other fine apparel scattered upon the floor. In the parlour, meantime, Bess found an apron that I had locked up in a closet two days previous. The key was yet in my pocket. The apron was rolled tight in its strings, that had in them seven knots. Bess, as I was told, found a flannel cap wrapped in the apron that my late mistress was fond of. After supper Mr. Haltridge called me to his study and says "I am a pretty lass but he must discharge me as the servants accuse me of working witchcraft in the house." "And before me they would blame the troubles on your own mother," I says. But he tells me only "hold my tongue" and give me my wages.

In my bed that night (for I would set out in the morning) a fit come over me. I saw and felt a knife run through my leg by a woman that I could not see. Margaret sat by me then and the fit soon passed, though scarce the burning. But at midnight seven or eight women seemed to crowd in, talking among themselves about how they would do me harm. "We will stick her all over with knives," says one. "No," cries another, "we will tip boiling oil into her ear as she sleeps," etc. The boy was among them the while, and even as they argued, they caressed him most lewdly, showing their asses to enflame him. They called each other by their names, so when they left I names them to Margaret: *Janet Liston, Elizabeth Sellar, Kate M'Calmont, Janet Carson, Janet Mean* (who twisted my tongue, and with her bony fingers and swelled knuckles pressed it so I could scarce breathe and would tear out my throat if she could), one they called *Latimer*, and a sly one they called but *Mrs. Ann.* I also give a strict account to Mr. Haltridge, who spoke to Reverend Sinclair and to Mr. Man, who sent for women answering [to] those names and fitting my descriptions and others besides. As each one come near the house I fell in a fresh fit, though I could not see them approach. When they brought in [Janet] Carson [a seamstress] I felt a most cruel pain in my knee. After[wards] they looked and found a fillet belonging to my mistress tied fast about it with seven double knots and one single. Mr. Adair [a local teacher] sent one [woman] and the fit come on again, driving a knife in my thigh, and when she come in I says, *O Latimer, Latimer* (which was her name) and she hit the description I give Margaret. In this way, out of thirty brought to me I found at first seven true witches. This, however, made them wrath[ful] and they swore they would carry me out the window but I called out to God in my mind and they let me drop. I was told after I had rose off the bed and sunk all outstretched to the floor.

At this time they begun to put things in my stomach and I to vomit them out again, viz. feathers, yarn, wool, pins, waistcoat buttons (five), hair, clippings of nails, mouse claws, and suchlike. These caused terrible torments in my guts. Also at this time I had suffering by a woman blind of an eye who told me they would hinder me hearing the curate's prayers for me, which they did. Three women blind of an eye were brought and they did not bother me. But when they brought [Jane] Miller near the house (though I did not know it), I fell a-sweating and thought I should faint and when they brought her struggling in the house, I fell in such fits that two men said they could not hold me, and [I] cried out, "For Christ's sake, take the Devil out of the room!" This creature was possessed, for she says to me, "If the plague of God is on thee, then the plague of God be on us all together, and if the Devil is among us God help us all. If God has taken thy health then God give thee health; if the Devil has taken it, then the Devil give it thee." She then stares like a madwoman about the room and cries in a loud voice, "O misbelieving ones, eating and drinking damnation to yourselves, crucifying Christ afresh, and taking all out of the hands of the Devil!" I heard no more, being made senseless by this talk. They took her from me and charged her. After this fit they found string tied round my waist that was not there before, with seven double knots and one single. Father O'Hare then advised Mr. Haltridge to write some words out of St. John. This paper Mrs. Haltridge would tie in an incle [i.e., length of narrow tape] knotted three times round my neck. The women [in my visions] refused, but in one of my fits she sneaked it on. I was then thrown in violent convulsions, being held down by three men, and a horrible pain struck through my middle. Seeking the trouble, Mrs. Haltridge discovered the incle tied now round my waist, with seven double knots and one single, my hands being held fast the while.

On Sunday the 28th [of] February Mr. Haltridge would have them carry me to church to partake [of] the sacrament, but the women [in my visions] declared I would not go over [the] threshold of that chamber. Several times did the men attempt to lead me out but as often was I thrown in fits. They then took up the threshold but were immediately struck with a horrid stench of brimstone that reeled them back and spread through the house causing their stomachs to rise up and confounding [their] brains. When the stench come I heard a great loud laugh from the boy (though I could not see him) and after the fit passed I could hear it still echoing for many minutes together.

Between the 3rd and 24th [of] March statements were took and the Mayor [of Carrickfergus] had arrested eight persons as you well know: Janet Mean, of Braid Island; Jane Miller and Jane Latimer of Irish Quarter, Carrickfergus; Margaret Mitchell, of Kilroot (called by the others "Mrs. Ann" but found out by my description); Catherine M'Calmont, Janet Liston (called Sellar), Elizabeth Sellar, and Janet Carson, all of Island Magee. [The women were brought up for trial on March 31, 1711, before Judges Upton (recipient of this letter) and James Macartney, both natives of County Antrim.] Those [the accused] swore to me privately that I should have no power to give evidence in court and indeed I did not know there where I was and could not speak being afflicted without mercy by three persons I never seen before, brought before me by the boy. These held me steady while he whispered me every manner of filth and lewdness.

The accused women had no lawyer, and the mental state of Mary Dunbar not being considered at that time a medical matter no such testimony was taken. All eight women strongly denied being witches, Jane Miller calling loudly for God to witness that she had been wronged. The court heard evidence concerning their characters, most of which was fairly damning, though this seems to have been more a result of their physical unattractiveness, the abrasiveness of their characters, their minority status (as Presbyterians), and the maliciousness these factors can give rise to in a small community, than of any particular information brought against them. As one authority points out, most had recently taken communion, and several were evidently steady, industrious women; many were known to pray with their families both in private and in public, and most knew the Lord's Prayer, though it was generally said that because they were all Presbyterians, they must have learned it in prison. (Witchcraft trials make some of the most sobering reading on earth.)

Judge Upton concluded his summation by saying that though he had no doubt the matter was diabolical in the genuine sense of that word, he also had no doubt that the jury should refuse to find the accused guilty on the basis merely of the visions of the afflicted woman. He concluded by saying that for himself, he could not see how persons in compact with the Devil would be such "faithful attenders upon Divine Service." Judge Macartney, on the other hand, thought that the jury might very reasonably find them guilty. The jury agreed, and the eight women were sentenced to one year in jail, during which period they were to stand in the pillory four half-days. On these occasions, the mob pelted them with the usual stones, rotten eggs, and vegetables, causing Janet Mean to lose an eye and Janet Carson to suffer a concussion and broken nose.

My tormentors being locked away [Mary Dunbar's letter concludes], Mr. Haltridge says I must get well and be lady to his wife. I thanked him on my knees, and he is a warm, handsome gentleman, sure. But last night The Boy come to me and would squeeze my arm until I cried out if I did not let him in my bed. There he makes himself a cat (though large for a cat), which the Devil has taught him—indeed, I'd wonder not were he the Devil himself—and these tricks and more he will teach me if I behave and do as he tells, for, says he, "We have work to do." "My mistress?" says I. "No," says he, "that bitch can wait." Truly he is a droll, comely lad at base and blessed with [super]natural powers.

And therefore out of your great kindness [of] which we have seen such evidence of late, tell me, good Sir (now it is Fools' Day), how a poor girl is to deny one who makes so large and energetic a cat? And tell me beside why you would call her before everybody a "poor visionary wretch"? And when you have considered these questions I expect you will want to attend one of these Divine Services of which you speak so high, and so you should, because you will need every Ally that you can muster in the Long Night that is a-coming for you. Sir, I am

> Your most humble obedient servant,
> MARY DUNBAR

According to the Dictionary of Irish Biography, *Anthony Upton committed suicide on September 11th of the same year. The circumstances are not given. I have been able to discover nothing about Mary Dunbar's subsequent career in the household of James Haltridge, but I do think that warm Mr. Haltridge had better have watched his step.*

LOST THINGS POKE THROUGH MELTING SNOW

STEPHANIE | *Bolster*

Stunted remnants of plants, months-old dog shit, a single red mitten that belonged to a girl who'd been punished for the loss, one hand made to go bare the rest of that winter, reddened bright as the mittened other. When her mother, tending tulip shoots, found the mitten, she pinned it to the girl's chest, broke the skin so she would not forget. The next winter they found the girl's heart, grey and hard as stone, in the centre of a thrown snowball. It nearly blinded the boy. In the kitchen they set the heart beside the turkey wishbone, meatless and saved for later. Microwaved on low, stroked with new white towels, it thawed into the pumping of nothing through itself. In the hospital they returned it wrapped in sheets and anaesthesia, stitched deep, a gift she could not return. The next year she went walking in her red rubber boots until only a trail of hollow exclamation marks was left.

STEPHANIE Bolster

ON THE STEPS OF THE MET

When the first wasp would not stop flying near me I sat still
and let it stay. All thin legs and yellow, it did not find my skin
but the silvered mouth of the Pepsi can. It crawled inside

and then another joined it there. I let those two
fill themselves while I finished my greasy knish and thought
how I would soon not be here and how painful

not wanting anyone. One wasp staggered out
and flew, and then the other, and in Manhattan
they were two cabs on their way in one direction. Inside,

what I had loved most: the folds of the woman's scarf
in Vermeer's portrait, their depth of shadow,
how the fabric came so close to itself without touching.

SOLAR PLEXUS

ANNE *Fleming*

AT SEVENTEEN, CRAIG BROUGHTON looked forty. His hair was the hair of the balding—lank and thin, starting well back of his forehead, with a line of lean, combed-back fuzz running the middle course of his pate. His forehead was pale and often wrinkled in thought, his chin was soft and pudgy, his fingers stubby, his glasses dug ridges into his puffy cheeks.

Craig Broughton, at seventeen, removed the mirror from the upstairs bathroom. His sister, to whom he did not speak, and who did not speak to him, put it up again. He took it down. She put it up. He broke it. Their parents didn't believe in interfering in the relationship between brother and sister. If they fought, they fought; it was up to them to make up. They did not imagine that they never would.

Inside Craig's pudgy soft face was the soul of a burning lover. That was what Craig didn't see when he looked in the mirror. And if he couldn't see it, knowing it was there, who would, not knowing? His long pale lashes, his nondescript eyes, the blackheads on his nose. None of it said who he was, and yet he was he. His body was his. His body was him. He had not always believed so.

From twelve to fourteen, Craig was convinced he had a vocation for the priesthood. The family was not Catholic, but he was serious, they did not know how serious he was. When his mother offered that he might want to keep his options open, he rebuked her with fiercely pious stares—he was not the beatific type. "Goodness! Look at him, Pete. I'm afraid he's going to start flagellating any minute." Unbearable, this mockery, but bear it he must. He went to his room to pray. Also to masturbate.

Which led him in the end to think that celibacy was not his thing after all. He started to wonder if sex could be his thing. He read D.H. Lawrence and science fiction free-love daddy-o Robert Heinlein along with whatever glossy mags he smuggled home (looking older than one's years can have its advantages). Finally he found Henry Miller, and knew he'd found what he was looking for. A man who would take women from behind, or two at a time, a man who would get his cock sucked under the table at restaurants, a man who would call them cunts and they would come dripping, running, coming, coming. Unh.

His burning lover's soul had a particular object in mind. A girl he had had a single class with the year before. They had sat next to each other. He had made her laugh on several occasions. Once, when he noticed a classmate's finger-drumming was irritating her, he'd asked the offending student to knock it off, and had thus earned a precious smile.

Fiona Theosakis was not particularly pretty, or particularly popular. Or ugly, or unpopular. Her smile, when it graced her face, was lovely, her eyes sorrowful. She did her homework diligently. Craig suspected her home life of severity. What form this severity took, he didn't know. An autocratic alcoholic father, say, and a wan work-worn mother, maybe a snotty-nosed toddling brother left in her care.

She had a small group of friends, a tight knot of girls who went places together, the washroom, the corner store, the cafeteria. In grade twelve, however, Fiona was unlucky enough to find she had a different lunch from her friends.

Craig was not stupid. He didn't try to approach her in the cafeteria, a place he loathed in any case. (He would have preferred to hold the cafeteria in high disdain rather than loathing, but he could not keep his emotion at such a remove.) He ate in the hall, reading, leaning up, it just so happened, against her locker, which was in an alcove. "Sorry, am I in your way?" he said when she stood above him. Quick smile, slide over. Back to the book. The next day he sat a few lockers over, not to be obvious. The third day she asked what he was reading. "Nietzsche," he said. "What's it about?" she asked. He hummed for a minute. "The death of God and the birth of man," he said. "Okay," she said skeptically and walked off with her books.

But the next day she said, "Your name's Craig, right? I'm Fiona." Two weeks later she ate her lunch in the alcove, too. She believed in God, although sometimes she wasn't sure. Her father was dying of lung cancer, and where was God in all of that? Offering a just reward for smoking his whole life, for contaminating the holy temple of his body?

When she later found out Craig smoked—Gitanes, of course—she said, "Don't. Don't smoke. It will kill you." He could have kissed her feet, right there, the way she said it, though he wouldn't stop smoking.

Craig was careful not to let his adoration show. He would be a friend, a confidant. One day she would cry for her father, cry and cry, and she would accept his shoulder, his kisses, his gentle stroking of hair. Then she would turn wild with grief, needing to feel alive, alive, every nerve alive, and they would ravish each other. This would happen in a park or woodland, on a warm fall evening.

Fiona left school every day by the southwest doors, walking the three blocks to the subway sometimes on her own, more often with one or two of her friends. Each afternoon, Craig sat on his motorcycle at the mouth of the teachers' parking lot, waiting to see if she'd be alone and if he'd have the courage. Each night he pictured their meeting, the graceful unfolding of fate: he pulling up smoothly beside her on his motorcycle, she turning to him instinctively, hair swirling like the softest skirt, hand wordlessly accepting the wordlessly proffered helmet.

The next time she was alone—about a week and a half after he'd started watching her—he did have the courage, gently easing out of the parking lot about a block behind her. But there was nowhere to pull up. Every parking space was taken. She passed the bus stop in the second block. It was stop now and yell, or lose her.

"Fiona!" His voice sounded squeaky and muffled, even to him. She kept walking.

Lifting his visor, he yelled again. "Hey, Fiona!"

She turned. Oh God, her hair, the swirl of it. It was exactly as he'd imagined. But she gazed blankly at the street with the wary, embarrassed look of a person unsure she'd heard right, and turned away.

Again he called her name. Another perfect swirl. Another unrecognizing scan of the street. He waved, fumbling with the strap on his helmet with one hand while ripping off his glasses with the other. Everything blurred, including her uncertain look. By the time he got his helmet off and glasses back on, she was coming towards him, smiling.

He was gelatinous all of a sudden, boneless. He had no bones. Somehow he managed to talk anyway. She wasn't going home, she was going to the hospital. She'd love a ride. She loved motorcycles, her uncle had one. She'd love a ride.

He handed her his spare helmet and she swung her hair—swoosh, swoosh—over her shoulders before putting it on. She straddled the motorcycle. His bones grew back into the hollows they'd left when they disappeared.

He took her to the hospital often after that. Not every day, not even every day she was alone. But often. He waited outside the hospital for long stretches before riding off. Sometimes he saw his reflection in store windows as he rode by. With the helmet and black jacket, he looked like he *could* be someone's fierce tender lover.

Once, he waited across the street until she came out again, her mother leaning on her arm in her flowered rain-hood and cheap plastic boots. Her younger sister lagging behind with a yo-yo. They got on the streetcar and went east.

For a week in late October, she did not come to school. For another week her friends skipped their lunchtime classes, a warm concerned knot around her again. When he said hi in the halls, they asked who he was, and she said nothing until he was out of earshot.

Friday afternoon the following week, she found him at his locker. "Take me for a ride," she said. "I want to go fast." So he took her up Highway 48 to Lake Simcoe. She was shivering when they stopped. He gave her his jacket. They went down to the water, and she started to cry, just as he'd imagined it, but when he put his arm around her, she pulled away and walked quickly down the beach. She sat down with the jacket around her knees. He followed and sat next to her. She shook. Her chin chattered up and down. He tried his arm around her again, lightly, then tighter. She felt thin and strong. All her muscles were tense.

He kissed her hair. Comfortingly, he thought, though surely she sensed the passion curled up in it. With each kiss, he smelled her hair, some ordinary shampoo forever destined to mean her and her alone. His nose, his sight, his sense of touch, everything seemed sharper than ever. Time seemed slower, it sat there on the beach like driftwood growing white. He tried a kiss on her cheek, half turned away. It turned no further. She swung the jacket from her knees to her shoulders.

He put his hand on her chin, to draw it to him. She let him. Her eyes were the fullest he'd seen. The only ones he'd seen this close up. "Don't," she said. He didn't think she meant it, but how could he know?

Henry Miller would know. Henry Miller could see through all the subterfuge of the words before sex. Henry didn't have to assess, he just knew, from how much he wanted her, she must want him, too. Craig put his lips to hers, moved his hand inside the jacket to her breast, the briefest flicker of tongue, tiny taste of bliss, the unbelievable weighty sphere against his fingers. And then a crack like an anvil across his chest and he lay back, winded. Jesus.

"Don't," she said again, voice tense, on her feet, fists at the ready. "I'll walk home if I have to."

He sucked at the air, furious but too stunned to do anything about it. Who'd have thought an elbow could hurt so much. She marched towards the road, clearly prepared to be true to her word. He wanted to chase after and tackle her, to punch her stomach, to knee her groin, to beat her and pound her and carry her away. His breath back, he panted. He wanted to hurt her any way he could, and he lay there knowing that, until he was stiff and cold and it was gone.

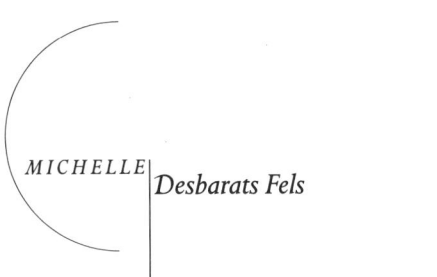

MICHELLE Desbarats Fels

FAIR

When the aliens came to town
they'd set up a fairground with rides,
names like the Galaxy Swing,
the Comet. There was a ride that resembled
a ferris wheel but it had stars
all over it, they lit up in the dark
so it looked like a circular section
of the night sky whirling around.
When the aliens came to town they
set up booths selling food called
space travel burgers and
milky way cotton candy. You could buy
a drink called lightspeed that looked
and tasted like lemonade
only sweeter, faster.
When the aliens came to town they all
had fuzzy hair like Albert Einstein,
like cotton candy, they all wore
muscle T-shirts with low hanging arm holes,
they wore jeans, the legs greasy from wiping
wrenches after tightening bolts.

Everything looked different
even outside the fairgrounds,
stop signs glowed like white-lettered poppies,
grass whispered next to sidewalks in the dark.
Money pressed into the pockets of our pants,
we put on pretty blouses leaving one more button
undone. We shivered as strange heavy
fingers pulled worn lines of leather
or black rubber across our hips,
the only protection for rides bringing
us a little closer to the stars.
Afterwards we'd wonder if the aliens loved us,
we'd search their faces,
laugh, move away from their moist grins.
Sometimes a girl went too far for love,
after the rides disappeared and the night had
lifted back into outer space
a half-human, half-alien child
would be left, growing in the ground
of her stomach,
a child to be afraid of.

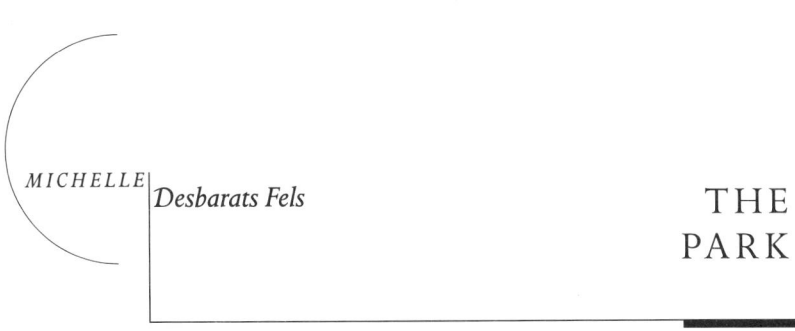

MICHELLE *Desbarats Fels*

THE PARK

Don't ever tell your mother this, said my aunt
but once when I took your little sister to the park
I turned my back, just for a moment
and she was gone,
where she'd been was sidewalk, grass, trees.
There were three directions I could go
to find her, I knew I only had one chance,
one choice, I took a deep breath and walked
toward the corner. I didn't run
because I knew if she was around it she would be there
and if she was not, it wouldn't make any difference.
And there she was, in her yellow sunsuit
walking, as proud as could be, along the sidewalk.
I was so happy, said my aunt, I think I cried.

As I listen to her tell me this I read in her face
what the years in between
have not removed.
A part of my aunt died that day as surely
as the other two little girls, yellow dressed,
who went walking down those other paths
and were never seen again.

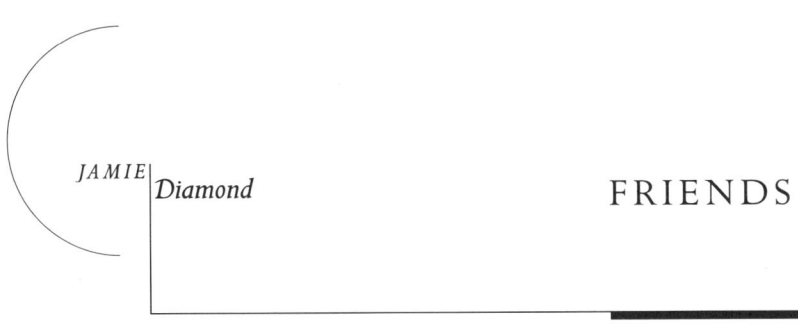

JAMIE Diamond   FRIENDS

A FEW MINUTES AFTER the Santa Monica library opens, Lindy sees a man who reminds her of Sam. He doesn't look like Sam. But there's something about the curve of his spine, the muscle twitching under his cheek.

Before she realizes it, she's out of her chair.

The aisles between the grey-metal library shelves are wide; she can easily pass behind the man. And as she does, she places her hand against his back, that simple gesture allowed of strangers when they need to get by.

Her palm takes in his body's warmth.

"Excuse me," she whispers.

The man steps forwards, without turning around to see who has touched him.

When she reaches the end of the row, she turns and walks back down the same aisle. She cannot stop her hand from brushing against his back once more. Once more, he steps forwards, accepting her touch without seeing her.

At Sunset Beach, she watches Richard Sullivan trying to find her. She peers over her sunglasses to make sure it's him, but he's an easy target. His profile is like Alfred Hitchcock's; he's wearing a pair of lime-green clam diggers and has draped a hot pink towel around his shoulders.

She waves.

"There you are." He shakes out a watermelon-patterned towel that floats to the sand like a sheet on a bed. He sinks down on it. "I found you."

"How was the water?"

He shrugs. "Not bad."

Lindy has known Richard for less than a week, but she knows he's afraid of the breakers. He's recently moved to Los Angeles from New York and cannot swim. He comes to the beach to get a tan and watch the men.

He squints at her. "Did you go in?"

"A while ago."

"And?"

"I swam for an hour." Sometimes it makes her feel better to lie.

A wave of air that smells like a Mounds bar floats by, but she knows it's suntan lotion. She watches a man holding a magazine disappear into the darkness of the public men's room. She pours hot sand from one palm to the other.

"Why do men take magazines to the bathroom?"

"Make use of the time, I guess."

The sand has cooled. "Sam used to piss on his cigarettes," she says. "He'd toss them into the toilet and piss on them."

"What for?"

"I don't know. Battleships in the ocean. He could make them burst apart at the seams."

"Such fond memories."

"I wish I didn't have any memories at all."

A small cluster of perspiration drops has gathered in the hollow between her breasts. She wipes the sand off her hands and stands up. "Let's get something to eat."

They pass Latin couples who sit in the sunshine, the men in long-sleeved shirts, the women in tight-fitting dresses. Purple-haired teenagers, also fully clothed, lie on the sand, resting on comic books spread under their heads.

At the snack bar, she orders from a young man wearing an apron smeared with tomato-sauce hand-prints. His eyebrows are sunbleached and his eyes are the turquoise of swimming pools. He tells her he'll call her number when her order is up. She watches him reach into a shimmering oven, lift out a pizza, and set it on a table. He wipes off his upper lip with the crook of his wrist and smiles when he notices her staring. She smiles back.

Richard is on about some bar he went to last night; she's not listening.

"Number fourteen?" The young man says, looking right at her. She starts to say yes, but she can't find her voice.

Richard reaches for his wallet.

"I'll get it," she says quickly. She gives the young man a five-dollar bill. He touches her fingers when he takes it. When he counts back her change, he looks into her eyes and lays each coin slowly and separately onto her open hand.

"That's fifty, seventy-five, and a dollar," he says. And with the last quarter, he draws his fingers slowly across her outstretched palm.

Then he looks behind her. "Next," he says.

"Do you think he's too young for me?" Richard says.

She turns. "Who?"

"Him," he gestures at the man behind the counter.

"Of course he's too young for you," she says.

By the time she gets home, she's a ball of nerves. Rainclouds hang low in the sky, but she's too jumpy to stay indoors. A long expanse of grass awaits her—a park on the bluffs above the ocean. She'll start slowly, stretching out until she finds her pace, and then she'll run, another force pulling her besides her flying feet, as if a shadow Lindy jogged tirelessly around the park just waiting for the flesh Lindy to come outside and join up.

The wind shakes the trees and makes them sound like the ocean. Why did she wear shorts? Her teeth start to chatter. Thunder claps overhead; an instant later the El Niño rain storm begins.

Raindrops, warmed by her scalp, roll down her face like tears. In only a few moments, the ground beneath her turns to mud. She wants to run faster to get warm, but the slippery earth won't provide traction. She's on a treadmill, going nowhere. She's not tired, she's not going to get tired.

She makes it back to her apartment, hugging herself, picturing a hot shower. She fumbles with the key, gets inside, and squishes to the bathroom. By now she's shaking. She steps into the shower with her clothes on and turns on the hot water. But she's still cold. Because she's left the bathroom door open, clouds of hot steam billow into the living room and set off the smoke alarm.

She turns off the shower.

It's just not going to work.

She reaches for the phone. "Richard, what are you doing for dinner?"

"Anyway," he says between bites, "I dragged him with me to buy cigarettes because the cigarette machine throws off the strongest light in The Elephant."

She fidgets. "I didn't know you smoked, Richard."

Strands of melted Swiss cheese escape through his Reuben sandwich and drop between his fingers. "I don't." He licks some cheese off his knuckles. "I had to get him into the light to make sure he didn't have warts or anything." He rips open five Sweet 'N Low packets and pours them into his iced tea. "Anyway," he says, "we made out by the cigarette machine. It was so romantic. But then he blew it. He stuck his tongue into my mouth. Would you like that on a first kiss?"

"How's your sandwich?"

"It's all right," Richard says. "Would you?"

She doesn't answer but Richard doesn't seem to notice.

"It started out so sweet," he says. "He put his finger under my chin, looked into my eyes, and slowly turned my face to his." Richard's expression is dreamy. "He looked into my eyes a moment longer, and we both knew what was going to happen next. He kissed me real soft. Then he ruined everything by jamming his tongue down my throat. Why couldn't he have waited until we were in bed, at least?"

She rolls her paper straw-wrapper into a little ball.

"I have something to admit," she says.

"What?"

"It's hard for me to have pictures like that."

He waits.

"Of men doing that to each other," she goes on.

He laughs. "Why?"

"I'm funny that way. I'm sorry. But I still want us to be friends. Can we be?"

"Of course." He nods at her, his mouth full. "Tell me what you did with Sam."

"What do you mean?"

"You know what I mean."

"No, I don't."

"You know. What did he like you to do?"

"This is too embarrassing."

He squints his eyes. "Aren't we friends?"

"Yes."

"Then there's nothing embarrassing about it."

"The light's too bright."

He says, "One little detail?"

Over his shoulder, she watches a homeless woman walk up to the counter, pour a container of cream into a dirty glass of ice water, and gulp the mixture down.

"Just one little detail?"

The woman looks around, wipes her chin, and shuffles out of the deli into the rain.

Lindy opens her mouth. She wishes she were wearing her sunglasses.

"The skin on his penis is smooth. Like baby's skin."

Richard stops eating.

"Sam doesn't like me to say it's soft. He likes me to say it's smooth."

Richard looks at her.

"It's smooth. I like it by my face. I like the way it smells."

Richard puts down his sandwich.

"More?" she says.

His voice is husky. "More."

She unclips her earrings, lays them on a paper napkin, and goes on talking.

It's past noon when she wakes up the next day. She draws back her curtains. The rain is gone.

Outside her window, just a few feet away, a shirtless telephone man shinnies up a cinnamon-coloured telephone pole. The veins on his arms bulge. Sweat glistens on his back.

Her hands play along the ropes of the curtain pull. She knows exactly what he smells like: freshly sawn lumber, Camel cigarettes, and grease.

He's close enough to touch.

She opens her window.

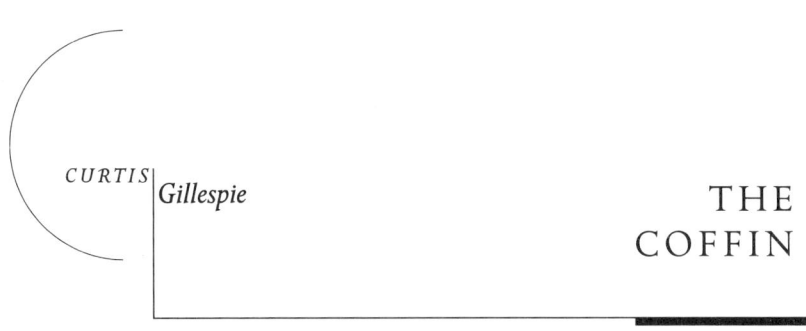

CURTIS *Gillespie*

THE
COFFIN

O N J A N U A R Y 4 , 1 9 6 0 , the French philosopher and novelist Albert Camus died in a car crash on the way from Lourmarins to Paris. January 4, 1960, was also the day, so I'm told, that my parents conceived me in Calgary, Alberta. I was made aware of this coincidence around the age of eighteen by my paternal grandfather, Neil, whom I lived with in Edmonton after the death of my father.

"What do you make of that?" Neil asked me when he told me about the coincidence. "Strange, isn't it?"

I was just another kid who didn't want to go to university, though, because of Neil's urging, I did read philosophy. I didn't mind philosophy, but I wanted to be a woodworker.

"That's pretty cool," I said. "Was he cool?"

"He most certainly was," said Neil. "French, good-looking, and dynamite with the ladies."

"All right," I said approvingly.

I lived with Neil for eleven years. My parents died in separate car accidents, and I was in the car on both occasions. My mother died when I was nine, my father when I was thirteen. Both crashes left me unscathed physically, and emotionally I have healed as much as I am going to. The only visible hold-over is that I do not drive. But this is largely at the insistence of Neil, who pretends to believe that I am the incarnation of the spirit of Albert Camus.

Neil was a natural with wood, though he earned his paycheque teaching philosophy at the University of Alberta, and it was from him that I learned the beautiful symmetry of working with wood. I also learned from him that philosophy and woodworking are just different sides of the same coin. Both are about construction, about imagination interwoven with system. The rendering of elements into a coherent structure. There is a design at the heart of everything, Neil used to say, whether with oak or knowledge or people. The artist is the person who can find it. I believed him to be right and earn my living as a woodworker today.

One evening my wife came out to the garage, which I have converted into a woodworking studio. It was about ten thirty, past our bedtime, but we had just returned from visiting at the hospital and I had gone straight out to the garage. She came in, bringing the cool fall air with her, and stood by the door, considering my latest project, the pieces of which I had up on a waist-high 8' x 2' trestle. She was looking, not talking. Just watching me work the palm sander. I saw her and turned it off, propped my safety glasses on my forehead.

"Honey," she said. "Don't you think it's just a bit morbid?"

I put the sander down. "Neil wants to be buried. In a coffin. I'm making it."

She kept watching me, her arms wrapped around her ribs. "Does Neil know? Have you told him, I mean? That you're building him a coffin?"

"No," I said. "It hasn't exactly come up."

Neil had been admitted to Oncology at the University of Alberta Hospital the previous week. The doctors had said he'd go soon, that his thoracic cancer was inoperable and would eat him from the inside out. The doctors also told us that we should prepare for him to die at any moment, and they told us this as if it is a kind of preparation we have been schooled in.

Anne kicked at some sawdust on the floor. "Do you want a ride to work tomorrow?"

"I'm taking the day off," I said. "I'm going to spend the morning with Neil and come back here in the afternoon."

"Oh," Anne said. "I can give you a ride to the hospital, then."

"Sure."

I knew I was being a little uncommunicative, but I was anxious to get back to work on the coffin. I picked up the sander. It was going to be a beautiful piece. Simple yet elegant. Solid mahogany. I was going to stain it with a light oil to highlight the long smooth grain, which had the pattern of soft waves emanating from a disturbance at the centre of a still pond.

I looked back to Anne. "Are you going to stand there all night?"

"I was saying a prayer for Neil."

"Oh."

"What about you?" she said.

"Prayers?"

"No, are you going to stay here all night?"

"No," I said. "I just want to finish this section."

She nodded. "I'll make some tea."

"Sure." I turned on the sander and its whine precluded further conversation. I put my safety glasses back on and went back to the piece I was edging.

Neil and my grandma had a good relationship. I understood this as a kid, just by being around them, but Neil talked a lot about Grandma after she died. They had fun together, he said, and even though they often argued, about anything, there was always an element of play to it, as if they were just teasing each other and knew it. I do remember sitting at our kitchen table when my own parents were still alive, listening to the four of them talk. Neil, my father's father, was logical, wordy, and secular; Grandma was common sense, tell-tale facial gestures, and deeply Catholic.

Neil became a much more serious man after Grandma died. Every November thereafter, on the anniversary of her death, he carved or built out of wood crucifixes and little churches and once even the tablet of the Ten Commandments. Every year it was something different. Grandma had always wanted him to convert, but he never did. The making of these things was his apology.

Anne took me to the hospital the next day on her way to work. I went to Oncology, but they had moved Neil to Intensive Care. When I got to ICU, there were different visitor-entrance criteria, and it took me ten minutes just to get through the doors and then into his room, which he was sharing with one other patient. When I walked in, three doctors were standing over Neil's bed. I went and stood at the edge of the group.

"You must be David," said one of the doctors. I said I was and they introduced themselves. They were all young, which bothered me immediately. They didn't look much older than myself.

Neil was conscious. He was lying on his back with tubes up his nose and an IV needle in his arm. I smiled at him and he gave me a feeble nod.

"Why has he been moved from Oncology?" I asked, still looking at Neil. I ran my hand over his hair and forehead.

The doctor who was obviously in charge didn't look at me, only at Neil. "Well," he said, in a cheerful voice, "we just thought it would be nice for Neil here to have a change of scenery. Isn't it better here, Neil?"

Neil's mouth was open, trying to breathe as best he could, so he didn't say anything, but he looked at the doctor and moved his head deliberately from side to side. The three doctors laughed heartily.

"No lack of spirit," said the one in charge. "We like having you anyway, Neil." He patted Neil on the leg. They made a show of closing some flipcharts they had in their hands, and started towards the door. I followed them out into the hallway.

"We moved him late last night," said the doctor in charge, half to me and half to the other doctors. "He's got a bad infection, maybe pneumonia. We're pretty sure he aspirated some vomit at some point last night."

"Which means?"

"That he's going to have an even tougher time. I'll be honest, he could be in for a rough ride."

I looked at the three of them in turn. "He knows he's going to die," I said. "Please don't be so condescending to him next time."

I went back into the room. Neil had his eyes closed but opened them when I said his name. I put my face close to his. His breath was wretched and he had blobs of mucus in the corners of his eyes, which I cleaned out for him. He needed a shave. He closed his eyes again when he knew I wasn't going to leave right away.

"Hey, Neil," I said softly. "How're they treating you here?"

He took a deep breath and spoke as he exhaled. "Same as other place," he hissed.

"That bad, eh?"

He nodded. We sat in silence for a couple of minutes. He opened his mouth as if he was going to speak, so I put my face closer.

"I'm old, aren't I, David?" he said. "Eighty-two, you know." He said it as if no one else knew.

I smiled at him. "Yes, I know, Neil. You're an old coot."

"An old coot," he laughed and hissed air out. "That's right." He stopped laughing and fixed his look at me though he kept his eyes closed. "We don't die, you know, David. Did you know that? We don't."

"Why's that?" I asked.

He let his eyes open. "Better to die on one's feet than live on one's knees. Camus said that."

"I know," I said, smiling. "I haven't forgotten."

"You're not driving are you, Albert?"

"No," I said, somewhat taken aback. I couldn't tell if he was joking.

He looked at me then as if he did not know me. He closed his eyes and appeared to fall into a sleep. A moment later, a nurse bustled noisily into the room, and his eyes flashed open at her like klieg lights. He looked terrified and he shut them again right away. After a couple of minutes, he drifted into a very restless sleep, moaning loudly, muttering about his head, his stomach. I spoke to the nurse and she gave him a Tylenol injection, which calmed him slightly. I sat at his bed and watched him for the next three hours. Occasionally, he spoke in his sleep, saying somebody's name. Once, he lifted his arm and went through the motions of writing something, a letter perhaps.

Sitting there, I thought that my life, from this point forwards, would be well spent directly emulating him. He was a kind and thoughtful man who lived his life with integrity. A man whose legacy ought to be having people emulate him.

I left the hospital around lunchtime and spent the afternoon working on Neil's coffin. When Anne got home, she saw where I was and came out.

"How's Neil?" she asked.

I leaned on the trestle. "He's not so great," I said. "Not making a lot of sense. They've moved him to ICU."

She didn't say anything but stepped forwards and ran her hand over one of the corner pieces of the coffin, then all the way down the edge to where I was standing. She lightly touched other parts of the coffin, then sifted her fingers through my hair and patted it down. "I know how much you want to give him something," she said softly. "I'm going to go see him after dinner. Will you come with me?"

I ran my sleeve over my eyes and nodded.

"Good," she said. She looked at the coffin and then me, as if she were going to say something about it but changed her mind. She kissed me and went back to the house.

After dinner, I collected some shaving materials so that I could give Neil a shave that evening. At the hospital, I got a bowl of hot water and a couple of towels. Anne helped me put the foam on his face and he tried to joke with us, but it cost him a lot of energy so he stayed quiet.

"Here we go, Neil," I said, as I drew the blade down from his sideburns to his chin. I took a few more strokes and then had to stop for a minute, my hands were shaking so badly.

"Are you all right?" Anne whispered.

I bent my head forwards. Neil had heard Anne.

"Don't nick me," he said, air whistling lightly out from between his teeth.

Anne and I smiled. She leaned over and gave him a kiss on the temple. "You hear everything, don't you?" she said. He gave one nod.

We finished shaving and rinsing him, and then I put some aftershave on him. He turned his mouth down as best he could. "I smell funny," he whispered. Then he tried to smile. He was in obvious pain, and Anne went to get a nurse to give another injection.

When Anne left the room, I bent close to him.

"Neil," I said into his ear. "Neil, can you understand me for a few minutes?" I drew my head back and looked at him. He didn't say or move anything, but he opened his eyes and squinted hard at me, as if to fight the pain.

"Neil, I've made you something."

He kept looking, his eyes were starting to water, and he wasn't blinking.

"I got some beautiful mahogany. Gorgeous panels." I stopped for a second. "I'm just finishing it and I wanted to tell you."

I began to describe it to him and he closed his eyes. He looked asleep, but he kept his arm up the whole time, placing his palm against my chin and cheek, then gently rubbing it over my face, touching my ears. Once or twice, he made a small little fist and lightly tapped me on the chin. I held on to his other hand.

He never said a word until I stopped. He closed his eyes and took a breath. He barely got it out, and only did because it was an exhalation. It was too faint to hear, but it didn't matter. I knew what he was saying. I was certain I would never again feel the way I felt at that moment, that I could not ever again feel anything so much. I would have traded him places if I could have.

Anne returned with a nurse who was carrying a tray full of bottles and needles and cotton swabs. The nurse gave him an injection, but it didn't seem to do him any good. He moaned and moved his head from side to side. He kept trying to roll over but couldn't.

A nurse came in at about ten o'clock. "You can probably go, you know," she said kindly. "He's been like this every night. Not that that's a comfort, I know, but you won't do yourselves much good sitting here. Go have a good sleep."

Anne thanked her and then talked me into leaving.

Neil and Anne had been fond of each other from the first time they'd met and were fast friends even before it was clear that Anne and I were going to stay together and be serious. I think that they would have stayed friends even if Anne and I hadn't married. Neil was like the proud father at the wedding, and Anne asked him to give the toast to the bride, which he did magnificently.

"Tell me something else about your wife," Anne always asked Neil whenever there was a lull in the conversation. At first, she asked out of politeness, but later out of interest and respect.

"Well, Anne," Neil would say. "She was funny. That's the best thing I remember about her. She was really funny." Then he would tell an anecdote or two, and the way he told them always made us laugh. The one thing he always told Anne was how much she was like Grandma. When Anne and I fought, he usually took her side; he would listen to me afterwards and then tell me I should be more considerate of her.

"You should thank your lucky stars you have someone like that. There are billions of unhappy people out there."

Anne's parents lived in Toronto, and she only saw them on holidays, though she talked to them on the phone regularly. But Neil, she always said, was her resident father.

We got a call early the next morning, and the nurse asked us to come in as soon as we could because Neil was struggling. On the drive over, we were mostly silent.

"Are you okay, David?" Anne asked at one point. "For what might happen?"

I didn't respond. I was holding the shoulder strap of the seat-belt with both hands, zinging it in and out of the slot. We took 114 Street, the main road heading north to the hospital and the university. I watched the morning traffic and people waiting at bus stops. The sun had just come up on our right, and it followed us to the hospital like a big yellow eye.

When we got to the hospital, Anne dropped me off at the Emergency door and went to park the car. I walked slowly to ICU and on the way to Neil's room passed a couple of nurses who offered me cheerful good mornings.

The nurse in Neil's room was doing something to one of the tubes in his nose. She looked up when I came in and acknowledged me, but she didn't offer any other sort of greeting.

"What's happening?" I said.

She spoke as she worked, taping a tube over his nostril. "He's not doing so hot. His coma score dropped badly overnight."

"Coma score?"

"Indicators," she said, not looking at me. "Predictors."

I looked at him lying on the bed. He was unconscious and he looked visibly worse than when we'd left him the night before. His skin had no colour and his forehead was clammy to the touch, feverish but cold.

"He's dying," I said to the nurse. "Is he dying?"

She looked at me directly but didn't say anything. Anne came in and saw me.

"The doctor," said the nurse, "is on the way." She turned and left the room.

Anne went over to Neil and stroked his forehead. "Oh, Neil," she said. She took a deep breath. "Oh, poor Neil."

A doctor arrived a few minutes later, not the doctor in charge but a junior one, and told us that Neil was going to die that day, that if he didn't, it would be both a miracle and a curse.

"You don't have to stay in the room, if you don't want to. Many people don't," he said. "He will have staff around him all the time and it might be easier for you."

I said nothing and looked at the floor the whole time he spoke. It was up to us, he said, and obviously we could stay in the room if we wanted.

We went back into the room, and it wasn't more than fifteen minutes later that Neil had a spasm and lunged for breath, held it, then coughed up a mouthful of mucus. He lunged again and this time his breathing stopped altogether. It started again after a few seconds. Anne and I were beside him on either side of the bed. She held him and I had my palms flat lightly across his chest.

He was completely comatose now, no longer able to feel pain, operating only on the orders of his central nervous system. Every breath was harder than the last, and each one diminished him as if he were a sandcastle going under a slow tide. Anne held him and whispered, "We love you, Neil. You know that. We all love you. David and me. We won't ever stop."

Neil didn't breathe when he should have, then started again in a different pattern. The veins in his throat were throbbing wildly.

"Anne," I said, quietly. "I ... I can't. Oh Jesus."

"Go," she said, turning her head towards me, but still holding Neil in her arms. "It's okay. I'm here with him."

She turned back to Neil and started whispering to him again, with her head right by his ear. He stopped and started breathing. I could hear strands of mucus bubbling in his throat when he struggled for air.

I went out into the hallway, sat on a plain metal chair, and held my head. My mind ran from thought to thought, finding reason or solace in none of them. A few minutes later, two nurses went into the room together and re-emerged almost immediately, one of them going one way down the hall and the other the opposite way.

Sitting upright in the hard metal chair, I saw my white knuckles gripping the armrests. People milled about the hallway, going into this room, leaving that one. A family was gathered in discussion with a doctor outside the room next to Neil's. Better to die on one's feet than live on one's knees, Camus had said. It sounded hollow and possibly even untrue.

I was no longer conscious of time or my surroundings and did not know how much later it was that Anne came out, found me in the chair, touched my head. It might have been hours. She let me sit for a moment longer and then asked if I wanted to go home.

This morning I'll go down to the Bow River
to wash my hands. In water I hear ripple
by the ice that still holds prints from the elk
and silver fox it supported last night.
With my clean hands, I'll carry away
the child that died inside you.

And the guilt you feel, I'll take that too.
Float it down the Bow, past the woodpecker
impregnating silence with hunger.
Into the mountains, where the measured breathing
of hibernating bears warms their hidden dens.
Guilt's heartbeat slows down too,
grows tired, sleeps awhile.

But I think sorrow is the bird
we must feed so it can fly away.
Throw food on top of the snow.
And when it returns, hungry again,
watch how this bird opens seeds,

the pattern of broken shells
it leaves on a crust
frozen to stay. Learn to listen
to its song.

LYNN *Davies*

BEFORE THE PHOENICIANS

Last night we lay under the stars with a map
and a flashlight, the lake beside us
reflecting passages we found in the sky.
Named by the Phoenicians—Draco the dragon,
the Dippers, and the shifting pole star, Thuban,
the pyramid builders used to orient their stones.
And someone said the fires we see up there
could be the light still travelling from stars
dead for thousands of years, finding our eyes only now.

I feel closer to the dead ones floating on the creek
    I paddle on this morning.
Those fallen stars that wake up as waterlilies,
the chosen ones, their afterlives burning white
in this dark pool. Such poise
after their long fall and burnout.
    For the damselflies
    and choirs of frogs they bloom,
    they live in the tiny currents
    spun by the sunfish and perch swimming below.

And I am here before the Phoenicians,
drifting among these fallen stars
that do not play tricks on me with time and light.
I find no constellations here,
do not whisper names to the white fires.
I follow the kingfisher downstream
to the lake where the lilies don't grow.

JANIS *Barlow*

THE
WHEEL

The fluorescent light above your bed
flickers and hums.
You lie like a chameleon
under the stiff white sheet and heaps
of plastic tubing. The rhythmical beep
and monotonous pattern on a screen
confirm you're alive. I need this (my back turned),
as I comb shattered glass from a dying boy's hair.

The raven moves through the halls,
putrid and moulting. He comes for the boy—his split
head rotten as old melon.
The wheels of the coffee cart turn slowly,
and the raven struts behind the woman dispensing snacks,
checking beds. Tonight, it's the boy,
and as always a part of me—some light
within the eye. A day, perhaps. A year.

I leave off combing as he pulls
his oily black wing over the child's face.
The alarm squeals from your bed, and the screen turns
interesting, chaotic. Momentarily, you slip
out of the pale spastic glove
of your body, take my hand.
Together we flee this cold narrow room, feel the sun
awakening. I am young again. You are whole.

JANIS Barlow

REFLECTION

Only twenty. When I look at her,
it's as if I were studying
myself in a trick
carnival mirror. With one eye closed, we become
each other's distortion, my own
twisted twin, half-
gone; sick
little sapling
wasting in the shadow
of my towering.

I want to escape
this room with its smell of old flowers,
radiation, scorched flesh.
My rubber-soled shoes
circle and circle
the scrubbed floor. On a west window,
curtains hug the bright glass,
anxious to cover up life
pouring in.

Six o'clock. Day's heat still
buzzes in the grass.
The sun is looking for a place to sleep.
As it drops from the sky,
the beige walls flare maroon.

I ask in the strained
voice of the inexperienced
if there is anything
I can do. Unspeaking—
her eyes the colour of ice—
she moves carefully,
pulling back her long black hair
so that a patch of light
settles on her cheek,
her face—distant
pale sliver of moon, craters and dark
rings,
and when she turns from me, slowly winding herself in sheets,
the bed keeps silent,
yet I can hear her bones
breaking.

CYNTHIA *Flood*

HALF-CENTURY

RECENTLY ONE OF OUR THREE CATS, the tortoise-shell, became very ill. Tests showed a fatal virus in her bloodstream. Retrieved from the vet's for a last day at home and decanted from her travelling box on to the living-room rug, the dying cat was prick-eared with pleasure. She sniffed, stretched, mewed, and pattered over to her favourite sunny window-sill to wash her face. This vivacity did not last twenty minutes. She crept then to my room. Anxiously, the calico came to smell her fur, and settled nearby; the tabby scuttled away, terrified. Curled on my bed, the tortoise-shell responded for a few hours to caresses but by nightfall to voices only. Next morning, back at the clinic, we stroked her stripes and said her beautiful name. The needle slid into her paw. Gracefully, the cat sank. The green brilliance of her eyes lost focus. "Counter, original, spare, strange"—she was gone.

This small death was the fifth death in my life this year, the year I turned fifty. All the other deaths were human: death from AIDS, from ovarian cancer, from cancer of the liver, from AIDS again. All the dead were roughly my age, all signified important seasons for me. Their deaths contrast with the life of my mother, who has reached ninety. My lover says gently, "I don't think she ever expected to live this long." No family members of her generation remain. Only a few friends linger, unaware, in nursing homes. "There is no one," my mother says, "who remembers the blue dress I had in 1933." Her own powers of memory falter, falter. She feeds her cats and her roses reliably but not herself.

My old friend, dying of AIDS this year, sneered at death. "My impending demise," he drawled. He made fun of his doctors, fought his nurses. Finally hospitalized, he lectured his visitors on current events in the Soviet Union and on the politics of AIDS research, while enduring his pain and appalling treatments as if they were vulgarisms no well-mannered person would acknowledge. He died a militant, this irritable gossipy pompous man. His life had seemed snarled in petty difficulties. Perhaps the grand horror of his death provided a stage on which his full nature could finally sound its voice? Perhaps I had never noticed what was in him? How will I die? What else have I not noticed, not known?

After the death of the tortoise-shell, the calico was at a loss, for all the days of her life had been passed in the presence of that other cat, her mother. She sat still on the living-room rug. We patted her, my daughters talked to her. Her yellow eyes stared at absence.

My mother is so pale. She doesn't wear lipstick any more. In her white summer blouse, at the white summer cottage where the family has convened to celebrate her ninetieth birthday, she is a living phantom. That blue dress—sky or Persian or indigo, linen or wool? In that year, her hair and eyebrows were black and high colour stood in her cheeks. Now it seems as if there's no blood for half an inch below the surface of her skin, almost transparent, shed snakeskin, a crisp cross-hatched veiling. In this year, my own blood's cycles are altering. I know this is right, it is the right time, but still I look disbelieving at the pad. Where is all my rich red blood, what are these rusty stains? That dress of my mother's: how were the sleeves? Long with buttoned cuffs maybe—she used to love unusual buttons—or short over smooth tanned arms? At the cottage, she used to swim every morning before breakfast, a strong breast-stroke from dock to beach.

Two women in my life died of cancer this year, this one a long-ago enemy, that other not quite a friend, and both part of my feminist context as I was of theirs. Three faces in the crowd of women. How many times had I seen this lopsided grin, that amused smile? Over two decades, the unfolding of feminism corresponded to the troubled or triumphant flowering of our own adult women's lives. Two decades: marches, motions, tears, protests, resolutions, victories, articles, rage, demonstrations, briefs, failures. These women were surely known to me? Yet at their memorials I seemed to hear thoughtful, loving reviews of books I'd skimmed, misread. Too late. Am I equally unknown? Two decades for disease to flourish in two women, to flourish in irony; these ovaries generated death, that liver failed in all feeling. My own body is not as it was. That smile, this grin— technological twentieth-century hospital deaths erased them both.

The expressions on my mother's once lively face are few. She looks sad, or cross, or uncertain. On one evening during our stay at the cottage, however, there arrived an unexpected visitor from a long-ago chapter: a friend of my father's. In this presence, my mother smiled. She sat up straight, heard everything that was said, ate all her dinner. She told stories, laughing, and drank her whiskies with enjoyment instead of resignation. Abruptly she faded, and, excusing herself with warm courtesy, she left the room. "Wonderful, your mother," said the guest later, getting into his car under the moonlit cedar trees. "Amazing for ninety." He drove off. With my daughters, I went down to the beach, to swim naked in the black-and-silver lake. My mother slept for thirteen hours and complained next morning about rude people who invited themselves to her house and overstayed their welcome.

Weeks after the tortoise-shell was dead, the tabby cat was still too frightened to enter our living room. She stayed close to what she knew— the upstairs, where the girls' rooms are. This tabby, a mature cat, is new to our household. Her old home no longer exists because of the fourth death in my life this year, the death of my ex-husband and the father of my children.

When I ended our sixteen-year marriage, I likened the pain to self-inflicted amputation without anaesthetic. A decade later, that metaphor will not do. I search for a new one during his final days, when our daughters tell me, on the phone from his far-away city, that the lesions of Kaposi's sarcoma now lie thick on their father's flesh. Crying, I search. How can I say the meaning of this major character's exit from my story? At last, it seems that only the old figure of the voyage feels right. With his death, I feel as if a great ship alongside which I've moved for years has suddenly slipped back, slipped away into watery utter darkness. The stars dislodge into disorientation. For years, he and I travelled together, and separately, through seascapes that transformed our lives, into revolutionary politics and those of sexual liberation, and into parenthood. We marched together, and separately. In my presence, he came out of the closet; in his, I gave birth to our children. We went through savage storms. We called them down upon ourselves, upon each other. My ship moves forwards. No one else remembers those radiant days when the daughters came. I feel the pull of the blank unreachable dark.

The calico and the tortoise-shell used to have the evening cat-crazies together. They raced round the house, lashed their tails, and lurked and sprang and pounced on the ping-pong ball. Now we toss the ball for the calico and the girls show her how to pat it. Her paw touches the tiny globe. She walks away.

My mother and my ex-husband disliked each other intensely. For years they fought over me, in contorted nasty ways that took me years more to understand, and when he died my mother did not speak condolences. Instead, she phoned long distance repeatedly to enquire about the welfare of his tabby cat; after his death, one of our daughters brought this much-loved puss from California to live with us. Torn from all she knew, the tabby hid for weeks under this daughter's bed, and, amid the terrible grieving of children for their father, we all worried about her. Would she ever feel at home? I took to spending a little time each day in my daughter's room, hoping to accustom this precious animal, this link with the vanished home of the father, to my presence and to her new dwelling. I lay reading on the bed. Finally, one day, furry movement stirred on the rug nearby. I stilled, and then she was on me, on my chest, a big cat lying down heavily to gaze at me with unreadable golden eyes. Just so she must have lain on him in his desperate solitary illness, gazed so. I could not bear thinking of the comfort she must have been, and whispered to her, "You don't know who I am." To my mother I reported, "She's getting friendlier." "Good," said my mother, relief in her voice.

Some years after my ex-husband and I parted—though the severance was never complete because of those two new voyagers, the children—I fell in love again. In the dazed first days of this love, I wondered: Can this be happening to me? Can I feel solid earth underfoot? I did not believe that I could be loved, me with my ugly married proud-flesh, nor that I could love so. I thought that capacity was dead, buried under pain. But this man moved into my house with me and began to plant flowers. He planted irises, peonies, bee balm, poppies, alyssum, phlox, daffodils, clematis, lupins, fragrant fireworks of nicotiana. He planted many roses. They flourish. They all flourish.

A few evenings ago, the calico fluffed up her fur and ran through the rooms by herself, finishing with a wild pursuit of her own tail. Then, as if surprised at herself, she washed very hard and quickly for some time.

When my ex-husband died of AIDS, I remembered those days of wondering new love, remembered in the light of new wonders: Would I now die of AIDS? Had he, in a last act of revenge, in our last miserable act of love, taken up arms to invade my bloodstream? Had he made death? Could this be happening to me? I looked at my daughters, numb or frantic with grief for their father. If their mother should die too ... I went for tests. While I awaited the results, his memorial gathering took place. His photo was displayed at the front of the crowded room, among flowers. My young handsome husband smiled.

He is gone. My mother is a shadow. I am here, with this man and with these girls. The tests showed negative; I will not die in that particular way. I am ashamed that I thought of my ex-husband in those terms, but I did. The fact sums up for me both the marriage and the death. I never knew all of him—our daughters, through their life with him in their city, saw prisms never turned to me—yet I knew him as no other, as my other. I would not be who I am now if I had not, through him, had to claim my own unknowns: cowardice, ruthlessness, meanness, anger, strength.

The tabby cat still does not feel safe in the living room, but she has delightedly discovered the garden. As she sits under the peony with her paws curled, the mix of shade and earth and sunshine integrates her tabbiness into this small landscape. For her, my lover has installed a cat door.

Sometimes on the downtown streets, I see my dead ex-husband. Instantly I cry, "The girls! You don't know about the girls! They're ..." It isn't him. I walk on. I have called aloud, and other pedestrians look at me. He was so proud of them, they who mourn him with an intensity that marks them as his daughters.

They are with me now. We are swimming in the moonlit water on the last night of our time at the cottage. Now in her ninety-first year, my mother has successfully endured her gigantic family birthday party. Just before she blew out her candles, she had been speaking of her husband, my father. "How strange all this is," she said, looking about the veranda at babies and teenagers and young adults. "If he were here, he wouldn't know who most of you are." Now, she is asleep. My lover is up at the cottage, building a fire for the girls and me to come back to after this midnight craziness. The cedar cottage will smell of burning pine. The flannelette sheets and the Bay blankets will enfold us two in the old double bed that squeaks.

We three are alone in the striped water of the bay. The moonlight washes over my breasts, over their young ones. In the not-quite-autumn sky, the stars are sharp. Floating on my back, I raise my arm so as to watch the silver run down over my skin; the moon shows me the faint cross-hatching, there on the forearm. My daughters are nearby in the black-and-silver water, visible as rippling blurs, audible as splashes. I have no idea what they are feeling or thinking, nor what they will remember of this time. I love them. What I am feeling is gratitude for my life, at fifty.

MARY Cameron

THE
PADDLE

Wet from the paddle's curved end
spills on the smooth surface of the lake,
the drops falling back as we glide

through lilies, fish, turtles—their sinking
shells through the green—a release of the lake
back into the lake, perceptibly

joining itself from a brief
drop-from-drop separation we slip through—
Wet at the tip, warm

at the core, this is something
like holding you, holding a breath
in the stroke, a breath—the paddle's release from the lake

curved on all shores, it fills
every hollow with lake—you slide into the
grip of the paddle, your fist and your palm—

and the wood of the woods surrounding us fills
every hollow with lake, every
part of us, parts and fills.

MARY Cameron

HONEY

Sometimes we come
straight
unfold aloud
like honey
down from the knife tip
fall through a thought
without a thought
and in falling, spin
translucent self to bare
thread, gold line
to bread
where we lie
tangled, melting

CALVARY

"HILDA BISHOP, BROKEN HIP." Mama was clinging to my arm, her fingers clawing my sleeve, as we inched across the icy parking lot. Her eyes fixed on the slippery ground ahead, she catalogued the disasters possible with each precarious step. "Been in hospital two months now. She'll never get out of a wheelchair, you know, and she's only seventy-two."

We made shuffling progress between the parked cars before she started up again. "Ruth Cooper's mother, collarbone. Fell in the produce section of FoodKing. Can't even do up her own brassiere."

I contemplated Ruth's mother, bra-less and stricken among the broccoli and cantaloupe. The parking lot curb was just ahead, almost hidden by the snow. "Careful, Mama," I said. "There's a step."

She glared. She always glared when she thought I was on at her about wearing her glasses instead of letting them dangle on the gold chain around her neck. Then again, she could have glared because I'd called her Mama. On my last birthday, she told me to call her Audrey. She said she wasn't going to have people thinking she was old enough to have a daughter of forty-five.

When we reached the door to Turner's Fine Foods, she dropped my arm and straightened, carefully adjusting the handle of the patent-leather bag over her arm. She held her handbag like the Queen Mother, her left arm bent at the elbow and the strap across her wrist. Head high, eyes straight ahead, she marched into the store, favouring customers and clerks with a slightly imperial nod and a vague smile. I scrabbled in the bottom of my shoulder bag for a quarter, slugged it into the slot to a free shopping cart, and took a deep breath before I followed her.

Every Thursday morning for the past three years, since Mama stopped driving, I'd been bringing her to Turner's Fine Foods. She'd called me that morning at eight o'clock, just as she did every Thursday morning.

"You sound foggy, Ruby. Did I wake you?"

"I'm always up at seven, Mama. You know that."

She sniffed. "Well, at least you get your rest. It's been weeks since I've been able to sleep through the way you do."

I took a bite of toast and made a muffled sound of agreement through the bread.

"You sound like you're getting a cold, Ruby. Maybe you should stay in bed."

I held the receiver away from my mouth and swallowed the last bite of toast. "I'm not getting a cold."

"I can always ask Mrs. Kersky's boy. He's so good to his mother."

Mrs. Kersky's boy is a fifty-year-old dentist whose mother is Mama's next-door neighbour. When Mama and Mrs. Kersky compare notes on their children, I'm sure the dentist comes out ahead. "I'll be there at nine, Mama."

"I made a reservation for us at Carlo's. We can have a lovely lunch."

Carlo's, Mama's favourite restaurant, had waiters who dressed like failed lounge singers and a cream sauce on every dish. I looked down at the soft bulge of my belly stretching the cotton-knit nightgown. My annual January quest for thinness would have to wait another day. "Fine, Mama. See you at nine."

When I hung up the phone, I carried my mug of cold milky coffee into the bathroom and stared in the mirror. My face was sallow and morning-puffy, my hair needed cutting and grey strands were showing at the roots. Mama would notice. Her own hair was still naturally as dark and thick as a girl's, while mine was fly-away and mouse-coloured. I ran a brush through it and slopped on some make-up, grabbing the tube of lipstick that came free with my purchase of Oil of Olay. It was bright scarlet, the kind of lipstick Lana Turner might have worn, but on my mouth it turned a ghastly orange-red, making me look pale as a corpse. Flipping over the lid on the toilet seat, I plunked myself down and contemplated my life. That's what Thursdays did to me, left me ruminative and melancholy.

"Everyone has a cross to bear, Ruby," my father told me once. "Your mother is mine." Daddy always pulled on his ear lobe when he talked. "She's a trial. There's no getting around it. But you got to learn to eat what's on your plate, Ruby."

That had been Daddy's way of telling me I should give up my furnished room on Howland Street and my job in data entry at Metropolitan Life and go back to Terry, my husband of six years and the father of Timmy, age five, who asked after me every night in his prayers, according to Daddy.

That was seventeen years ago, and I never did take Daddy's advice. Back then I wasn't as good at doing the things I should as I am now. Before Daddy passed on four years ago, I'd moved to a sunny new apartment and left Met Life for a job at the Carlingwood Children's Library. Terry had married, then divorced again, and Tim had become a handsome, clever twenty-two-year-old, turning women's heads at his college in Montreal. It was only on Thursday mornings that I wondered if I should have paid more attention to Daddy.

Dom phoned as I was rummaging through my closet to find something Mama would approve of. Behind his voice, I could hear the roar of the heavy trucks he supervised on the construction site. I'd known him for years, ever since he brought his young daughter into the library one day, but we'd only been seeing each other for the three months, since his wife had left for Saltspring Island to find herself. We were having adjustment problems. It'd been a long time since either of us had been with another person, and while it was comfortable enough going to movies or dinner or skating on the canal, so far we'd avoided the question of bed. I'm not sure what was behind Dom's reluctance, probably some male potency thing, but I wasn't ready to give him a glimpse of my pallid forty-something body with its dimples of cellulite and stretch marks. Still, it was getting increasingly difficult to make excuses to each other, and we both knew the time was coming.

I complained to Dom about having to go to Carlo's. "The food's so rich, and there's always so much of it."

"Just order a salad."

I thought longingly of Dom's comfortable bulk. I liked to put my head on his round belly, feeling it smooth and hard as a pumpkin. He'd never ordered just a salad in his life. "She'll get upset," I said. "She likes to see me eat."

"So order a pasta but just eat a few bites."

"If I haven't got anything in my mouth, then I might say what I think. It's safer just to stuff myself."

Dom sighed. I imagined him standing in the phone booth, lifting his yellow hard hat, and running his hand through his thick salt-and-pepper hair while he tried to find the right thing to say. He wasn't a complicated man and I was starting to think I liked that.

When I hung up the phone, I chose a severe grey skirt and jacket. Mama would be sure to offer me one of her scarves to brighten it up. As I pulled on my last good pair of pantihose, a wide run snaked down the outside of my leg. Maybe with my winter boots and long coat, she wouldn't notice.

She was waiting, pacing the small lobby, when I drove up. I got out to open the passenger door for her. She looked good, not just good for her age, but really handsome, a deep rose scarf setting off her grey Persian lamb coat and brush of purple eye shadow bringing out the blue of her eyes. As I helped her into the car, I breathed a whiff of *l'Heure bleu* perfume. She must have worn it the day I married Terry because I suddenly remembered her white linen suit and the large black hat and black gloves she'd worn to the wedding. She had a habit of drawing attention to herself with her clothes, like the shocking pink suit she wore to my father's funeral. People talked about it, but never to her face.

By the time I'd slid back into the driver's seat, she'd spread a packet of Kleenex, a bottle of aspirin and a tube of cough drops on the seat beside her. "I brought some things for your cold, Ruby." She patted my arm. "Don't forget to take them."

I felt my hands clenching. "I don't have a cold."

She looked me up and down. "Well, you seem pale. No colour at all in your face. It must be the lipstick."

I navigated through the heavy suburban traffic to Turner's. When I was growing up, these rows of strip malls and tract houses had been pasture and market gardens, and Turner's had been the centre of a small village. Now the city sprawl surrounded what was left of the village, and Turner's old store with its wooden counters and sawdust on the floor had been replaced by an unremarkable modern supermarket. Still, Mama remained loyal.

As I drove, she hit the floor with her foot every time she thought I should brake. Even though she was wearing a seat-belt, she braced herself with both hands on the dash and watched the road intently, telling me when to change lanes or use my turn signals.

"You're driving too fast, Ruby." She pointed ahead to the stop-light. "The light's going to change."

I tried distraction. "Tim said he'd called you on Sunday." I'd worked out a deal with Tim. An increase in his allowance guaranteed Mama one phone call every week.

"Really? It seems much longer ago than that." She stared out the window as I braced myself for the question I knew was coming. "Have you heard from Terry?"

"He calls to talk to Tim, that's all."

"I don't understand why you two couldn't get along. He's such a lovely fellow."

I let it hang in the air. Since leaving Terry, the only thing I'd learned for sure was to avoid that question.

Just before we got to Turner's, she said, "I'm thinking of buying a house."

I kept my eyes on the road, my voice even. "We've been through this."

"You just don't understand my situation."

"You don't like living in an apartment. You can smell all the neighbours' cooking. You want a garden. You want a cat." By the end of the list, my voice was starting to get louder, and I knew without looking that she was twisting the ends of her scarf round and round in her hands.

Her tone was petulant. "What's wrong with that?"

"It's not realistic." I pulled into the parking lot at Turner's and clicked off the engine. "First, you can't afford it. You can't manage a house. Who'll clean? Who'll cut the grass or shovel snow? And you'll be nervous all alone in a house at night."

"I could get a dog. A big dog."

I smacked my palm against the steering wheel. "A dog? And who's going to walk your dog on a day like this? You can't even get across this parking lot without help."

Mama made little pursing motions with her mouth, but she didn't say anything.

I hated my own meanness, but before I could think of a way to take it back, she gathered up her gloves and handbag and with one quick smack swept the Kleenex, aspirin and cough drops onto the floor of the car.

"Well," she said. "Are we going shopping today or not?"

Inside Turner's, Mama shopped erratically, without a list, picking up and setting down several brands before deciding which she wanted. She compared prices, squeezed fruits and examined cans for dents. I followed along with the cart and got things down from the top shelves for her.

As we passed along an aisle full of pickles and relishes, she stopped so quickly that I ran into her heels with the cart.

"There," she said, pointing to the bottom shelf. "Reach down and give me a bottle of those."

"Pickled onions?" I picked up the jar and showed it to her. "Since when did you like pickled onions?"

"I've always liked them. In fact, when I was expecting you, I once sent your daddy out in a rain storm to get some."

"I'm surprised he came back." I said it in a voice just too low for her to hear, but she picked up that I was being smart-mouthed.

"You're always mumbling, Ruby."

"I said it's a big jar for just one person."

She snatched the bottle from me. "Now I suppose you're going to tell me what I can eat." She cradled the bottle in her arms like a baby and started towards the butcher counter, then turned back to look at me. "And watch where you're going with that cart."

Young Mr. Turner, as Mama liked to call him, was behind the counter. He wasn't a day under seventy, but he'd taken over from his father when Mama had first started coming to the store thirty years ago. Now his grandsons were managing the business, but he came in a few days a week. He and Mama compared notes on prime rib and loin of pork while I leaned on the cart waiting. As usual, she was buying too much, enough for a family. Young Mr. Turner wrapped the roast and the chicken breasts and pork loin in pink butcher paper and began to pass the packages over the counter to her.

"Are you sure you need all that, Mama?"

She wheeled on me, still holding the pickled onions. "Unless I'm mistaken, I'm the one who's doing the shopping. I'm quite capable of choosing my own groceries, whatever you think."

I put my hands up in a gesture of surrender. "Just trying to be helpful."

"If you want to be helpful, take this." She shoved the jar of pickled onions towards me, and I juggled it crazily before getting a grip on it. "Don't drop it, for heaven's sake."

I held the jar and watched Young Mr. Turner handing her the pink packages over the meat counter. Her hands seemed suddenly small and frail, her skin old and blue-white against the rows of red meat in the display case.

Mama took the wrapped roast in both hands, turned and put it in the cart, then reached back for the other two packages. As she did, one foot suddenly seemed to slip from under her and she skidded sideways in a sort of jig, grabbing the side of the cart to keep from falling, then righting herself.

"Are you all right?" It had happened so quickly I hadn't had time to reach for her.

She stood very still, her feet a little apart, her hands still clutching the side of the cart. Her mouth was hanging open and her eyes were wide and horrified, staring first at me, then down at the floor below her. A small puddle spread between her feet, streaks of wet running down her stockings and into her winter boots.

Almost before thinking about it, I stretched out my hand with the bottle of pickled onions in it and let the jar drop on the hard floor just in front of her. It shattered, onions rolling around, the pungent juice splashing her boots and wetting her stockings. The puddle between her feet disappeared into the pickle juice.

Young Mr. Turner came running, followed by a boy with a mop, and between all of us we got Mama out to the car. I kept apologizing for being sloppy, Young Mr. Turner kept fussing about the slippery floors, and Mama said nothing, her face very white except for two high spots of colour on her cheeks.

I went back and paid for the groceries, loaded them into the trunk, then got into the car beside her. She was sitting very straight, her Persian lamb coat pulled under her, her seat-belt tight and her hands gripping her bag in her lap. The car smelled of brine and urine. I rolled down the window and pretended to adjust the side mirror in order to get some fresh air.

"Let's take the groceries home, you can change your stockings, get rid of that onion juice, and we'll go to Carlo's." I tried to make my voice normal, but it came out sweet, the kind of voice you'd use to talk to a balky child.

"I'm not up to Carlo's. I'm tired." She didn't even make the effort to look at me.

We drove back to her apartment in silence. I let her out at the door, then parked and carried the bags up to her apartment. She wasn't in the living room or kitchen when I came in, so I put the groceries away and waited. After a few minutes, I called to her, but she didn't answer.

I went down the hall to her bedroom. The Persian lamb coat was sprawled across her bed, her boots lying on their sides on the floor as if she'd kicked them off at the same time as she'd dropped her purse. It was yawning open, her lipstick and Kleenex and pill bottles spilled on the carpet. The bathroom door was closed, and there was no sound.

I knocked on the door. "Mama? Are you okay?" There was no answer. For a panicky moment I thought of calling Dom, then I jiggled the door-latch until it opened.

She was sitting on a low plastic shower-stool, her skirt heaped in the corner and a pair of pantihose and underpants wadded up in the sink. She sat splay-legged, a washcloth in her hand, her bare bottom on the pink plastic seat, and her belly folding flaccidly over her scanty grey pubic hair. There were wet streaks across her face. She didn't look at me.

"Mama?" I stood holding on to the doorknob for support. I hadn't seen her half-naked since I was a child, and I'd never seen her cry. Not when I told her I had to get married, not when Terry and I separated, not when she told me Daddy had died. Not even at his funeral.

"Do you know something, Ruby?" Her voice was suddenly soft, like a girl's. "Your daddy never touched me. In the last years, I mean. Never laid his hands on me, not even a pat to say good morning or good bye." Her tone had taken on a note of wonderment, as if she herself couldn't quite believe what she was telling me. "It was an angry thing between us, in the end. I couldn't forgive him, you see. I just couldn't get over it."

I knelt down on the floor beside her and took the washcloth out of her hand. It was warm and soapy and smelled of violets.

She kept talking as if she'd forgotten I was in the room. "And he would never use my name. Just called me Mama. It's a terrible thing never to hear your name." She looked down at her empty hands lying limp across her belly. "My name is Audrey Anne Elizabeth. There's almost nobody left who remembers that."

Kneeling beside her, I clutched the washcloth in front of my chest with both hands, as if I were going to present it to her as a gift. "I remember it, Mama," I said.

She looked at me then for the first time. It was the look of a woman who had been disappointed in life and would not let her disappointment go. "Hand me the towel, Ruby," she said, getting to her feet. Her voice was the old Mama's voice again, and she turned her back to where I was still kneeling on the floor. "And phone Carlo's and tell them to hold some veal scaloppine for us. You need to eat something if you're going to get rid of that cold."

REBECCA Fredrickson

RUBY

Three years dead, and already I can't remember you.
I won't go back to your last years in institutions,
where you slugged a nurse and refused to eat
anything but chicken in a mug and soda crackers.
Before death, we can boil down to what has been
the worst in us and then our grandchildren
must be trusted to forget.

Ruby, I'll go way back to the raspberries,
colour of your name, colour of your nose,
and your bad thumb, thumb you ruined with a thorn
while picking the ripe, red ones.
You fed us bowls filled with fruit
and crawling with short, white worms.
Afraid to make a fuss in front of you,
I piled on white sugar and the canned milk
you kept out all day on your slick Formica table.

Ruby, your beautiful name, a jewel,
birthstone for July, a hard hard rock
like the one that grew in your heart.
Eleven children and not one of them
named something gorgeous.
Eddie, Sam, Irene, and my father, Billy.
As if you knew better than to give
names that could refract light,
roll pleasure and possibility off the tongue.
Charlie, Bobby, Raymond, and Grace,
humble enough to forgive their father
for the sting of a willow switch.

You married a barrel-chested butcher, settled
in Valhalla, Alberta, to make leftsa and rosettas,
lutefisk for Easter and Christmas.
You'd whisper bible stories in Norwegian,
till he'd fall asleep, then lie awake,
thinking what paradise might really be like:
not gold and the thick white wings of angels,
but Boise, Idaho, and the Irishman who kissed you there,
whose hair smelled of pipe smoke.
He was studying to be a doctor
and you could have had him *just like that,*
you told me—your hip broken
the time I went to see you in the hospital.

Ruby, I never did figure out what happened to your leg,
why it was stiff at the knee, straight as a cane.
Something to do with the raspberry thorn
in your thumb, the infection that went through you.
I mean to look up the name in a doctor's book,
but you're buried now, just outside of La Glace,
in your brown stockings and flowered house-dress.
Most days I don't remember to think of you.
I have one portrait, looking down;
it shows off your eyelids and lashes.

I used to get angry when they said we looked alike,
but it's our eyes, the wideness of our faces.

Born again in your twenties,
you built your life around the prophecy
that all your children would be saved.
You were visited once by an angel
who accepted fresh-baked buns and jam
and spoke with you in the Norwegian
you hadn't heard for years—
your husband, Valhalla, gone.
You asked neighbours about this
great, tall man who had come on foot,
but they shook their heads. Only you had seen him.

Ruby, I'd like to ask you more about the angel.
When he looked into your eyes, did he mention
how they could bend light in ripples around the room?
Were his hands rough from the field, or soft, like a child's?

BOSTON YWCA

BILLIE *Livingston*

It smells institutional in here
this asylum they've created
smells insane like nerves and fear
and poverty
like fat and acne and found-lumps
under skin that doesn't care anymore
I leave room 227 and try not to
shuffle like the others
to the disinfected tiles
of the second-floor bathroom

Washing in the very last sink
is a ghosty string-of-a-woman
her spidery hands scratching
each other's wet back—
eyes dart up at my intrusion
and I am unnerved
by that part of her that reads
Permanent Resident.
I splash and brush furiously

in time to my mantra: S'onlytemporary
and patter back to 227,
    Pick your feet up 'n
    don't   shuffle
    and   don't
breathe in the slumping   don't
breathe 2nd hand memories   don't breathe

I wonder where the
Young Christian Women
of this Association are
Glad they're not here
Avert your eyes—shun the desk drawer
for fear of bibles
The door closes heavy behind me

and I am faced with my room.
Pushed against the only
electrical outlet is the stick-width bed
its single flat pillow flashing neon—"We're not getting any."
Stuffing myself between tight sheets
I cringe to feel my limp hands dangle
over either mattress edge
and listen

The tiny rasp of TV has scraped
under someone's door and is scratching
its way down the hall
Twitchy and hollow
I force myself still and imagine her
face radiated by a black-and-white box
sitting on that white aluminum stand—
I bet she's got the same one and she's
shoved the plug between the bed and wall
jammed its two sparking prongs
into the wall's two slits.
She must feel smug.
I would.

THE ONLY GOOD POLITICIAN IS A DEAD POLITICIAN

YANN *Martel*

THE FUTURE WAS LUIS GALAN, presented as the saviour of democracy, the cleaner-up of corruption, the sacker of nephews and cousins, the terror of drug dealers, the redeemer of tarnished ideals, but unfortunately he was assassinated the day before the election. Out of anger, despair, and disgust, the population nonetheless voted for him and the dead candidate was elected President by a landslide. There was consternation among members of the Electoral Commission, but the people had spoken, and loudly. So Galan, with the hole in his forehead masked over by make-up and the absent back of his head cleverly camouflaged by a hairpiece (regrettably, nothing could be done about the grimness of his expression, only his cheeks made gay by a touch of rouge), Galan, we repeat, was sworn in and given the Seat of Honour in the Great Hall of the Casa Roja, the presidential palace. Then, the Prime Minister, a dull but capable workhorse who had taken on many of the executive duties in the weeks after Galan's election (because the constitution made no provision for a vice-president), died of a heart attack while being serviced by his favourite prostitute. By dint of his very dullness, the Prime Minister had become popular and, to appease the population, the ruling Conservative Revolutionary Party and the opposition Reactionary Liberal Party agreed not to remove him from office. And so effective power fell into the hands of the President of the Senate, an old man blind in one eye and stiff in one leg who had been head of the upper chamber for fifty-three years, a miracle of continuity. But, having just reconfirmed the members of the Cabinet to their duties, his very first act, the President of the Senate tripped over his grandson's eldest daughter and fell from his balcony and impaled himself on the fence below before being crushed by a bus whose driver had lost control of his crowded vehicle moments earlier. "Don't touch him!" —this was the cry from the people. The President of the House of Deputies, next in line, was a younger man, but he was also a *bon vivant* and not two weeks after taking over the affairs of state, he was overly ambitious in cutting his third steak during a dinner and he choked to death on a morsel. Sadly, the Chief Justice of the Supreme Court had been wasting away of cancer for some time and he only had the strength to ask the members of the President of the House of Deputies' Cabinet to stay on, before he died. Next in seniority on the Supreme Court were two Associate Justices who had been appointed at the same time some years before. They were lean and hungry men and both lusted for power. Quickly, they turned to violence and one killed the other with a knife, by this very act disqualifying himself from consideration. The next Associate Justice had no ambition other than to be a good judge and a good family man. He had recently lost his beloved wife and daughter in a traffic accident, the very one, in fact, that had killed the President of the Senate, and this, coupled with the new responsibilities of directing the destiny of the nation, was too much for him and he committed suicide, leaving a note in which he reappointed to their portfolios the members of the Chief Justice's Cabinet. In normal times, there would have been five other Associate Justices, for a total court of nine, but these had been killed shortly after the presidential election in a particularly nasty grenade-and-machine-gun assault by an idealistic Marxist group backed by drug dealers. The Minister for Foreign Affairs assumed power. His first problem was a purely practical one: where could he meet with members of the Associate Justice's Cabinet and get on with the task of nation-building? The stumbling block was a point of pathology. A body, once it has died, goes through three stages before it gives itself up to decay. They are, in order of occurrence, *algor mortis*, in which the temperature of the body falls to that of the environment; *rigor mortis*, in which skeletal muscles become rigid; and *livor mortis*, in which parts of the body—usually the back, the buttocks, and the back of the legs—become purple-red as a result of the settling of blood. When Galan was elected President, he was well past *algor* and *rigor mortis* and would have quickly gone on to *livor mortis* if not for the wild celebrations one naturally associates with a smashing electoral victory and a presidential inauguration. But once seated (with difficulty) in his Seat of Honour, he settled down to the settling of his blood, which naturally meant to his legs and feet, the amazing swelling of which could be testified to by his staff, who went into the Great Hall as little as possible and greatly restricted access to it, which was fine, because Galan after all *was* President and part of the aura of heads of state lies in the exclusivity of the company they keep. Now fate (and his sexual proclivities) would have it that the Prime Minister had died in the Cabinet Room, and the Cabinet, under the chairmanship of the President of the House of Deputies, found it increasingly difficult to meet in his presence. His fixed gaze, rigid expression, grey-white pallor were trying enough—the Minister of Defence once momentarily lost his nerve and tried to remove the naked Prime Minister from his seat, but he held on with all the strength of his *rigor mortis*—and the inward sinking of his eyes would have been too much had not the Prime Minister toppled forwards onto the table, and it was not even this, the beginning of thorough-going, out-and-out decomposition, with its accompanying bloating, flatulence, and liquefaction, that drove the Cabinet away; it was when, in one of those moments when a slow imperceptible process results in a sudden dramatic action, the members of the Cabinet saw with their own eyes both the Prime Minister's ears, at exactly the same moment, detach themselves from his skull and fall to the table. They hit the table with a light knocking sound that echoed in their ears for the rest of their lives. Screaming, throwing back their chairs, and pushing at one another, they evacuated the room, vowing never to return. So the Great Hall and the Cabinet Room were no longer possibilities. The Private Dining Room in the Parliamentary restaurant would have been ideal, except the President of the House of Deputies had choked on his steak there and the members of the Cabinet were not prepared to go through with him what they had gone through with the Prime Minister. The Ministry of Education had a meeting room of suitable size and elegance on its first floor and the Minister of Foreign Affairs decided that they would meet there. As an aside, the Cabinet was made of the poorest wood, so to speak, ability having been of distant consideration in the appointment of its members, far behind considerations of family, wealth, constituency, ambition, and danger. They were all equally corrupt except for the Minister of Housing, who was corrupt in specific areas only, one of them being, however, the handing out of government building contracts, which was unfortunate, for the very day when the Cabinet was meeting at the Ministry of Education, the capital suffered a minor earthquake that was noticed only by those in poorly constructed buildings where the safety standards had been shamelessly disregarded during their construction, the Ministry of Education for example, whose cement foundations gave way like sand, which is mostly what they were. The building collapsed like a house of cards, squashing to death the Minister of Foreign Affairs and his entire cabinet—except for the Minister of Sports, who was a jogger and away from the capital that day for the opening ceremonies of a soccer tournament; and the Minister of Culture, who was a drinker and was inaugurating a museum at a seaside resort. The Minister of Sports was the more senior of the two and, upon being informed of the circumstances that had raised him to the supreme office of the land, he called the Minister of Culture and they agreed to meet in the capital. The Minister of Sports arrived first, which was his loss, because before meeting with the Minister of Foreign Affairs' Cabinet, that is, with the Minister of Culture, he decided to go for a relaxing jog, which would have been fine on any other day except this one, for the Minister of Culture had had one too many to drink that morning and upon seeing a jogger while driving to meet his colleague, he decided to have himself a little private fun and run the jogger over. Clearly, he didn't recognize the jogger as the Minister of Sports, for if he had he would have remembered that he was a superb athlete and would not be an easy jogger to run over. Indeed, the Minister of Sports was endowed with sufficient athletic ability to put his hand on the hood of the car and jump and somewhat avoid the full impact of the speeding car, but no athletic ability in the world could have saved him from crashing into the car's window, which he did most violently; in fact, with such violence that he was cruelly and clearly cut into two by the roof of the car, his distraught upper body pursuing its outside course while his hips and legs joined the Minister of Culture inside the car. One might say that the Minister of Sports had his revenge, however, for his right knee kicked the Minister of Culture in the face so hard that his neck snapped.

The car hit a utility pole and they were killed again, and then the shirtless poor and their pigs set upon them, killing them a third time, a clear example of the dehumanizing effects of poverty.

In the ensuing elections four years later, in spite of the near-complete elimination of government corruption and a spectacular improvement in the economy, the Conservative Revolutionary Party was swept out of office. They had presented Luis Galan and his team again, but they could do nothing against the star candidates of the Reactionary Liberal Party, who put forwards Simon Bolivar for President and Christopher Columbus for Prime Minister.

BRIAN Bartlett

GRANITE ERRATICS

To personify If—But—And ...
—HAWTHORNE, *The American Notebooks*

1

I*f* has a tail shaped like a questionmark.
Among meshed branches, it floats from spruce
to pine, pine to birch. The playful one. Furred
with conditionals, its nimble feet twitch even in its sleep.
If *if* weren't with us, the brain might be little more
than a register, the sky a sealed roof.

What if anti-gravity always kept us an inch
off the earth—if frontier artists heard the truth:
    being painted shields you from bullets—
if the curator didn't exaggerate a bit
    when he said, "A toad is in heaven
    with a breakfast of earwigs and June bugs"—
if the cat obsessed with reflections speeding up the wall
    leapt, and at its touch lightbeams became birds.

2

"But," said the wounded, wide-eyed sailor, "but ... "
seeing the surgeon pull off his wig and lift out
his own glass eye.

        "But," said the seventy-year-old woman
buried under earthquake rubble, refusing to come out,
"but I'm naked, and people will say I have no shame."

But rears its scaly head, blinks. Now it hisses,
cantankerous; then, makes the mouth's subtlest upturn.
Alert, *But* finds the generous thief, the sour pit
in the sweetness, the lighthouse killing blinded birds.

Where would we be without *But?*—under a government
whose voices all huddle into one, on a planet
        without shadows or valleys.

3

And is *And* the greatest of these?
                Ever-migrant,
at home anywhere, winged and gilled. Eyes bloodshot
with smoke, sea-water, cave-air. Its diseases many, its beauties
contradictory. The generous one. Finds it hard to say *no.*

We have mosses that live 2000 years—a year
and a year and a year—and vireos that sing
20,000 times a day—a song and a song and a song.
We have birds' feet, forgotten by many,
poor cousins to feathers and wings—
                           a grackle's (black)
grasping a wire fence, and a guillemot's (red)
backpaddling, and a willet's (blue) crisscrossing sand.

And crosses the spaces between this and that.
On the coast, step among the granite erratics—
boulders pushed from other latitudes by glaciers
aeons ago, monoliths on wind-flattened plateaus—a rock
and a rock and a rock. Totem to nothing,
each claims a place
                      among the haphazard many,
there, inescapable,
                      immovable for the meantime.

SACRED PINE
(FOR DONNA)

ARMAND

*Garnet
Ruffo*

This morning the shape of trees
swing me past Voltaire's house
where I stoop to pick a pine cone,
look up at the huge windows,
heavy doors, remind myself tomorrow
I'll visit the museum inside.
Much too interested in just thinking
of his old enlightened words:

    all humans are formed by their age
    and very few
    rise above it.

This is Geneva, and I am on my way to search
the newspapers and magazines
for something on what they are calling the Oka Crisis.
There's not much. Two short columns.
(a little affair on a world scale)
It won't last long. The army has been called
to quell the terrorist Mohawk warriors.
Back home
    in the so-called Peaceable Kingdom.

There was a time when Voltaire
called Canada nothing
but snow and ice, trying to dissuade the French
from such a foolish adventure.
Makes me wonder what he was really trying to tell them?
Perhaps if they believed it was worthless
they might leave well enough alone.
Nothing but speculation.

The one certainty the fact of families
protecting their heritage, their land.
    (During the stand-off, the army shrouded the area
    in barbed wire in case the Mohawks tried to flee,
    unable to comprehend they weren't going
    anywhere.)
And the power of a pine cone
in the palm of my hand.
The tree of peace,
rooted in earth extending to sky,
a sacred connection
to the Mohawk people.

HER
WOMAN
SONG

ARMAND | Garnet
Ruffo

There was a song I sang when we met, an old song I had learned at the kitchen table. I couldn't have been much more than ten and she would come over in the afternoon with a bottle of Golden Wedding and light sinking into her eyes, flaming across her dark face, swelling her shrunken heart. The song had to do with ships though we lived nowhere near the sea. Instead, we would look past the torn blinds to the tips of a river of trees and imagine the wind as waves. All we had to do was climb aboard and sail away. The music didn't come easily, my little fingers strained through the chords, trying to make sense of the dissected sound. But the afternoons were long, an eternity, which would end only when the Golden Wedding was finished, and her magical fingers turned to fists, a song turned to a cry.

Remember. I played it for you that first afternoon we met and then later played you. (Or was it you who played me?) The next morning I had to steal back to my own place, locked out by a room-mate who thought I had gone on a bender, taken to the street. Well I had, kind of. I swear I was intoxicated. I remember you were making cut-outs. Pictures from glossy magazines strewn all over your room, pinned to the walls. A head here, an arm there, legs and eyes, breasts and thighs, a neck lying in a heap of coloured light. (Or shall I call it delight?) What I know for certain, if anything, is that for the moment we were still whole, my hand still connected to my heart, to yours, your touch still to brain and skin and laughter.

When I played you the song, you thanked me and I confessed I had never thanked her for teaching it to me. And at that moment I wished I had more than anything. But I was young and growing fast and never thought much about the song or her, both far too tragic and old-fashioned. Besides, the crunch of bone, teeth, and eyes blooming like bluish violets played their own song that rode the wave of her life until the day she died. You loved tragedies you said and asked me to play her one small cry over and over on a mattress on a floor of a white room. As for the cut-outs, you said they were a project in communication, as you spread your limbs like a bird in flight. It was only when we got into each other and couldn't get out, found ourselves pinned, and slapped and cried and sliced, until we too were strewn all over that I finally understood what the song meant, what release she had been singing for. As I now come back to you, the bandages long removed, the wounds but faint scars to sing.

MESOPOTAMIA

JOAN Skogan

A RIVER HAD ENTERED INTO HER BODY, Marianne thought once. She had felt the water slipping over the dry hills in her head, soaking into the desert lying dark between her ribs.

She was in Turkey by then, but not noticing, only day-dreaming out the windows of the bus belonging to the theatre company from Istanbul. The actors had found her at the hotel in Eregli the morning after their performance, sitting on the front steps beside her bags, looking as if she were watching a walnut tree, she supposed, but not seeing the tree and not thinking, What next? Without words, Abdullah and the Last Rose and the others knew this. They pointed to the window beside the double seat she could have to herself on their bus and made soft bird sounds in Turkish until she got up and went with them.

On the bus, apricots were handed around, and paper cones of new almonds that squeaked between the teeth. There was tea in tulip-shaped glasses from stands by the side of the road in the long afternoons, and sometimes knife-cheeked government men who searched the bus and demanded papers. Marianne floated in shallow daytime sleep with her head on the pillow provided by the ingenue who looked like blackberry pie, she thought, her flesh sweetly round and dark, her dimples and shining eyes glittering and winking like sugar on a baked crust. When the road swooped and curved and she opened her eyes, she saw the oval blue eye of Allah swinging in its small arc above the head of Mahmoud, the driver. Inshallah, the eye whispered. In God's hands. Oh easily, and Where else? Marianne wrote in a notebook she forgot in a field where they stopped to buy honey in the comb.

In the evenings, she sat behind dusty curtains in theatres in Tarsus and Mersin and other towns, waiting for the performance to be done, and dinner and sleep, keeping company with the wedding dress costume, the general's uniform, and the plastic pistol; befriending the military hats and skull caps stacked in order of their appearance in the play, resting with her now beside a string of worry beads and a thick stage-prop book crowded among sugar-crusted tea glasses and Maltepe cigarette packets.

Three towns cancelled performances, and after Iskenderun, there was no dinner and no bed, only the bus loaded again, turning away from the coast. To Diyarbakir, Inshallah, Abdullah muttered before he covered himself with a grey blanket and sank down in his seat across the aisle. The road unwound in the cooling night while the bus ran fast, whirling its soft Mediterranean air out the edges of the doors and windows into a new sharp darkness. One light, another hours later, flickered and vanished far from the highway until the cool blue of a Turkpetrel station gleamed from a rise in the road.

The bus engine sighed as it stopped and Mahmoud grunted softly, heaving himself from the driver's seat. Marianne got off to sit beside him at a tea table within the circle of fluorescence around the fuel pumps. Soiled white ducks prospected the asphalt at their feet while Mahmoud drank his tea and she looked up Diyarbakir in *The Lands of the Eastern Caliphate: Mesopotamia, Persia, and Central Asia from the Moslem Conquest to the Time of Timur*, published in 1905.

Nasir-i-Khusraw, the Persian pilgrim, passed through Diyarbakir in 438 (1046), and wrote a careful description of the city as he saw it.

The town was two thousand paces in length and in breadth, and its black stone walls also surrounded the overlooking hill. In the centre of the town, a great spring of water, sufficient to turn five mills, gushed out; the water was excellent, and its overflow irrigated the neighbouring gardens.

The Friday mosque was a beautiful building, of black stone like the rest of the town, with a great gable roof and over two hundred columns, each a monolith, every two connected by an arch ... The ceiling was of carved wood, coloured and varnished. In the mosque court was a round stone basin, from the midst of which a brass jet sent up a column of clear water, which kept the level within the basin always the same.

Near the mosque stood a great church, built of stone and paved with marble, the walls finely sculptured. Leading to its sanctuary, Nasir saw an iron gate of lattice-work so beautifully wrought that never had he seen the equal thereof.

Marianne was certain the sanctuary gate's iron lattice had been shaped into flowers, tulips *turkestanica* twisting their petals and stems towards roses, then unbearably, intimately, turning back upon themselves. The marble on the floor of the tenth-century church would have been cream-coloured, threaded with green streams before the altar. People had thought the springs in the centre of town would water their gardens forever.

A truck without headlights screamed past the Turkpetrel station. Mahmoud stood and motioned to her to get back onto the bus.

The sky was brightening now over a wide plain without people or villages, without wooden carts or Massey-Ferguson tractors with blue beads strung around the exhaust pipes, where stones the size of a man's head were piled by the side of the road, and flocks of small brown birds flung themselves into the air as the bus passed. Marianne set her pillow against the window and tried to sleep in the empty land, but she feared the dark behind her eyes. She sat up again and again, seeing only the stones and the startled birds until black walls rose matchbox-height in the distance.

The highway broke into the basalt walls and Mahmoud stopped the bus before a narrow door marked Dicle Nehri Hotel. The actors went to their rooms and Marianne walked down the street carrying *The Lands of the Eastern Caliphate*.

The walls of Diyarbakir were pierced by gates, namely the Water Gate, the Mountain Gate, the Bab-ar-Rum (the Greek Gate), the

Hill Gate, and the Postern Gate (Bab-as-Sir, used in time of war). The line of fortified walls included the hill in their circuit, and in the fourth (tenth) century, the geographer Mukaddas says that the Moslems possessed no stronger or better fortress than Diyarbakir on their frontier against the Greek Empire.

This description of the magnificence of Diyarbakir is borne out by the anonymous annotator of the Paris manuscript of Ibn Hawkal, who was here in 534 (1140). He notes also that the markets were well built and full of merchandise. In the seventh (thirteenth) century, Yakut speaks of the city as then covering a great half-circle of ground, surrounded by magnificent gardens.

The afternoon was half gone when she came upon the walls of the city again, to surrender beneath a stone arch deep enough to create a shadowed passageway, knowing that she could not tell if this was the gate called Hill or Mountain or Water or War, and that she would not find the iron flowers leading to the sanctuary now. Where is the museum? she asked a tea boy, and the child set his tray at her feet and ran off, crying, Aziz, Aziz, English.

Marianne had forgotten that English could be spoken in sentences. The museum is forbidden now, Aziz said, thin and in his twenties, anxious under his smile.

Why forbidden? Marianne asked, meaning, Is that so? and I don't believe you, and It hardly matters.

There is the house of a dead poet, Aziz said, watching her. Also forbidden, but possible to see. A Kurdish poet.

Aziz raised his hands in supplication to the guard who cracked open the door of the house along a dusty lane. His arms were slender, Marianne saw, without enough flesh and muscle for a man. She passed him some lira and the door opened.

The poet's home was arranged around a courtyard containing a plane tree, airy rooms lined with worn silk carpets, edged with cushioned benches and low tables. Between the shutters hung photographs of a woman with deep pool eyes and bobbed hair, holding the arms of her daughters, helpful and serious on either side of their mother. The man who stood behind them, and alone in other pictures, turned his head from the camera, so that neither his eyes nor his expression was ever entirely clear. His desk was polished hardwood fitted with a multitude of drawers and brass-finished pigeonholes, all empty. Dozens of poems written with black ink in Turkic script on stiff cream paper had been framed and mounted on the wall behind the desk. Marianne took *The Lands of the Eastern Caliphate* from her pocket and wrote a description of the desk and the framed poems on the front flyleaf.

Aziz stood in front of a portrait of the writer's shaded face, his head turned at the same angle as the man in the photograph. It was a secret that this man was a poet, until he died and the poems were found, he told her.

What was his name? Marianne asked.

You are a writer also, Aziz said.

What was his name? Marianne repeated.

Writers are shot sometimes in these days, Aziz said. For security. The writers of newspapers and other things. Some people made a petrol fire for burning them. I don't know all the dead names.

Aziz's words fell in fragments among the leaves of the plane tree whispering together outside the shutters. Marianne listened hard to hear water running through his sentences over stone somewhere beyond the courtyard.

She made Aziz talk about himself on the way back along the lane, about how he was sometimes hired to work with the Shell Oil survey of the land between Diyarbakir and the Iraqi border; how the boss said all of his boys must try to work perfectly for the company, to make no measuring or drafting errors; about the thousand-year-old caravanserai where his uncle sold carpets, only foreigners did not come to buy them now.

Let me take you to the play tonight, Marianne said at the place where they had begun. Aziz's eyes widened, then his shoulders hunched and he made no reply. Seven o'clock, she said, Dicle Nehri Hotel, and she turned away from him.

The street was already dark, lit only with the tiny flames tended by the men selling roasted hazelnuts from wheelbarrows, and by bigger fires burning rubbish on the pavement. Small boys gathered around these bonfires, laughing soundlessly as they poked one another and dodged away. They were eight and nine and ten, she thought, the same age she had been when she saw her first fire out of doors at night. At church camp, she had stared into flames and had not been watched or asked why. The counsellors told campfire stories about Artaban, the fourth wise man from the fabled east, the one who had dilly-dallied on his way to Bethlehem and missed the Christ child.

At twenty minutes to seven, Marianne came out of the hotel to buy hazelnuts and found Aziz already pacing the street. His eyes were alight with excitement, Marianne thought, but his mouth was set determinedly straight. He looked importunate, Marianne decided, and she made him wait while she went around the corner to find a nut man. They did not speak in the taxi to the theatre. Men with guns were at the door when they arrived and Aziz hesitated, but she jerked his arm and pulled him inside, then left him in the lobby while she went backstage to collect their tickets. For the first time, she was to see the play from the audience.

When she returned to Aziz, more playgoers had gathered, but they stood apart from him. Two men in black suits were at his back and his face had gone still. She gave him his ticket and took hold of his arm, more gently now, feeling his body tremble, urging him towards their seats in the front row. Looking back, she saw that the men in black were gone, leaving behind them a sense of indrawn air, a space where they had stood that others still avoided.

Aziz's voice was cracked and dry. I tell you they watch every moment that I am in this place. They are somewhere watching now. The theatre was less than half-filled with people whose faces were as smooth as the polished leather of their coats.

Who are these people? Marianne asked. Government? Oil?

I have not come to this place before, Aziz answered. No one I know has come here.

Ah Biz Esekler, a voice announced. We Are Donkeys, Aziz murmured, a comedy. Abdullah appeared onstage, small and fingering his worry beads exactly as he did in his seat beside Marianne on the bus, but more bewildered now, ready to convince the audience that he was an ordinary Turk, hopeful but confused about *demokrasi*.

The blackberry-pie ingenue wearing the wedding dress and then the veiled *chador;* the big man in the general's glittering costume who usually helped Mahmoud carry the lights and props; the Last Rose waving a schoolroom pointer; and the actors who used the thick book first as a bureaucratic rule manual, next as the Koran—all these presences whirled across the stage, tricking and humiliating Abdullah's trusting little man. Beside Marianne, Aziz leaned forwards to catch each word of dialogue, laughing soundlessly like the boys around the street fires.

Even I did not know a play could be such as this, Aziz whispered to her, making circumspect dancing motions of his fingers in the direction of the stage. He did not seem to hear the repeated padded slap of the swing door as people behind them left the theatre.

The big man became a politician, babbling thunderous words even Marianne knew were not Turkish, but nonsense syllables. Some nights he said Canadadadadadacanada to make her laugh backstage. The politician was surrounded by the young actors who sat at the back of the bus, transformed into bodyguards who shoved the cheering Abdullah hard enough to make him fall.

Ah, *demokrasi, demokrasi*, the entire cast sang at the end of the play.

Aziz translated: The prime minister changes, but nothing else is new. Don't be fooled by sugar *demokrasi*.

Sweet, Marianne said. Don't be fooled by sweet democracy.

She's not for me and you, Aziz finished, his words suddenly loud in the silence as the curtains slid together and the actors vanished. The house lights came on immediately.

Aziz looked more boyish than ever, blinking in the electric glare, Marianne thought, but the men in black had not shown themselves again, and she was hungry, afraid the actors would forget to take her with them to dinner. She stood up and shook Aziz's hand, cold and brittle in her grasp. I must go. She waved towards the stage door.

But you will return here? he asked. She shook her head and left him crouched in his seat.

She opened the stage door and stepped into darkness as it closed after her. Her hands moved forwards, raising themselves to search the dark air. She half-turned to find the door again, to find Aziz and help him get home, to ask him to help her. Then the Last Rose's voice rippled out in a muffled flow, guiding her through the curtains in the wings into the every-night dismantling of the play. Only the haste and the absence of laughter were new. Mahmoud and the big man were rushing down the back stairs with the lights. The wedding dress and the other costumes already hung on their racks. Marianne wandered among the actors and their props until she came to the familiar stack of hats, the worry beads, and the stage book. She carried them out to the bus and took her place.

The streets were empty, lit only by Mahmoud's headlights. The bus stopped several times while Abdullah leaned from the window and answered questions from men Marianne could not see. No one else spoke.

The restaurant will be bright, Marianne thought. Everyone will talk and laugh again, and some of the dishes will smell like flowers. There might be lamb with yoghurt and mint, or the salad made from green olives, walnuts, and pomegranates. The bus stopped at the hotel, where lentil soup and rice gone cold waited in the grey twilight of the basement.

Wide awake in her room, Marianne walked back and forth between the bed and the window. Diyarbakir was entirely still around her. She took out *The Lands of the Eastern Caliphate* and wrote on the back flyleaf:

1. Cancelled performances. Small audiences everywhere. Walk-outs here.
2. Government men. Questions, rifles, black suits. Search bus. Guard theatres.
3. Television. Black and white, usually hotel desk or lobby. Not in Diyarbakir. TV images seen: none. Not interested or fiddling with money. Sounds heard: men's voices, neutral and explaining, or adamant and loud. Once in English (which town?), the words there are not Kurds, only mountain Turks. Shots. Explosions. Keening, brief.
4. The forbidden museum.
5. The dark streets.
6. Aziz. His words about writers. Shot sometimes. Fire to burn them.

She understood that Aziz might have got home safely, that she would not now and not in the morning and not ever know for sure. Too tired to undress, or even to take off her jacket and boots, she lay down on the bed, but even with the overhead light on, the blanket beneath her became a dry field encompassing the width of her body, stretching out on either side of her under a darkening sky.

At dawn, shrieking birds with wide, crooked wings came down on the field, and she ran to the window to escape them. Helicopters drifted above the heads of people already in the streets. No one looked up into the scream of their engines. She sat down on the edge of the bed and was still sitting there when the Last Rose came to find her, to put *The Lands of the Eastern Caliphate* into her bag, and to lead her to the bus.

At the broken place in the black basalt walls, Mahmoud took the highway east to the mountains, away from the coast. Marianne did not look out the window, and she stayed in her seat when the bus stopped and the actors got out. The Last Rose and the blackberry ingenue stood in the aisle beside her. Dicle Nehri, they said, and when she did not move, they reached for her hands.

The Dicle Nehri Hotel might have loosed itself from its moorings in the city to drift here, Marianne told herself, but there was only a river running deep and fast over black stones. Abdullah handed her a piece of paper on which someone, the hotel clerk perhaps, had written in wavering capital letters DICLE NEHRI = BLACK ARROW = RIVER TIGRIS.

Marianne stood at the edge of the bank and saw that the river water carried Aziz, still asking her if she would return, and herself, still shaking her head, No, and leaving him. The Tigris carried the actors and blue-centred gasoline flames, and the government men in black, along with Artaban, bearing his gift of a great pearl, seeing the men and women and children whose hunger caused him to hesitate, then to sell the pearl, to halt his journey under the distracting star again and again to give food and water and coins, each delay, he thought, moving Bethlehem farther beyond his reach.

Marianne remembered that when she was a child, the Tigris River had decided to join the Euphrates and make a cradle to rock a rich green land called Mesopotamia. She felt in her handbag for the weight of *The Lands of the Eastern Caliphate*.

> Beyond the city lies the chief source of the Tigris, which Mukaddasi describes as flowing with a rush of green water out of a dark cave. At first, he says, the stream is small, and only of sufficient volume to turn a single millwheel; but many effluents soon join and swell the current. The beginning of the Tigris River, according to Yakut, was distant two and a half days' journey from Diyarbakir, and he, too, speaks of the dark cavern from which the waters of the Tigris gush forth.

Thirty-eight writers, poets, dancers, and academics died in a fire set by Islamic funda-mentalists at a hotel in the central Turkish city of Sivas in 1993. The victims had gathered to commemorate the death of sixteenth-century Turkish poet Pir Sultan Abdal, hanged for his opposition to religious oppression. Aziz Nesin, who wrote the play Ah Biz Esekler, *escaped because the firemen mistook him for a police lieutenant.*

AUTHOR BIOGRAPHIES

KRISTIN ANDRYCHUK Kingston writer Kristin Andrychuk attended the 1989 and 1997 Writing Studios and the 1990 Radio Writers' Workshop. At Banff in 1989, Andrychuk worked on poetry and prose, starting what became her first novel, *The Swing Tree* (Oberon 1996). At Banff in 1997, she finished her yet-to-be published second novel, *Crystal and Crown Derby*.

JANIS BARLOW Poet Janis Barlow grew up in Windsor. She became a registered nurse and also earned a BA in English (University of Western Ontario) and an MFA in English and Creative Writing (Mills College, California). Her poems have appeared in publications including *Poetry Canada Review, Midwest Poetry Review, Mediphors*, and *Walrus*. Barlow attended the 1988 Writing Studio and now lives in Michigan.

BRIAN BARTLETT Brian Bartlett's most recent poetry collections are *Granite Erratics* (Ekstasis Editions 1997) and *Underwater Carpentry* (Goose Lane Editions 1994). A participant in the 1993 Writing Studio, Bartlett won *The Malahat Review* Long Poem Prize in 1991 and again in 1997. He also writes fiction, and has published essays, journals, memoirs, and other prose pieces about poetry. Bartlett teaches creative writing and literature at Saint Mary's University in Halifax.

VEN BEGAMUDRÉ At the 1990 and 1991 Writing Studios, Ven Begamudré worked on his novel *Van de Graaff Days* (Oolichan Books 1993) and story collection *Laterna Magika* (Oolichan Books 1997). *Laterna Magika* was a best book finalist in the Canada-Caribbean region for the Commonwealth Writers' Prize. Begamudré served as writer-in-residence in the University of Calgary's Markin-Flanagan Distinguished Writers Programme, the University of Alberta's English Department, and the Canada-Scotland Exchange. He now lives in Regina.

ASTRID BLODGETT Astrid Blodgett lives and works in Edmonton. Her short stories have appeared in *Prairie Fire* and *Pottersfield Portfolio*, and have been produced on CBC Radio's *Alberta Anthology*. Blodgett is now polishing her first collection of short stories, which will include "Learning to Speak." When she is not writing, she plays Renaissance recorder and wanders through the Rocky Mountains. She attended the 1997 Writing Studio.

RONNA BLOOM Born in Montreal, Ronna Bloom now lives and works in Toronto as a writer, a psychotherapist, and sometimes a photographer. A participant in the 1994 Writing Studio, Bloom has published poems in numerous journals. Her collection *Fear of the Ride* (Carleton University Press 1996) was shortlisted for the 1997 Gerald Lampert Award for best first book of poetry.

STEPHANIE BOLSTER Stephanie Bolster's recent work includes *White Stone: The Alice Poems* (Signal Editions, Véhicule Press 1998). A winner of the 1996 Bronwen Wallace Award for Poetry, *The Malahat Review* 1997 Long Poem Prize, and the 1998 Mother Tongue Press Chapbook Competition, Bolster has also published in journals including *Breathing Fire, The Malahat*

Review, and *The Backwater Review*. A participant in the 1994 Writing Studio, Bolster was born and raised in Burnaby and now lives in Ottawa.

MARY BORSKY "Ice" first appeared in Mary Borsky's short story collection *Influence of the Moon* (The Porcupine's Quill 1995). Borsky attended the 1992 Writing Studio. Her stories are included in *The Third Macmillan Anthology, Best Canadian Stories '93, The Journey Prize Anthology*, and *Two Lands, New Visions* (Coteau Books 1998), a Canadian-Ukrainian anthology. She now lives in Ottawa.

MARY CAMERON Mary Cameron's poetry has appeared in many publications, including *The Malahat Review, The Last Word*, and the American journal *The Thrashing Dove Review*. A former poetry editor of *Prism: international* and editor of *Quarry* (1994 to 1997), Cameron holds an MA in Writing (University of British Columbia). She participated in the 1991 Writing Studio. *Clouds Without Heaven* (Beach Holme/Press Porcepic 1998), a collection of poems, is her most recent published work.

WARREN CARIOU Expatriate Saskatchewanian Warren Cariou now lives in Vancouver, where he is a post-doctoral teaching fellow in the English Department at the University of British Columbia. "Puerto Escondido," written during the 1993 Writing Studio, first appeared in *The Malahat Review*. Cariou's stories are included in *Coming Attractions '95* and *Due West*. His first book,

Convictions, is forthcoming (Coteau Books 1999).

MARLENE COOKSHAW Marlene Cookshaw is the author of two chapbooks and two full-length collections, including *Coupling* (Outlaw Editions 1994) and *The Whole Elephant* (Brick Books 1989). "South Island" was written at the 1997 Writing Studio and is included in the forthcoming *Double Somersaults* (Brick Books 1999). Cookshaw is associate editor of *The Malahat Review* and lives on Pender Island, British Columbia.

LYNN DAVIES In 1995, Lynn Davies attended the Writing Studio and won the Lina Chartrand Poetry Award. "Before the Phoenicians" originally appeared in *Pottersfield Portfolio*. Davies's first book of poetry, *The Bridge That Carries the Road*, is forthcoming (Brick Books 1999). She lives in McLeod Hill, New Brunswick.

JAMIE DIAMOND Jamie Diamond lives in Los Angeles, where she is working on her second novel, *Los Angeles Times*. A journalist, she is the West Coast editor of *Mademoiselle*. Her short stories have appeared in *Ploughshares*, *Ark*, and *The Quarterly*.

MARILYN DUMONT Originally from northeastern Alberta, Marilyn Dumont has published in journals and anthologies, including *Writing the Circle* (NeWest Press 1990), *The Road Home* (Reidmore Books 1992), *The Colour of Resistance* (Sister Vision Press 1994), *Looking at the Words of Our People* (Theytus

Books 1994), and *Miscegenation Blues* (Sister Vision Press 1994). Her collection of poetry *A Really Good Brown Girl* (Brick Books 1996) won the 1996 Gerald Lampert Award for best first book of poetry and earned an honourable mention for the 1997 VanCity Book Prize. Dumont holds an MFA in Creative Writing (University of British Columbia) and teaches English and creative writing in Vancouver.

DEIRDRE DWYER Deirdre Dwyer's "That time of month" was first published in *The Fiddlehead*, and her collection of travel poems, *The Breath That Lightens the Body*, is forthcoming (Beach Holme 1999). Dwyer holds an MA in English and Creative Writing (University of Windsor) and participated in various Banff writing programs in 1982, 1984, and 1995. She lives in Halifax.

MICHELLE DESBARATS FELS Michelle Desbarats Fels attended the 1997 Writing Studio and was a finalist in the 1996/97 CBC/*Saturday Night* National Poetry Contest. In 1998, she received an Ontario Arts Council–Works in Progress grant. Her book *Last Child to Come Inside* is forthcoming (Carleton University Press). Fels now lives in Ottawa.

ANNE FLEMING Anne Fleming teaches at Emily Carr Institute of Art and Design in Vancouver and is currently working on a novel. Fleming participated in the 1997 Writing Studio. Her first book of stories is *Pool-Hopping and Other Stories* (Polestar 1998).

CYNTHIA FLOOD Cynthia Flood's "Half-Century" originally appeared in *Geist*. Her short story collections are *The Animals in their Elements* (Talonbooks 1987) and *My Father Took a Cake to France* (Talonbooks 1992). Flood attended the 1996 Writing Studio, where she began her novel-in-progress, *The City Where the Deer Sleep*. Flood's awards include the 1990 Journey Prize and the 1993 Western Magazine Gold Award for Fiction.

REBECCA FREDRICKSON A participant in the 1996 Writing Studio, Rebecca Fredrickson has published poems in *Grain, Prairie Fire*, and *The Fiddlehead*. Fredrickson wrote "Ruby" in Banff, and she is now finishing a poetry manuscript, tentatively titled *A Secret Envy of the Unsaved*. She lives in Victoria.

BILL GASTON Bill Gaston writes fiction, poetry, and drama for stage and screen. His novels include *Tall Lives, Bella Combe Journal, The Cameraman*, and *The Good Body*. His story collections include *North of Jesus' Beans* (Cormorant 1993) and *Sex is Red* (Cormorant 1998). "Try a Younger Man" is from his poetry collection *Inviting Blindness* (Oolichan 1995). Gaston has lived and taught writing across Canada, for ten years in New Brunswick. He now lives in Victoria with his wife and children, and teaches at the University of Victoria.

JOANNE GERBER Joanne Gerber attended the 1994 and 1996 Writing Studios. Her first book, *In the Misleading Absence of Light* (Coteau Books 1997), received several awards, including the 1998 Canadian Author's Association

Jubilee Award for Short Story Collection and the 1997 Saskatchewan Book Awards for Fiction, First Book, and City of Regina (shared). It is also shortlisted for the 1998 City of Toronto Book Award. Gerber lives in Regina and is currently working on a novel and a chamber opera with composer David L. McIntyre.

CURTIS GILLESPIE Curtis Gillespie is the author of *The Progress of an Object in Motion* (Coteau Books 1997), which won the 1998 Writer's Guild of Alberta Henry Kreisel Award and the inaugural 1998 Danuta Gleed Prize from the Writer's Union of Canada. Gillespie has lived most of his live in Alberta, and now lives with his wife and daughter in Edmonton.

SUSAN GOYETTE Sue Goyette grew up on the south shore of Montreal and now lives with her family in Cole Harbour, Nova Scotia. Her work has appeared in numerous periodicals, and she has published a collection of poetry, *The True Names of Birds* (Brick Books 1998). Goyette is now working on a second manuscript of poems.

GP GREENWOOD GP (Gail) Greenwood attended Banff in 1979 and 1980. Her poems and short stories have been broadcast on CBC Radio and have appeared in magazines and anthologies, including *Celebrating Canadian Women* and *Glass Canyons*. Her first book of poetry is *Buying Space in the Lifeboat* (Childe Thursday Press 1993). Greenwood lives in Mill Bay, British Columbia, and recently completed an MA in English (University of Victoria).

GAIL HELGASON A participant in the 1993 and 1996 Writing Studios, Gail Helgason lives in Edmonton and is working on a novel. Her short story collection *Fracture Patterns* (Coteau Books 1995) was shortlisted for the 1996 Writers Guild of Alberta Best First Book Award and the 1996 City of Edmonton Book Prize.

GREG HOLLINGSHEAD Greg Hollingshead has published three collections of stories and two novels, including *The Healer* (HarperCollins 1998). His work has won numerous awards, among them the 1995 Governor-General's Award for Fiction. "The Mary Dunbar Letter" first appeared in *Descant* in 1986 and was revised at the 1988 Writing Studio for publication in the author's second collection, *White Buick* (Oolichan 1992). He lives in Edmonton.

SALLY ITO Sally Ito is from Edmonton and attended the 1993 Writing Studio. Ito's first book of poetry, *Frogs in the Rain Barrel* (Nightwood Editions 1995), was first runner-up for the 1997 Milton Acorn People's Memorial Award. Her most recent book is a collection of short stories entitled *Floating Shore* (Mercury Press 1998).

DAYV JAMES-FRENCH Born on Prince Edward Island, Dayv James-French now makes his home in Ottawa. In between, he has spent time in England, Israel, Europe, and every province except Saskatchewan. A participant in the 1994 Writing Studio, James-French's short story collections are *What Else Is a Heart*

for? (Beach Holme 1998) and *Victims of Gravity* (The Porcupine's Quill 1990).

JANICE KULYK KEEFER The author of nine books of poetry, fiction, and literary criticism, Janice Kulyk Keefer has twice been nominated for a Governor-General's Award, and twice won first prize in both the CBC Radio Literary Competition and the National Magazine Awards. She participated in the 1985 and 1986 Writing Studios. Keefer teaches at the University of Guelph and lives in Eden Mills, Ontario.

CATHERINE KIDD After releasing her book/cassette of performance pieces, *everything I know about love I learned from taxidermy*, Catherine Kidd began work on the novel *Bestial Rooms*, to be published by Patrick Crean. Her performance work has been featured in venues across Canada and her written work has appeared in journals including *Matrix* and *Tessera*. Kidd attended the 1997 Writing Studio, completing her MA (Concordia) the following spring. She lives in Montreal.

BILLIE LIVINGSTON After poet Billie Livingston attended the 1994 Writing Studio, she received grants through the Canada Council's Explorations Program and the Barbara Deming Memorial Fund to begin a novel. In 1996, she was awarded a residency at the UCROSS Foundation in Wyoming, Sheridan, to continue working on her novel, now titled *Going Down Swinging*. A chapter from this novel won the 1996 *sub-TERRAIN* Short Fiction Contest. Livingston's work is included or upcoming in *Imago, One Step Beyond, Atom Mind, TickleAce,* and *The Capilano Review.* She lives in Delta, British Columbia.

YANN MARTEL Yann Martel's published work includes a collection of short stories, *The Facts Behind the Helsinki Roccamatios* (Alfred A. Knopf Canada 1993) and a novel, *Self* (Knopf 1996). He is now working on his next novel, about an Indian family that runs a zoo. They decide to immigrate to Canada. Big mistake. Martel lives in Montreal.

JULIE MASON Ottawa writer Julie Mason, a participant in the 1996 Writing Studio, has published in *Canadian Forum* and the anthology *A Room at the Heart of Things* (Véhicule Press 1998). She is completing her MA in Writing at Antioch University. Her story "Calvary" was a finalist in the CBC Radio Literary Competition, the Glimmer Train Short Fiction Awards, and the International Short Fiction Competition of the Writers' Workshop in Asheville, North Carolina.

ALLY MCKAY Ally McKay attended the 1983 Writing Studio and later participated in the 1985 and 1986 Writing Studios. "The Storms Are on the Ocean" formed part of her collection *Human Bones* (Oberon Press 1988, re-issued in the Canadian Library Series, HarperCollins 1990). She lives in Victoria.

BARBARA NICKEL Barbara Nickel's first book of poetry, *The Gladys Elegies* (Coteau Books 1997), won the 1998 Pat Lowther Memorial Award, and her young adult novel, *The Secret Wish of*

Nannerl Mozart (Second Story Press 1996), was shortlisted for the Mr. Christie Book Award. A participant in the 1994 Writing Studio, Nickel also won *The Malahat Review* Long Poem Prize in 1995, and her work is included in *Breathing Fire: Canada's New Poets.* "Three Poems for Violin" originally appeared in *Event.* She lives in St. John's.

ARMAND GARNET RUFFO Born in Northern Ontario, Armand Garnet Ruffo is the director of the Centre for Aboriginal Education, Research and Culture, and a lecturer in the English department at Carleton University. A participant in the 1989 Writing Studio, Ruffo is strongly influenced by his Ojibway heritage. His first collection of poetry, *Opening in the Sky* (Theytus Books 1994), and the creative biography *Grey Owl: The Mystery of Archie Belaney* (Coteau Books 1997) reflect his abiding interest in the complexities of Aboriginal identity in a multicultural society.

JAY RUZESKY A participant in the 1989 and 1992 Writing Studios, Jay Ruzesky has published in Canadian and American journals and magazines, including *Caliban, Prism: international, Saturday Night, Descant,* and *Border Crossings.* His books include *Writing on the Wall* (Outlaw Editions 1996), *Painting the Yellow House Blue* (House of Anansi 1994), and *Am I Glad to See You* (Thistledown Press 1992). He lives in Victoria and teaches at Malaspina University-College.

JEAN RYSSTAD Jean Rysstad began writing fiction in 1985. She attended the 1989 Radio Drama Program and returned to Banff to work on fiction in 1993. "Contiguous" was written at the 1986 Writing Studio and first published in the *Windsor Review*. The stories in her collections *Travelling In* (Oolichan Books 1990) and *Home Fires* (Harbour 1997) are primarily set on the north coast of BC, where Rysstad has lived for twenty-three years.

DIANE SCHOEMPERLEN A participant in the 1976 Writing Studio, Diane Schoemperlen is the author of *Double Exposure* (Coach House 1984), *Frogs and Other Stories* (Quarry 1986), *Hockey Night in Canada* (Quarry 1987), *Hockey Night in Canada and Other Stories* (Quarry 1991), *In the Language of Love* (HarperCollins 1994), and *Forms of Devotion* (HarperCollins 1998). "Stranger than Fiction" was originally published in her collection *The Man of My Dreams* (Macmillan 1990), which was shortlisted for both the Governor-General's Award and the Trillium Award. Schoemperlen lives in Kingston with her son.

JOAN SKOGAN Joan Skogan has written features for CBC Radio, *Saturday Night*, and other magazines. Her first novel, *Moving Water* (Beach Holme 1998), grew from "Mesopotamia," which was written at the 1995 Writing Studio. Skogan's other books include *Voyages at Sea with Strangers* (HarperCollins 1992), and for children, *The Princess and the Sea Bear and Other Tsimshian Stories* (Polestar 1990), *Grey Cat at Sea* (Polestar 1993), and *The Good Companion* (Orca 1998). She lives on Gabriola Island, British Columbia.

MICHAEL WINTER Most of the stories in Michael Winter's *Creaking in their Skins* (Quarry Press 1994) were edited in the 1993 Writing Studio. Winter is also the author of the story collection *One Last Good Look* (The Porcupine's Quill 1999) and a yet-to-be-published journal of personal observation, *This All Happened*. "The Distance" originally appeared in *Event*. Winter lived in St. John's for thirty years, where he co-edited *TickleAce* for six. He is now living in Toronto and working on a novel, *Must*.

ABOUT THE EDITORS

EDNA ALFORD Recipient of the Marian Engel Award and co-winner of the Gerald Lampert Award, Edna Alford has published two collections of short fiction, *A Sleep Full of Dreams* (Oolichan 1981) and *The Garden of Eloise Loon* (Oolichan 1986). Her work has appeared in numerous journals and anthologies. She was co-founder and co-editor (with Joan Clark) of *Dandelion Magazine* for five years and fiction editor of *Grain Magazine* for five years. She has served on the editorial board of Coteau Books since 1988 and has edited many short fiction collections as well as co-editing (with Claire Harris) the anthology *Kitchen Talk* (Red Deer College Press 1992). She is Associate Director of the Writing Studio at The Banff Centre for the Arts.

DON MCKAY Don McKay has published eight books of poetry, including *Birding, or desire* (McClelland & Stewart 1983); *Night Field* (McClelland & Stewart 1991), which received the Governor General's Award; and *Apparatus* (McClelland & Stewart 1997). His work has also received the National Magazine Award and the Canadian Authors Association Award. Since 1975 he has served as editor and publisher with Brick Books. He taught creative writing and English literature at the University of Western Ontario and the University of New Brunswick for twenty-seven years before resigning to write and edit poetry full time. From 1991 to 1996 he edited *The Fiddlehead* magazine, and he has also served as a faculty resource person at the Sage Hill Writing Experience and The Banff Centre for the Arts, where he currently holds the position of Senior Poetry Editor.

RHEA TREGEBOV Rhea Tregebov was born in Saskatoon, raised in Winnipeg, and now lives in Toronto. She has four collections of poetry: *Remembering History* (Guernica Press 1982), which won the 1983 League of Canadian Poets' Pat Lowther Award; *No One We Know* (Aya/Mercury Press 1986); *The Proving Grounds* (Véhicule Press 1991); and *Mapping the Chaos* (Véhicule Press 1995). She has also published four children's picture books and edited the anthologies *Frictions* (1989), *Frictions II* (1993), and *Sudden Miracles* (Second Story Press 1991). Tregebov was co-winner of *The Malahat Review* Long Poem Competition in 1994 and also received the 1993 Readers' Choice Award for Poetry from *Prairie Schooner* (Nebraska). She teaches creative writing for Ryerson's Continuing Education program and works as a freelance editor of adult and young adult fiction and poetry.

RACHEL WYATT Rachel Wyatt emigrated to Canada in 1957. Her four novels were published by The House of Anansi. Her most recent book is *The Day Marlene Dietrich Died* (Oolichan 1996). Her stage plays include *Geometry, Chairs and Tables,* and *Crackpot.* She has written many radio dramas for the CBC and the BBC. Her new collection of stories is to be published by Oolichan Books in Spring 1999. She was on faculty at the Banff Writing Studio in 1993, 1994, and 1996 and is currently Director of the Writing Studio at The Banff Centre for the Arts.

PERMISSIONS

All contributions to this collection are published with the permission of their authors.

"Granite Erratics" by Brian Bartlett was previously published in *Granite Erratics* (Ekstasis Editions 1997). Reprinted by permission of the publisher.

"Indian Cooking" by Ven Begamudré was previously published in a longer version in *Laterna Magika* (Oolichan Books 1997). Reprinted by permission of the publisher.

"The Blue Raft" and "The Job of an Apple" by Ronna Bloom were previously published in *Fear of the Ride* (Carleton University Press 1996). Reprinted by permission of the publisher.

"On the Steps of the Met" by Stephanie Bolster was previously published in *The Malahat Review* (No. 120, Fall 1997). "Lost Things Poke Through Melting Snow" by Stephanie Bolster was previously published in *The Backwater Review* (Vol. 1, No. 1, Spring/Summer 1997).

"Ice" by Mary Borsky was previously published in *Influence of the Moon* (The Porcupine's Quill 1995). Reprinted by permission of the publisher.

"Puerto Escondido" by Warren Cariou was previously published in *The Malahat Review*, *Coming Attractions '95*, and *Due West*.

"Before the Phoenicians" by Lynn Davies was first published in *Pottersfield Portfolio*.

"Friends" by Jamie Diamond first appeared in *ARK*, the Literary Review of New York University.

"a hard bed to lie in" and "It Crosses My Mind" by Marilyn Dumont were previously published in *a really good brown girl* (Brick Books 1996). Reprinted by permission of the publisher.

"That time of month" by Deirdre Dwyer was previously published in *The Fiddlehead* (No. 189, Autumn 1996).

"Solar Plexus" by Anne Fleming was previously published in *Pool-Hopping and Other Stories* (Polestar 1998). Reprinted by permission of the publisher.

"Half-Century" by Cynthia Flood first appeared in *Geist*.

"Listening to the Angels" by Joanne Gerber was previously published in *In the Misleading Absence of Light* (Coteau Books 1997). Reprinted by permission of the publisher.

"The Coffin" by Curtis Gillespie was previously published in *The Progress of an Object in Motion* (Coteau Books 1997). Reprinted by permission of the publisher.

"This Stone of Knowledge" by Susan Goyette was previously published in *Grain* (Vol. 24, No. 3: Winter 1997).

"Bluffing" by Gail Helgason was previously published in *Fracture Patterns* (Coteau Books 1995). Reprinted by permission of the publisher.

"The Mary Dunbar Letter" by Greg Hollingshead was previously published in *White Buick* (Oolichan Books 1992). Reprinted by permission of the publisher.

"Honeymoon" by Sally Ito was previously published in *Floating Shore* (Mercury Press 1998). Reprinted by permission of the publisher.

"...because" by Dayv James-French was first published in *What Else is a Heart for?* (Beach Holme 1998).

"*Virgin and Child with Spoon—Gerard David*" by Janice Kulyk Keefer was previously published in *The Malahat Review* (No. 116, September 1996).

"Boston YWCA" by Billie Livingston was first published in *Quarry*.

"The Storms Are on the Ocean" by Ally McKay was previously published in *Human Bones* (Oberon Press 1988). Reprinted by permission of the publisher.

"Three Poems for Violin" by Barbara Nickel was previously published in *Event* magazine (Vol. 25, No. 2) and in *The Gladys Elegies* (Coteau 1997). Reprinted by permission of the publisher.

"Sneaking into the Stephen Hawking Lecture, Then Sneaking Back Out Again" and "Roller Coaster" by Jay Ruzesky were previously published in *Painting the Yellow House Blue* (House of Anansi 1994). Reprinted by permission of the publisher.

"Contiguous" by Jean Rysstad first appeared in the *Windsor Review* and *Travelling In* (Oolichan Books 1990).

"The Distance" by Michael Winter was first published in *Event* magazine (Vol. 26, No. 1, 1997). It was later translated and published in Mexico in *Anthologia de cuentos canadienses contemporaraneos*, edited by John Metcalf.